Baltimore Symphony Orchestra

A CENTURY OF SOUND

Michael J. Lisicky

foreword by Leon Fleisher

1916–2016

Editing
Edited by David Sullivan.
Additional editing by Paul Meecham.

Photography
The majority of photographs in this book belong to the
Baltimore Symphony and are carefully housed at the
Baltimore City Archives. A special thank you is due to
the City Archives staff members Anthony Freeman,
Rob Schoeberlein, Saul Gibusiwa, and former staff member
Amy James.

Design
Glenn Dellon, Dellon Design
dellondesign.com

Printing
Schmitz Press
schmitzpress.com

ISBN
978-1-4951-7326-4

Library of Congress Control Number
2015950825

Michael J. Lisicky is an internationally recognized
department store historian, lecturer, and author. His books
have received critical acclaim by the Washington Post,
Boston Globe, Baltimore Sun, and the Philadelphia Inquirer.
In addition, he has been featured on National Public Radio,
in Fortune Magazine, and on the CBS Sunday Morning
television program. Mr. Lisicky is also an oboist with the
Baltimore Symphony Orchestra.

Note from the author: Remarks in quotations, especially
during the early chapters of the book, are largely taken from
the following sources: The Baltimore Sun, The Evening Sun,
and The Baltimore News American. The musician roster was
hand-compiled from printed programs and should be used
as a guide. Apologies are given for any incorrect or missing
personnel information. A sincere thanks goes to every person
who gave an interview or facilitated a conversation for this
book, especially Miryam Yardumian, Karen Stahl, Patrick
Chamberlain, and Lee Kappelman. Additional gratitude is due
to the staff at the Baltimore City Archives, the Peabody
Archives, the Maryland Department at the Enoch Pratt Free
Library, and the library staff at the Baltimore Symphony.

The Baltimore Symphony Orchestra
bsomusic.org

Contents

5   Introduction

6   Foreword

---

8   **Chapter One**
1914-1920

18   **Chapter Two**
The 1920s

28   **Chapter Three**
The 1930s

46   **Chapter Four**
The 1940s

62   **Chapter Five**
The 1950s

70   **Chapter Six**
The 1960s

90   **Chapter Seven**
The 1970s

104   **Chapter Eight**
The 1980s

126   **Chapter Nine**
The 1990s

142   **Chapter Ten**
2000-2006

158   **Chapter Eleven**
2007-2016

---

174   Epilogue

---

177   Leadership

178   Musician Roster

188   BSO Discography

192   Happy Birthday

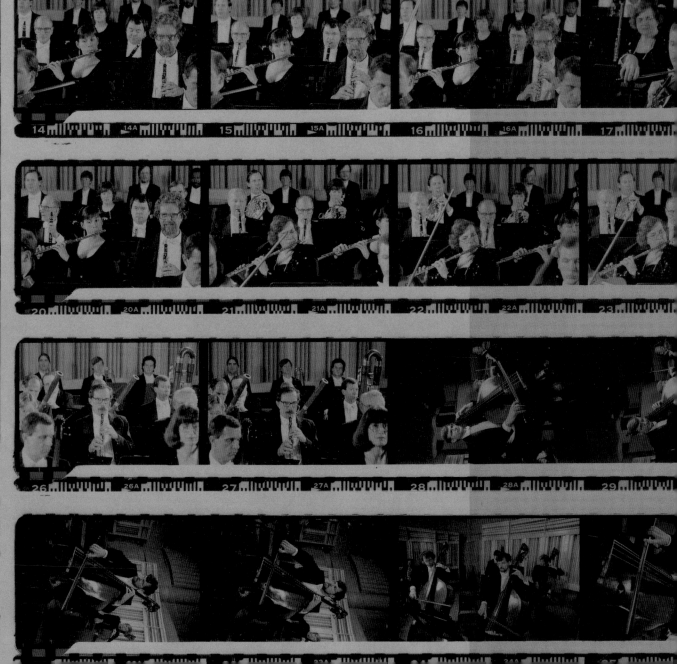

Introduction

The occasion was one that will remain long in the memory of all who were present, for in a sense this concert marked a turning point in the musical life of Baltimore. With the encouragement and sympathy that the Baltimoreans will undoubtedly give this new venture, the Baltimore Symphony Orchestra will soon develop into a notable feature of our civic life. It is not too much to believe that in the course of time an orchestra that will take its place with the most important organizations in the country will result from the beginning that was made at the Lyric last evening.

Baltimore Sun, February 12, 1916
describing the first performance
of the Baltimore Symphony Orchestra

Foreword

Despite being born in San Francisco and spending my first decade in the thrall of the Golden Gate, I have this long, curious, almost karmic connection with Baltimore.

The wife of my San Francisco benefactor (one James David Zellerbach, West Coast industrialist, who was later named as Eisenhower's ambassador to Rome) was a Baltimorean, née Hannah Fuld. In fact my very first trip to Baltimore was to visit her one fateful day in 1941, December 7.

My first professional trip to Baltimore was in 1954 to play the Brahms B-flat concerto with then music director Massimo Freccia, followed by multiple appearances with each succeeding music director ever since. My first formal teaching position was here in Baltimore at the Peabody Institute under director Peter Mennin in 1959, where I have been ever since, having the pleasure of working with such extraordinary talents as André Watts, Yefim Bronfman, Jonathan Biss, Louis Lortie, Alon Goldstein, amongst many, many others. Also in 1959, I met my second wife, Rikki Rosenthal, a Baltimore girl. We resided in Bolton Hill, had two children, Paula and Julian, who went respectively to Bryn Mawr and The Park School.

In 1970, I further cemented my connection to the area by accepting an invitation to start a new career that of conductor, proffered by the Annapolis Symphony Orchestra, a stint that lasted some twelve years. That was followed by an invitation from Sergiu Comissiona to become an associate conductor of the BSO. Sergiu Comissiona was, in my opinion, just about the greatest conductor of non-German music that I have ever known. Without question, he brought the BSO to the highest point of its history up to that moment, to a truly international level.

If you think a great professional football team is a thing of beauty and wonder, just multiply that by ten or eleven times and you'll get a vague idea of the precision and artistic involvement in the creation and maintenance of a great orchestra. So when the 1981 lockout occurred, threatening the dismemberment, the very existence of what Sergiu spent years to do, I felt something drastic needed to be done. Calling on two intrepid friends, Julie Alderman and Gordon Becker, we formed *The Friends of the Baltimore Symphony Orchestra* and, with negotiations led by Ron Shapiro, committed ourselves to raising the difference between what the orchestra felt it needed and management felt it could offer.

Leon Fleisher and Sergiu Comissiona at the piano in 1975.

In 1982, I had the joy of participating as soloist with the BSO in the opening of the Meyerhoff Symphony Hall, while making my return to the two-handed repertoire. The BSO reached new pinnacles in 1985 with the advent of David Zinman, a former "mentee" (as was I) of the great French maestro Pierre Monteux. David's mastery of the German repertoire brought the BSO to the edge of greatness. As for our flirtation with Temirkanov, it was just that; a mutual seduction that ended with Yuri's return to his true mistress, St. Petersburg. Marin Alsop is now taking the next giant step of bringing this jewel in Baltimore's cultural crown out into the community and back into our educational system.

Also in 1982, Katherine Jacobson, a former student of mine at Peabody, agreed to become my "Eroica," and gave me a last chance at getting it right. Despite being confronted with an entire stepfamily including Deborah, Dickie, and Leah from my first marriage, she has managed to juggle said five children with countless rescued animals, as well as helping form The Fleisher-Jacobson Duo, a four hand piano team (mostly one piano) that has performed all over the world, from Beijing to Rio to Paris, in addition to making two records with Sony. We have resided in Roland Park for the past 30 odd years, and I look forward to continuing this strange and wonderful journey.

See you all with the BSO in January 2016 at the Meyerhoff.

~ Leon Fleisher

CHAPTER

1914–

ONE
1920

While today's Baltimore Symphony Orchestra (BSO) traces its roots back to 1916, the *history* of classical music in Baltimore can be traced back well before that time.

The Peabody Institute was founded in 1857 as the nation's first conservatory of music and the school maintained a regular schedule of free performances. However, symphony orchestras were slow to develop in the United States. Most of the earliest presentations of classical music were presented by brass bands since instruments and supplies were difficult to obtain. In order to give a better "symphonic sound," woodwind instruments were added by the mid-1850s, followed by strings a few decades later.

Some large cities, such as New York, Boston, and St. Louis, were fortunate to have hometown symphony orchestras. Yet in the mid-1880s, symphony performances were still seen as anomalies, not a part of America's young and unestablished culture. The first documented symphony orchestra performance in Baltimore was on March 14, 1849, at Washington Hall on Baltimore Street. Billed as "A Grand Concert of Music," the event, conducted by a Mr. A. Mutie, also featured several Chinese dogs and an African monkey as a way to stimulate interest. In 1873, the Peabody Institute established a student orchestra and provided symphonic opportunities for its students six times a year. But as the 1800s developed, general interest in classical music did not. In response to low attendance at performances by the city's Oratorio Society, the Baltimore Sun complained of how "the vast majority of the people of Baltimore care nothing for the better and the higher grade of music." Some

prominent and wealthy citizens were already working to change that perception.

In 1887, the Boston Symphony Orchestra, under the direction of Wilhelm Gericke, accepted an invitation that established a regular concert series in Baltimore. Its initial appearance that February, held at the Academy of Music, featured 68 musicians and music by Weber and Beethoven. These initial concerts were well promoted by word of mouth and through the press, and began a long-term relationship between the Boston Symphony and the city of Baltimore.

In 1890, a local "energetic and enthusiastic businessman and musician" named Ross Jungnickel laid the groundwork for the formation of a Baltimore Symphony Orchestra. Jungnickel gathered together 45 musicians and established an ensemble under that name. He served as the group's conductor, manager, and visionary. The ensemble debuted on Feb. 5, 1890, and Jungnickel worked to establish a steady concert series with grand plans for growth. His stated purpose was "to foster and elevate the standard of musical culture" in Baltimore. Jungnickel solicited donations from public and private sources, but his goal of 70 salaried musicians who worked 32 weeks a year with an annual salary of $1,500 never fully materialized. In 1894, Jungnickel, frustrated by financial struggles and "public apathy," left Baltimore and moved to New York. But he returned to Baltimore in 1896 and restarted his orchestra. Jungnickel and his Baltimore Symphony

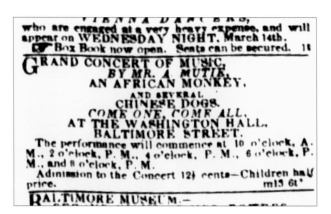

Orchestra attempted a Tuesday afternoon concert series at Washington's National Theater. Jungnickel's appearances in Washington featured such artists as violinists Alexander Petschnikoff and Leonora Jackson, but the series was abandoned in March 1900 due to poor attendance. Concerts continued throughout 1900, until Jungnickel left town and the ad hoc group disbanded. This early attempt at a local symphony orchestra battled not only apathy but also competition from out-of-town orchestras. The Boston Symphony had firmly established its series of concerts, and was joined by a regular Philadelphia Orchestra series in 1907 and a New York Philharmonic series in 1911.

In 1905, an organization called the Orchestra Club was formed with the intention of becoming the next Baltimore Symphony Orchestra. The Orchestra Club desired to create an ensemble that "would develop into one of sufficient ability and strength" and would make the city proud. Within one year, the club grew to more than 20 musicians, whose repertoire included Haydn's Symphony No. 6 and Beethoven's *Egmont* Overture. Under the leadership of violinist and composer Abram Moses, the Orchestra Club suffered from waning interest and was shortly disbanded.

From 1911 to 1917, the Florestan Club, at 522 N. Charles St., was a popular social club that catered to the city's professional and amateur musicians along with some of Baltimore's most prominent leaders. Among the club's members were H.L.

Top left. An advertisement for Baltimore's first orchestra concert, held on March 14, 1849, appeared in the Baltimore Sun.

Top right. Orchestra concerts were held at the Academy of Music before the Music Hall,

later named the Lyric Theatre, opened on October 31, 1894.

Bottom right. The first Baltimore Symphony Orchestra, led by conductor Ross Jungnickel, debuted on February 5, 1890 and continued for about a decade.

Mencken; Frederick Gottlieb of the Gottlieb, Bauernschmidt, and Straus brewery; and Harold Randolph, Peabody's longtime director. After a Boston Symphony performance in October 1914, some members of the Florestan Club discussed the establishment of a municipal orchestra that would be fully supported by the city "in order to broaden the scope of musical interest." Frederick R. Huber, a member of the Peabody faculty and the Florestan Club, spearheaded the effort and presented it to Mayor James H. Preston in December 1914.

The initial proposal called for the establishment of a municipal band at an expenditure of $8,000. Preston enthusiastically supported the plan and saw the foray into municipally-supported music as "a progressive step" toward the city's identity and cultural growth. "We are providing playgrounds for children. We provide bands for the parks out of that fund. It has occurred to us that in the early spring, summer and fall months there is always a very considerable population remaining in town without amusement and entertainment, and we have thought that a municipal band at times playing on a portable stand in the central section of the city… would not be an unwelcome diversion for those months." Preston noted that other American cities had bands but that none were fully subsidized by local government.

Preston felt strongly that Baltimoreans should be exposed to many forms of "culture." He frequented many European capitals, such as London, Paris, and Rome, and was eager to develop the city's cultural identity. "I do believe that my grandfather was always a lover of classical music," says Preston Rich, his grandson. "He wanted to develop a cultural life that would last beyond his administration." Mayor Preston had a good working relationship with Huber, who was also Peabody's summer school director. Huber was "used to taking orders from Mayor Preston," and in early 1915 he suggested to the mayor that the words to songs be projected onto a screen during band concerts. While the Municipal Band played accompanying music, audience members, assisted by a choral group, could sing along. Preston enthusiastically agreed to the idea and the relationship between the men strengthened over the next several years.

The Municipal Band gave its first performance on July 13, 1915, on a storm-filled night under Baltimore's Washington Monument. Over 1,500 Baltimoreans attended the performance, from Mayor Preston "down to the street urchins, who encircled the Monument at its base and sat through it all." The concert featured selections by a community chorus that included "Dixie" and "Old Folks at Home," to the delight of the mayor. The concert's success persuaded Preston to expand upon his vision of municipally-funded music programs.

The mayor also expressed a desire for a municipal anthem. A contest was held for poems that could be set to music. The program fell on the heels of the city-wide "Star-Spangled

Those of us who were his colleagues will remember him at the height of his powers – a leader of men, an inspired teacher, and a lovable friend.

REGINALD STEWART, 1953, DISCUSSING GUSTAV STRUBE (PICTURED)

Opp. Left. The Peabody Institute as it appeared in the early 1900s.

Opp. Right. Founding conductor Gustav Strube, Mayor Preston, and Frederick Huber pose in Mt. Vernon Square in 1919.

Banner" celebration in 1914. Over 800 poems were submitted for approval and the poem "Baltimore, our Baltimore," written by Folger McKinsey, won the $250 prize. Preston wanted the poem to be arranged for band or orchestra. Mrs. Theodor Hemberger was selected to compose the music.

Preston then assembled an official committee to study the concept of a municipal symphony orchestra. Huber had already discussed the idea of a symphony orchestra as a means to create additional prestige for the city. Gustav Strube, head of the harmony department at Peabody and a former assistant conductor of the Boston Symphony, and J.C. Van Hulsteyn, Peabody faculty violinist and former concertmaster of the Lamoureux Orchestra in Paris, met with Huber and discussed the idea. The committee presented Preston with a plan that included a $6,000 allocation toward the formation of a municipal orchestra. Huber offered his services "without remuneration" in establishing the logistical aspects of organization. Huber, who also was concert director at Peabody, felt it was "his duty" to help with the project and stated that he was "grateful to the Mayor for making the organization possible."

Preston agreed to the plan and, according to grandson Rich, the mayor's wife, Helen, personally guaranteed the new orchestra's funding should there be a shortfall. Huber organized 54 musicians "recruited from jazz bands,

Baltimore Symphony Orchestra.

The Baltimore Symphony Orchestra is now an assured fact, for its first concert is announced for Friday evening, February 11, at 8.30 o'clock. Gustav Strube, who occupies the Chair of Harmony and Composition at the Conservatory, has been selected as the conductor, and J. C. Van Hulsteyn will be the concert-master. The soloist for the opening concert will be Mabel Garrison, a graduate of the vocal department of the Conservatory and now one of the prima donnas of the Metropolitan Opera Company of New York. W. G. Owst, a prominent local musician, will make the annotations for the printed programs. In order to make it possible for everyone to attend the concerts the scale of prices has been put at a very low figure. Fifty cents wil be charged for the first floor seats; twenty-five cents for the balcony seats, and fifteen cents for the gallery seats. Two other concerts will take place this season, one on March 10 and the other on April 14. The Orchestra will number fifty players chosen from among the local musicians. It is hoped that all the students will avail themselves of this unusual opportunity to hear good orchestral music at a price easily within reach of every one. The orchestra is being subsidized by the Mayor and City Council of Baltimore, which is one of the first of the larger cities to display so great an interest in the musical welfare of the community.

OUR BALTIMORE

Baltimore, where Carroll flourished.
    And the fame of Calvert grew!
Here the old defenders conquered
    As their valiant swords they drew.
Here the starry banner glistened
    In the sunshine of the sea,
In that dawn of golden vision
    That awoke the song of Key;
Here are hearts that beat forever
    For the city we adore;
Here the love of men and brothers——
    Baltimore, our Baltimore!

Top. Folger McKinsey was awarded $250 in gold for his poem, "Baltimore, our Baltimore."

Opposite page. The program booklet from the February 11, 1916 Baltimore Symphony debut stated that the ensemble was, "Established and Maintained Exclusively by the City of Baltimore."

theater orchestras, the Peabody faculty, brass bands and players in musical sections of fraternal societies," and named Van Hulsteyn the orchestra's concertmaster and Strube its conductor. Rehearsals for the new Baltimore Symphony Orchestra began in January 1916.

On Feb. 11, 1916, the Baltimore Symphony Orchestra gave its debut performance at the Lyric Theatre. Strube and Metropolitan Opera "prima donna" and native Baltimorean Mabel Garrison, along with 53 instrumentalists, played for a crowd that "overflowed into the aisles." The concert began with a "spirited" performance of Beethoven's Symphony No. 8 that included "some delightful things from the players." The Sun reported: "It was indeed a brilliant and inspiring occasion, in many respects the most important event that has taken place in the local musical world in our time. For with the founding of this little orchestra composed of Baltimore players the morale of the musical fraternity here seems in a way to have been suddenly placed upon an entirely different basis." The Baltimore Sun continued that Garrison "never looked so charming" and received "a supreme ovation" for her arias by Mozart and Delibes. The concert ended with Wagner's Overture to *Tannhäuser*.

The initial season consisted of three concerts, the second held on March 10 and the final on April 14. The newly organized orchestra also appeared at a special concert that

unveiled the city's new municipal anthem, "Baltimore, our Baltimore." Held on Feb. 22, it featured the symphony performing Offenbach's Overture to *Orpheus in the Underworld* along with a repeat of the *Tannhäuser* Overture. The Baltimore Symphony did not perform Emma Hemberger's musical accompaniment for the anthem because its involvement "was only suggested the day before."

The first season was declared a rousing success and Huber, as the organization's sole manager, received tremendous praise. Huber had budgeted a $1,000 cost per concert and the season ended with a $963 surplus. This surplus was able to help fund a presentation of George W. Chadwick's "Noël" the following December. The Baltimore Symphony continued its popularity and received such headlines as "Symphony Up to the Mark," "Symphony a Triumph," and "Symphony Gives Sympathetic Reading." Its growth elevated Strube's status in the city. Along with Mencken, Strube was a fixture at the Saturday Night Club, an upper-middle-class German social organization. According to Strube's great-grandson Carl Lee, members of the club frequently held goulash-making contests. Lee said that Strube "once blew off the door of his oven [at his house on Calvert Street] because he failed to ignite the pilot light!"

But in rehearsal, Strube was regarded as "stern, formidable, but sensitive." According to his greatgrandson, Strube once

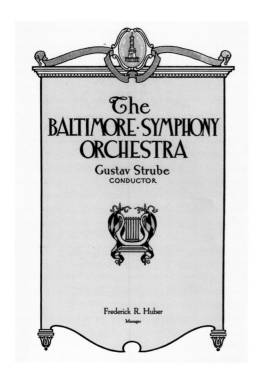

brought a symphony musician to the breaking point as he chastised him for a subpar performance. As the musician grew more upset, Strube told him, "You can't pay attention to me. I'm just a grumpy old man!" Former BSO violinist Louis Cheslock later recalled, "Strube was, above all, a disciplinarian…. Sometimes, during rehearsals, the sounds did not exactly correspond with the score. [I] will never forget Strube's acidity: 'Who is that genius back there?' – or 'my boy, you are crazy!' However, we soon learned that his bark was worse than his bite."

The symphony's mission expanded when the orchestra gave its first out-of-town concert on May 5, 1918, during World War I. Several buses transported the musicians to Camp Meade for a special concert. The musicians volunteered their services and gave a performance of Dvořák's Symphony No. 9 in E minor ("From the New World"). Cheslock recalled, "The attention of the soldiers was surprisingly serious and

quiet. During the famous Largo movement, however, some soft singing was heard from the men in the hall [barracks] to the words of "Goin' Home." The *William Tell* Overture followed the Dvořák and the soldiers became "unrestrained" during the final section: "The burst of cheers, the hearty hand-clapping and stomping of feet gave good evidence of the caliber of the men who were soon to go 'over the top' and win allied victory."

Mayor Preston was overwhelmed by the concert and gave Huber full credit for its success. Preston saw the Camp Meade concert as the ultimate example of municipally-funded music. Two weeks later, Preston appointed Huber as Baltimore's municipal director of music. Huber now had jurisdiction over the city's musical affairs both logistically and artistically. Huber, who had previously worked without compensation out of a sense of duty, reportedly received a hefty salary for this new position. The following spring, Preston did not seek a

third term and was replaced by William F. Broening. Preston had made municipally-funded music a cornerstone of his administration. When he left office, he was given "grateful recognition [for] his valuable services to the cause of music" in Baltimore. Huber worried that the change in city leadership would affect the musical programs. Once in office, Broening took time to study the Baltimore Symphony Orchestra and its structure. He supported the concept of a city-based orchestra but wanted to make sure that "the best interests of the orchestra" were in place. In late 1919, he decided to continue the city's funding of its musical programs and reappointed Huber as director.

Frederick R. Huber was one of the Baltimore Symphony's most controversial figures. Some saw him as a visionary, while others viewed him as self-serving. Huber enjoyed his power and did not want to share decision-making with others. As the symphony grew, so did Huber's control.

Huber was deeply involved in the Baltimore Symphony's artistic needs and managerial duties. He was committed to bringing music to as many Baltimoreans as possible. With his concept of municipal music, Huber found a way for musical organizations to weather financial challenges by being a line item in the city's budget, not totally dependent on ticket sales and donations.

But there was a cost. The Baltimore Symphony's budget remained incredibly small when compared with other peer-city symphony orchestras. The small budget, though, was easier for Huber to manage and control. Over the next decade, musicians and audience members rallied behind the orchestra but wanted artistic improvement. This continual debate weighed on Huber's shoulders for almost a quarter-century.

Opp. Left. Gustav Strube, with the tuba, second from the right, poses with the Saturday Night Club in 1925.

Right. Patrons line up at 8am outside of Albaugh's Ticket Agency on Charles Street during the symphony's early years.

Bottom. The symphony's first out-of-town concert occurred on May 5, 1918 at Camp Meade, MD.

Baltimore Symphony Orchestra -- Camp Meade, Md. -- Sunday Afternoon - May 5, 1918
Leonare Sparkes, soloist of the Metropolitan Opera Co.

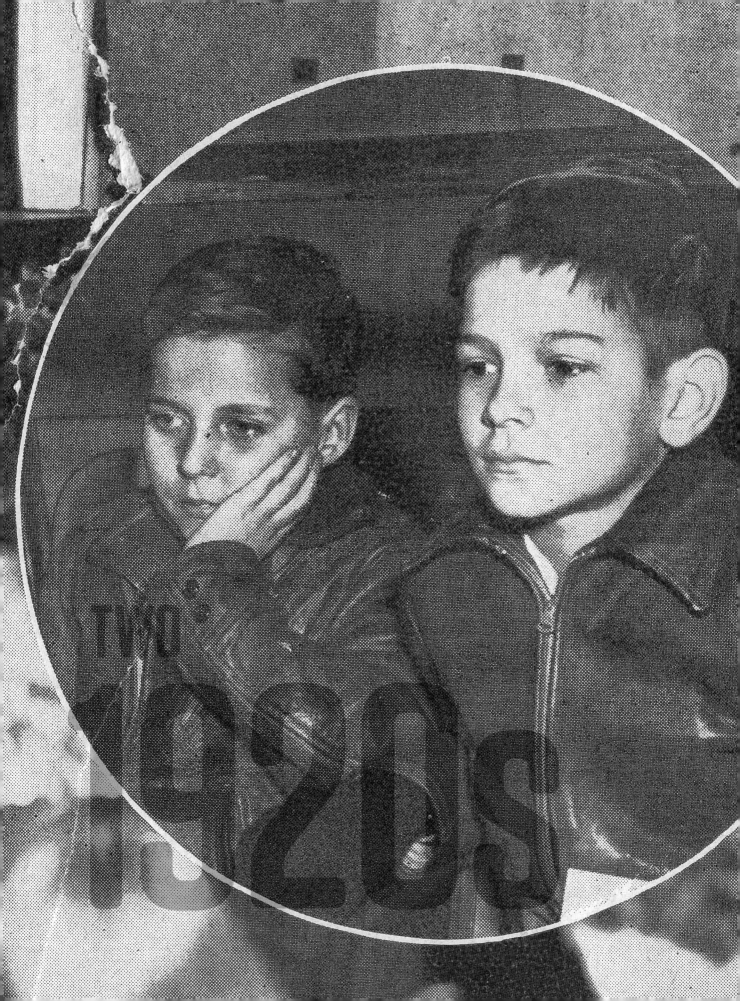

In July 1919, Baltimoreans had waited eagerly for Mayor William Broening's announcement about the continuance of the BSO.

The new mayor questioned the orchestra's current management and structure. The 1919-20 season announcement was delayed for almost two months because Broening needed more time to evaluate the situation. The Sun implored, "If the performances are to be acceptable to Baltimore audiences, the plans must be made at once." Elizabeth Ellen Starr, leader of the newly formed Permanent Committee for the Promotion of Music in Baltimore, asked Broening to at least maintain the orchestra's current standards and structure. The group supported both city music director Huber and conductor Strube, and thought that they should be kept in their current positions. They had organized the orchestra and knew its needs. Starr and her group did not want to see the orchestra's management put into the hands of local government officials.

Once the 1919-20 season was announced in early October, ticket sales were strong. Many people grew angry that they had to wait in long lines at Albaugh's Ticket Agency at Charles and Fayette Streets beginning at 8 a.m., only to be quickly turned away. They questioned how concerts could be sold out in under an hour and why a publicly supported organization such as the Baltimore Symphony did not offer enough seats.

The Baltimore Symphony was now embarked on its eternal journey of balancing financial stability with gradual artistic growth. The city-funded organization was a nationally regarded and admired orchestra model, but its very nature prohibited the necessary financial structure for growth. The symphony's musical leadership and its loyal attendees desired "more extended drilling," through more rehearsing by the musicians. Audiences applauded the "ambitious" programming of the young group, but critics made comments such as this from the Sun: "The brasses at times left something to be desired on the score of smoothness."

On March 29, 1921, Broening approved a plan that could place the Baltimore Symphony in the front ranks of American orchestras. Along with Huber, Broening promised to increase the orchestra's annual budget to $30,000. That would provide for two to three concerts a month and a weekly salary to musicians for six months. Huber said the orchestra should be afforded the same commitment of support as the public baths, which were also operated by the city. Broening and Huber stated that the object of the new plan would be to give Baltimore audiences "the best music attainable and an organization that would be second to none in the world."

This plan met with mixed responses. Musicians were not eager to sign on to six months of salaried work, since many were steadily employed in theaters and motion picture houses. Rumors abounded that city and cultural leaders were not confident in Strube's artistic leadership. The planned increase

Gustav Strube, with cigar in mouth, conducts members of the Sunday Night Music Club.

Strube poses in front of the Washington Monument in the late 1920s.

in artistic commitment also led to discussion of ending municipal stewardship and incorporating the organization.

The plan was never realized, even though city leaders wanted Baltimore to have an "adequate orchestra of its own." Orchestras from Philadelphia, New York, and Boston continued to make regular appearances in Baltimore. The visiting orchestras hampered the local group's artistic credibility in the community and frustrated Huber, who grew concerned that his musicians were growing restless. He said he hoped that "no [financial] demands will be made" by the musicians or "the Baltimore Symphony would be just a memory." The musicians were paid $3 a rehearsal and $8 a concert. Huber noted that orchestras in Philadelphia, Cleveland, Detroit, and Los Angeles were facing financial difficulties.

On Oct. 21, 1921, six musicians refused to perform in the opening concerts – the first labor strife at the Baltimore Symphony. They said they would not work for less than $40 a performance. Their action angered Huber, who thought that "the musicians cannot be replaced and that the orchestra would be unable to function" without [leadership]. All of the Baltimore Symphony musicians belonged to the city's Musical Union, but the union did not have any authority over musician pay and working conditions. Huber canceled the opening concert, and the situation between Huber and the

musicians grew "chaotic." Since the orchestra was under municipal leadership, no collective bargaining agreement was in place. Huber met with the 64 other musicians and gauged if they would work under the previous pay structure. He assured them that the winter concerts could be salvaged and that there had been "no final order of disbandment." On Nov. 7, the six musicians, under pressure from their colleagues, withdrew their demands. The delayed opening concert was performed on Dec. 11.

By 1922, talk of incorporating the orchestra had increased. The mayor initially withheld public support for the Baltimore Symphony while he assessed the benefits of allowing the orchestra to raise independent funds and solicit contributions. Incorporation would let the symphony travel and increase its visibility. Edwin Moffett and Shepherd Pearson, two of the previously anonymous six musicians who had refused to perform the preceding fall, publicly endorsed talk of incorporation, which included collective bargaining. But in the end, Broening decided that the best way to ensure the symphony's future was for it to remain under municipal leadership.

One of the greatest changes to the Baltimore Symphony occurred in October 1922. Huber proposed moving the Sunday afternoon concerts to Sunday evenings. That angered some leaders in Baltimore's religious community. The Rev.

Dr. William H. Morgan of the First Methodist Episcopal Church stated that the move was "just another wedge of the Devil to open things up here." He hoped that "a brick church meant more to Baltimoreans than the BSO." At the time, it was common for Protestant churches to hold services on both Sunday morning and evening. Pastors believed that Sunday evening was a time for religious reflection. Huber enlisted the help of Walter Damrosch, conductor of the New York Symphony Orchestra. Damrosch publicly encouraged local residents to accept the move. He told Baltimore concertgoers that symphony concerts were "spiritual food. … There is nothing like it. It is on par with any church service for the development of the spiritual soul." On Jan. 21, 1923, the Baltimore Symphony made the switch to Sunday evening concerts.

In early 1923, negotiations began to bring Siegfried Wagner, son of Richard Wagner, to Baltimore as a featured guest conductor. Wagner was to tour the United States in 1924. Huber said the engagement would mark "another milestone on the road to Baltimore's musical progress." Wagner's appearance on Feb. 3, 1924, put the city on par with cultural centers such as New York, Philadelphia, San Francisco, and Chicago. City leaders and concertgoers hailed Wagner's appearance, but critics wondered if the concert's popularity was based on his "musical labors or fame." To fund Wagner's appearance, musicians were asked to sacrifice their pay.

Back in 1920, the Baltimore Symphony had begun its educational outreach by holding rehearsals at Baltimore City College. These rehearsals included a discussion from the podium about each of the works. On Nov. 4, 1923, Huber announced his intention to make Baltimore "an artistic center where children from their infancy must be given the opportunity to hear good music, attend good plays, and see good pictures." Huber wanted children to

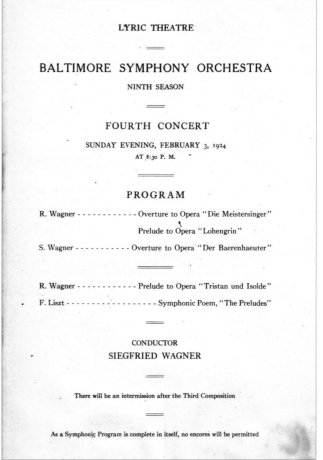

"receive a thorough training in music on entirely new lines." He envisioned concerts "designed where children, even those of no musical training, could understand." These performances incorporated group singing of nursery rhymes with "compositions of various levels of difficulty." The series of orchestral educational concerts was touted as "the first time such a movement has been tried in any city in the world." Huber's vision "to create love and harmony in boys and girls" was realized on Feb. 16, 1924. For only 25 cents, children heard such works as Haydn's Symphony No. 94 ("Surprise"), Mendelssohn's Song Without Words in A major (the "Spinning Song"), and Tchaikovsky's "March of the Toy Soldiers," in addition to the Peabody Children's Chorus. From this point forward, educational concerts and programs became a permanent mission of the Baltimore Symphony Orchestra.

Opp. Left. One of the symphony's greatest achievements to date was the appearance of Siegfried Wagner, son of Richard Wagner, as a guest conductor in 1924. At the time, Richard Wagner's music was one of the Baltimore Symphony's most popular composers.

Bottom. With cases piled in front of the stage, members of the Baltimore Symphony perform an educational concert at an area high school.

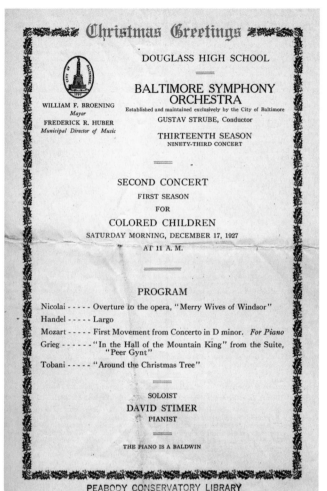

Top. Children's Christmas concerts in 1927 were presented separately for white and colored children.

Opposite. Former mayor James Preston and then-current mayor Howard Jackson sent congratulatory messages to the orchestra on its 10th anniversary in 1926.

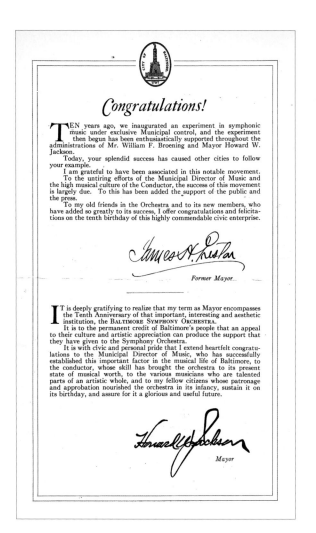

After World War I, Americans experienced a social revolution. The country was eager to develop its own identity and style, and present them to the world. A number of people questioned classical music's devotion to European composers and wanted to hear works by Americans. Since the Baltimore Symphony was a branch of the city government, some in the community wanted the symphony to only perform American compositions. A report in the Sun in February 1924 stated that 90 percent of symphony musicians working in the United States were European: "Europe sees us as unmusical, fundamentally barred from the highest fields of musical endeavor." It noted that since Baltimore was home of the country's first conservatory and musical publishing house, the municipally-funded Baltimore Symphony needed to be more "pro-American" by hiring more American musicians, performing American music at every concert, and becoming an organization that was more "of, by, and for the people."

To appease this emerging sentiment, Huber announced that the final concert of the following season would be part of "Baltimore Week." The concert would feature only works by Baltimore composers that had been "awarded prizes either in municipal, state, or national contests," or had been performed by other large symphony orchestras. According to the published rules, the compositions were to be "strongly tinged with the modern idiom" – as long as the composers "had not gone to extremes, thus making the works tuneless and bad sounding." Works by Theodor Hemberger, Louis Cheslock, Franz C. Bornschein, and Strube himself were featured in the first Baltimore Week celebratory concert.

On Feb. 14, 1926, Baltimore's "musical experiment" celebrated its 10th anniversary. The largest audience in the Lyric Theatre's history attended the anniversary gala concert. More than 800 people purchased standing-room-only tickets to hear an exact repeat of the orchestra's very first program. Soloist Mabel Garrison and 26 musicians who performed at the initial concert joined conductor Strube. Billed as a "Genuinely Baltimore Event," the concert promised "to be a musical event which will live long in the memory of music lovers of the city." Most of the anticipated excitement from this gala centered on Garrison's solo performance. But Garrison was stricken with laryngitis and spent the hours before the concert with ice bags applied to her throat. She issued a statement: "Tell the people out there that I shall try. I can't do more than that. In any other city or on any other occasion I would not appear under these conditions. But this is a special gift. I'll do it." Garrison sang cautiously, but to the delight of critics and the audience.

The symphony enjoyed continued artistic growth and its credibility with Baltimore music lovers increased. The Baltimore Week concert in April 1926 was broadcast live on WBAL radio and marked the symphony's first appearance on the new medium. The live broadcast also featured the premiere performance of "Baltimore, our Baltimore," composed by Emma Hemberger and described as the first municipal city anthem in the country.

LYRIC THEATRE

Baltimore Symphony Orchestra
FIRST SEASON

FIRST CONCERT
FRIDAY EVENING, FEBRUARY 11
AT 8.30

PROGRAM

Beethoven . . . . Symphony No. 8, F major, Op. 93
  I. Allegro vivace e con brio
  II. Allegretto scherzando
  III. Tempo di menuetto
  IV. Allegro vivace

Mozart . . . Aria from "Il Re Pastore." *For Soprano*
  With Violin Obligato

Saint-Saens . Symphonic Poem, Op. 51. "Le Rouet d'Omphale"

Delibes . . Indian Bell Song from "Lakme." *For Soprano*

Wagner . . . . . Overture to "Tannhaeuser"

SOLOIST
MISS MABEL GARRISON

As a symphonic program is complete in itself,
no encores will be permitted
Reprinted from Program Book, February 11, 1916

4

LYRIC THEATRE

BALTIMORE SYMPHONY ORCHESTRA
ELEVENTH SEASON
SEVENTY-FIFTH CONCERT

TENTH
ANNIVERSARY CONCERT
SUNDAY EVENING, FEBRUARY 14, 1926
AT 8.30 P. M.

PROGRAM

Beethoven - - - - - - - - - - - - Symphony No. 8 in F major. Op. 93
  Allegro vivace e con brio
  Allegretto scherzando
  Tempo di menuetto
  Allegro vivace

Mozart - - - - - - - - - - - - Aria from "Il Re Pastore." *For Soprano*
  Violin obligato played by Mr. Van Hulsteyn

Saint-Saens - - - - - - - - - Symphonic Poem, "Le Rouet d'Omphale"

Delibes - - - - - - Indian Bell Song from opera, "Lakme." *For Soprano*

Wagner - - - - - - - - - - - - - - - Overture to opera, "Tannhaeuser"

SOLOIST
MABEL GARRISON

There will be an intermission after the Symphony

As a Symphonic Program is complete in itself, no encores will be permitted

---

A November 1926 performance of Tchaikovsky's Symphony No. 5 received critical acclaim. The Fifth "requires an orchestra of considerable efficiency to give it an adequate production. Last evening was more than adequate. It was artistic and authoritative and manifested the conductor's keen comprehension of the work and his sympathy with the composer's intent," the Sun stated. Guest conductors such as Howard Hanson and Eugene Goossens, along with Beethoven and Schubert anniversary concerts, helped lift the orchestra's local reputation. However, the Baltimore Symphony continued to compete with out-of-town orchestras that maintained a regular concert schedule in the city. With its financial hands tied to the city's fiscal leadership, the symphony was unable to compete artistically with these larger organizations. Its budget did not allow for effective rehearsal time and competitive pay. Supporters of the other orchestras thought that even though the Baltimore Symphony deserved support, it did not possess the "impeccable virtuosity of the larger orchestras of long standing and permanence."

As the sole employee assigned to manage the Baltimore Symphony, Huber began to feel the stress of his role as the city's municipal director of music. When his musician representative, John Itzel, resigned from the symphony in March 1928 and became the supervisor of instrumental music in the city's schools, Huber grew frustrated and resigned from his city post. Huber had recently inaugurated a successful educational concert series for black public and parochial school children at Douglass High School. He thought it was time for somebody else to take on the orchestra position. Broening acknowledged Huber's importance in the community and begged him to reconsider. "I was the mayor's luncheon guest this afternoon. I was deeply moved by the request of the mayor and the tribute of Baltimore music lovers, particularly those who have followed the history of the Baltimore Symphony Orchestra, in asking

Opposite. The programs from the debut concert in 1916 and the 10th anniversary celebration in 1926 were identical in music, conductor, and soloist.

Right. A caricature sketch of Gustav Strube drawn by an unknown artist.

me to remain in office," said Huber. His decision to reconsider was supplemented by hundreds of letters and telephone calls. After receiving community support, Huber reconsidered and remained in his position despite having to "make personal sacrifice."

By the end of the decade, the city had begun to provide more musical opportunities for its "Negro" citizens. The Baltimore Symphony now offered seven concerts a year for white schoolchildren and seven for black children. In October 1929, the first Negro symphony orchestra in the country was formed in Baltimore. Charles Harris, director of the Negro Municipal Band, was hired as its conductor, and Strube served as musical adviser. The Negro orchestra was developed after a series of Baltimore Symphony concerts at Douglass High School. The city felt that the Baltimore Symphony's presence at Douglass "showed that Negroes should have every opportunity to hear and participate in symphonic music." Harris acknowledged that every instrument might not be represented, but said this

would be remedied by having white coaches and teachers develop local black talent. Over the next year and a half, Baltimore's Negro orchestra, also referred to as the City Colored Orchestra, prepared for its debut as another wing of the city's cultural department.

The Baltimore Symphony ended the 1920s with a bright future, and a record of artistic growth and increased visibility and respect. The final concert of the 1929-30 season was deemed "the most successful artistically and in attendance" to date. The Sun praised the orchestra's accomplishments: "The Baltimore Symphony has ambitions and, what is more, is measuring up to them."

THREE
1930s

Baltimore was not immune to the financial and social struggles brought on by the Great Depression. Before October 1929, Baltimore had experienced tremendous growth in population and construction projects.

The Port of Baltimore and the city's varied industries helped create an image of a prosperous yet hard-working community. But the Depression brought the same hardship to the city and its residents that it did to much of the world. Operated under the umbrella of municipal government, the Baltimore Symphony Orchestra did not feel the dire effects of the country's economic woes as much as other symphony orchestras throughout the country. Since it did not rely on ticket sales, public and private donations, and large endowments, the symphony operated on a relatively safe and stable financial footing.

Huber convinced the mayor that no cuts should be made to the city's musical programs. He believed that "music, more than any other diversion, will strengthen the morale and spirit of the community during these trying times." The New York Philharmonic and the Boston Symphony suspended their regular visits to the city, but public programs in Baltimore continued. On May 25, 1930, the City Colored Orchestra gave its premiere concert at Coppin Normal School. The 67 musicians presented a "simple program" but performed "with deep interest and keen zest." This orchestra operated as an outreach project of the city's efforts to reach

out to the city's black population. A $1,000 anonymous gift to the Colored Orchestra insured that it would have a future. The demand for tickets to these concerts was "so great that whites would be excluded from the concerts except for its ushers and attendants," according to newspaper reports.

On Oct. 14, 1930, the Baltimore Symphony suffered its greatest challenge to date when Gustav Strube announced his resignation as conductor. It was reported that he had been unable to negotiate a salary increase, and that he and Huber "parted as friends with no ill feelings." Huber had to quickly fill the position, and he turned to George Siemonn. Siemonn was a former composition teacher at the Peabody Conservatory and was well-known in the community. He was married to the singer Mabel Garrison, a Metropolitan Opera star performer who had been soloist in the Baltimore Symphony's initial concert in 1916 as well as its 10th anniversary presentation. Siemonn had given up his position at Peabody in 1913 to become his wife's full-time accompanist. He reportedly could "play nearly every instrument in the orchestra," and had studied composition, violin, and piano at the Leipzig Conservatory. But Siemonn had never formally studied

Top. George Siemonn poses in front
of the Baltimore Symphony after his
appointment in 1930.

Bottom. A program cover from
George Siemonn's conducting debut.

conducting, and Huber initially announced his appointment
as temporary.

Strube's departure angered many community leaders and
symphony supporters. Some called it "ignoble," "preposterous,"
and "a terrible wrong." Strube had led the orchestra from its
infancy on a shoestring budget. Letters flooded the newspapers
demanding that Huber reconsider Strube's request for a salary
increase, and asking Siemonn to step aside until the dispute
was resolved in the public's eyes. One letter to the Sun stated,
"Mr. Siemonn, with all honor due to you, return the baton to its
rightful owner and claim yourself a noble musician." The pleas
went unfulfilled as George Siemonn soon accepted the position
of conductor of the Baltimore Symphony Orchestra.

Siemonn made his conducting debut on Nov. 23, 1930. Mabel
Garrison joined her husband as the evening's soloist, singing
arias by Mozart, Rubinstein, Mussorgsky, and Tchaikovsky.
Garrison was reportedly "tense and nervous" as she watched
her husband conduct Mozart's Symphony No. 41 ("Jupiter")
from backstage. The concert ended with lavish praise for both
Siemonn and Garrison. Critics hailed Siemonn's leadership
as a "musician without ostentations or mannerisms." As the
season continued, Siemonn remained committed to the

The
BALTIMORE SYMPHONY
ORCHESTRA

George Siemonn
CONDUCTOR

NOVEMBER TWENTY-THIRD
NINETEEN-THIRTY
FREDERICK R. HUBER
Municipal Director of Music

Baltimore City Colored Orchestra

An anonymous grant of $1,000 paved the way for the formation of the Baltimore City Colored Orchestra, the nation's first Negro symphony orchestra. Initially referred to as an "experiment," the orchestra was funded as part of the Department of Municipal Music. Under the leadership of Montgomery County-based band conductor Charles L. Harris, the City Colored Orchestra first gathered in November 1929. Baltimore Symphony conductor Gustav Strube served as the group's official musical adviser.

The orchestra gave its debut performance on May 27, 1931, at Douglass High School. It consisted of African-American musicians of all performance levels, from professional swing band members to Douglass students and teachers. The City Colored Orchestra was an offshoot of the City Colored Band, formed in 1922, and helped in the establishment of a City Colored Chorus in 1932. The orchestra and chorus frequently performed together, and the two organizations played an important cultural role throughout the 1930s.

After the debut, Llewellyn Wilson, head of music at Douglass, took over the leadership of the orchestra and chorus. Wilson has been referred to as "the dean of Negro musicians" in Baltimore. He had taught Cab Calloway, along with *Porgy and Bess* singers Anne Brown (the title role in the original 1935 Broadway production) and Avon Long (Sportin' Life in the 1942 revival). Wilson was beloved at Douglass High, and taught music from his large room on the third floor, often as many as three classes at a time. "He was an outstanding and very comical person," recalls Theadosia Johnson Stokes, a former pupil. "But he didn't like you chewing gum! If he caught you, he'd make you walk to the trash can in front of the whole class while he played a little tune or a march on the piano. It was so embarrassing!" Stokes' father, Harvey Johnson, was the orchestra's principal cello. "He loved the cello and he enjoyed practicing in the kitchen. He was always telling us to get out of the kitchen," she says. Stokes was proud to see her father at concerts, seated right next to Wilson's podium. As a Douglass student, she recalls sitting in on the City Colored Orchestra's rehearsals. "It was part of our classwork," she says. "They used to practice on us and we enjoyed it."

The City Colored Orchestra performed about four concerts a year. Wilson once told the Sun that he chose "the light classics and finer things" for the group's concerts. "We don't use the tawdry kind of music." The group was sometimes referred to as the Colored Orchestra, the Negro Orchestra, or the Race Orchestra, but Stokes says the community called it the Colored Symphony Orchestra. "Their concerts were in the evening and we would dress up. It attracted a lot of people."

By 1935, the City Colored Orchestra had replaced the Baltimore Symphony's concert series at Douglass High because of its artistic "improvement." The orchestra and chorus continued through the 1930s, until Wilson faced pressure from the Colored Musicians' Local 543 of the American Federation of Musicians. The Local wanted the group to be a union organization and insisted Wilson join. He refused, but many of the orchestra's best trained and professionally hired instrumentalists obeyed the Local's orders. As the dispute played out, the orchestra diminished in size and stature, and there is no record of the orchestra past 1941.

The Municipal Department of Music said it funded the City Colored Orchestra, Chorus, and Band because it wanted to make Baltimore "a good place to live in" for its "colored citizens." However, the budgets of the municipally-funded Baltimore Symphony and the Colored Orchestra were by no means equal. In 1935, the Baltimore Symphony received an annual city subsidy of $30,000; the Colored Orchestra, $1,300.

The initial concerts of the City Colored Orchestra clearly stated in promotional material, "No Whites Will Be Admitted." "That's ridiculous," says Stokes. "They never would have entertained coming to these concerts. They had their own symphony orchestra." And in another statement of irony, the Baltimore City Colored Orchestra accepted both women and men into its ranks years before the Baltimore Symphony did.

Opposite. Conductor Llewellyn Wilson stands before the Baltimore City Colored Orchestra at Douglass High School.

symphony's educational mission and its efforts to feature American composers. Siemonn often programmed some of his own compositions, just as many of his successors would do.

After his first season as conductor, Siemonn traveled the world, and researched old and new music that could be introduced to Baltimore audiences. He developed relationships with musicians such as Percy Grainger, Efrem Zimbalist, Carlos Salzedo, and Hilda Burke, a Baltimorean and Chicago Opera star. However, the Baltimore Symphony's soloists frequently overshadowed Siemonn's own musical abilities. The orchestra was praised for its growing "depth and breadth of tone," but Baltimore's musical elite refused to compare its quality to that of the country's largest orchestras. As an arm of municipal government, the symphony had to stay within its "pitifully small budget." At the same time, this meant it "never had to scream for help in meeting a deficit" as the Depression wore on.

The ongoing discussion of public money being used to exclusively support Baltimore's cultural institutions came to a head in late 1932. An organization called the Taxpayers' War Council called for the elimination of funding for the Baltimore Symphony, the City Colored Orchestra, the Municipal Band, and the Municipal Museum of the City of Baltimore, known as the Peale Museum. Over 4,000 angry Baltimoreans attended a City Council meeting on Dec. 7,

1932, at which taxpayers booed and cheered at the proposed budget and its possible changes. Among a large number of contentious items, many were angered about the $40,000 appropriation to the Baltimore Symphony and the Municipal Band. One protester shouted, "It would be more music to my ears to hear that item [music] was out than it was in." Even though Mayor Howard Jackson did not attend the meeting at Baltimore Polytechnic Institute, he remained firm in his commitment to the orchestra. He said, "After 18 seasons, removing the Baltimore Symphony from the list of municipal activities would have been akin to abolishing the public library. Citizens need music as well as street lamps to maintain morale in the darksome night of world distress, as we all move steadily forward toward the dawn of a new and brighter economic day."

By 1933, the country's economic troubles were beginning to right themselves. The Boston Symphony, National Symphony, and Philadelphia Orchestra resumed their Baltimore appearances. As the larger orchestras returned to financial normalcy, the Baltimore Symphony reassumed its second-tier status to its hometown audiences. The visiting orchestras received preference in scheduling at the Lyric, as they needed to make plans well in advance of their appearances, and the Baltimore Symphony's season schedule was always dependent on approval of a municipal budget. The larger orchestras often duplicated their repertoire, and audiences complained about being "Brahms-ed and Tchaikovsky-ed to death." But that proved of little help to the Baltimore Symphony as it fought for artistic respect. When Percy Grainger, the composer and pianist, made a January 1933 appearance, a bat flew over the heads of the musicians and audience at the Lyric. As Grainger performed the Grieg Piano Concerto in A minor, the "flying mouse cut figure eights around the drummer's neck as women [in the audience] kept shelter behind coats, wraps, and programs." The Sun's review praised the bat's performance over the orchestra's. The review stated that the Baltimore Symphony's playing "reminds one of unpainted wood and that the orchestra might do well to visit a local bird sanctuary and lease a bat for all performances."

SUNDAY, EVENING, FEBRUARY 21, 1932
AT 8.50 P. M.

THIRD CONCERT
(SEVENTEENTH SEASON)

Baltimore Symphony Orchestra
GEORGE SIEMONN, Conductor

SOLOIST

CARLOS SALZEDO
Harpist

SALE OF SEATS OPENS
WEDNESDAY MORNING, FEBRUARY 10
ALBAUGH'S TICKET AGENCY
8 EAST LEXINGTON STREET

A program cover from 1932 states George Siemonn as the orchestra's current conductor.

In February 1933, the composer Ernest Schelling guest conducted the Baltimore Symphony in a performance of his fantasy, *A Victory Ball*. Schelling's work, based on his impressions of the World War through the eyes of an American soldier, was timely and well-received. The program also featured the English actor Robert Loraine in a recitation of the Alfred Noyes poem "The Victory Ball," before Schelling's work. After the performance, Schelling gave effusive praise to the Baltimore Symphony and its role in the community. He called the concert "the supreme consummation of all that symphonic music should be in the country," and said he had accepted the invitation to conduct his work because he "had heard reports of what was being done in Baltimore."

"Baltimore is showing a real understanding of conditions," Schelling said. "Orchestral music such as the city is providing is something soothing for the masses, for the people in these trying times. With your museums of art, your university, and the orchestra, you have a center of culture. I had only heard on and off what Baltimore was doing musically, but now, having seen, I shall be a missionary and tell it to the country." Even New Yorkers took notice of Baltimore's commitment to municipal music. The New York Times said Baltimore's yearly subsidy of $26,000 would equal $221,000 in New York when the population of the two cities was compared. It continued, "One wonders if the time has not arrived for Father Knickerbocker to emulate the excellent example of his relatively small neighbor to the south. … [At $221,000 a year] one could even afford a whole season of Toscanini."

In 1934, the City of Baltimore restored a 10 percent salary cut to the musicians of the Baltimore Symphony and the Municipal Band. The cut was made in 1932 to help balance the municipal music budget. Huber pushed the mayor to add more rehearsals and players to the orchestra as the city "returned to more prosperous days." He also sought a budget increase to help fund a greater variety in repertoire. Conductor Siemonn continued on his quest to bring new or lesser-known music to Baltimore audiences. By 1935, Siemonn had introduced Baltimoreans to works such as Strauss' *Don Juan*, Ravel's *Pavane for a Dead Princess*, Griffes' Poem for Flute and Orchestra, and Glière's "Sailors' Dance" from *The Red Poppy*.

George Siemonn, whose enterprise and cosmopolitan scholarship made the orchestra a medium for the introduction of much new music to Baltimore.

FREDERICK R. HUBER, 1935 DISCUSSING GEORGE SIEMONN (PICTURED)

The whole secret
is to make listening
to orchestral music
a recreation
and a pleasure –
never a chore.

ERNEST SCHELLING

Members of the Baltimore Symphony String Quartet, including concertmaster Frank Gittelson and cellist Bart Wirtz, perform in 1937.

Huber announced in late January 1935 that Schelling would return to Baltimore to conduct a March children's concert. Schelling was then well-known for his Saturday morning educational concert series at Carnegie Hall. He also had been presenting educational concerts in the Netherlands, Belgium, and England, and Huber was eager to bring him back. But just before Schelling was to appear, Siemonn abruptly resigned as conductor on Feb. 22. He gave no reason, but Huber stated that his departure "created no surprise." As with Strube, Huber called his relationship with Siemonn "harmonious" with "no discontent" between the men. Two days later, Siemonn led his final performance as conductor. He received several ovations from the audience and the musicians. His final concert brought modest praise for his work, according to newspaper reports. The papers gave equal attention to his departure and his choice of repertoire. His interpretation of de Falla's *El Amor Brujo* was not well received, and Zádor's *Sinfonia Technica* was defined as a "strenuous essay in organized noise."

Within a week of Siemonn's resignation, Schelling made his scheduled return for the children's concert at the Lyric. By May, he had been named the orchestra's new conductor. Schelling came to Baltimore with ambitious plans that challenged the orchestra's budget. He wanted to present more choral works, such as Beethoven's Symphony No. 9 ("Choral"), Brahms' *A German Requiem*, and entire acts

of Wagnerian opera. Though he had previously praised the orchestra's accomplishments, Schelling thought that the limited budget had "not kept pace with the development of the orchestra." He debated the issue of fewer concerts with more rehearsals to improve the orchestra's quality. His official debut as conductor on Nov. 24, 1935, was celebrated throughout the city at luncheons and receptions. The performance featured a repeat performance of *A Victory Ball* and included Tchaikovsky's Symphony No. 5. While critics said the performance of *A Victory Ball* was "poignant and thrilling," they thought the Tchaikovsky "exposed weakness" and proved that "there was still plenty of room for improvement in the orchestra."

Throughout his first season, Schelling was vocal about his desire to improve the orchestra's quality. He got the support of Baltimore's press, which supported his call for more rehearsals and higher pay for the musicians. Schelling and the newspapers continually stressed how orchestras such as Boston's and Philadelphia's had annual budgets "close to $1,000,000," while the Baltimore Symphony's "low-price concerts at the Lyric tapped the city treasury for a modest $25,000 a year." But Schelling received a setback when J.C. Van Hulsteyn, the orchestra's concertmaster since its inception, announced his resignation in June 1936, saying he wanted to concentrate on teaching. Schelling urged him to reconsider, but Van Hulsteyn's decision was final. Schelling told Van Hulsteyn, "[This] means that I lose the most valuable collaborator in the arduous and delicate task of building up the orchestra. … The loss of your sensitive musicianship and great artistry will be a difficult one to bear." Van Hulsteyn's departure was accompanied by rumors that Schelling would not return for a second season, since no mention of the next season's plans was released when the 1935-36 season ended. Huber soon announced that Frank Gittelson, concertmaster of Washington's National Symphony, would fill Van Hulsteyn's vacant chair.

Schelling did return for the 1936-37 season, agreeing to conduct five subscription concerts and five educational programs. The Baltimore Symphony's long-time educational mission was enhanced under his leadership. He earned the title of "Uncle Ernest," as "many a Baltimore child from a family possessing no interest in music became a lover of this form of art through [his] kindly influence." He was praised as the city's "Pied Piper" who led children "into the enchanted land of Beautiful Music, who charmed them not only through the orchestra but through the intuitive rightness of his explanatory remarks, in which he talked with them simply and with many a touch of humor." Due to Schelling's availability, the opening night of the season did not come until Dec. 20, with a performance of Franck's Symphony in D minor and Rimsky-Korsakov's *Scheherazade*.

As the season continued, Schelling began a search for stronger talent. "When [Ernest Schelling] needed a viola player and wanted to find somebody who could play, he hired my mother," says Maurice Feldman. Schelling selected Feldman's mother, Sara Feldman, along with Vivienne Conn as the newest members of the Baltimore Symphony Orchestra. They were the first women to join the orchestra, and their addition was met with protest. Huber initially said he was against their hiring, but the biggest roadblock was with the other members of the orchestra and the Musical Union of Baltimore. "When she joined, the men went on a walkout," says Maurice Feldman. The union, under the direction of Oscar Appel, questioned whether women should be members of the orchestra and whether Feldman and Conn had followed the proper procedures to join the union. Since its inception, all members of the Baltimore Symphony were members of the union, a practice that continues today.

Three other women were also selected for symphony membership, but the union halted their appointment until it was assured that "no male member of the orchestra would be dropped after the women were admitted." Huber could not offer that assurance. He stated, "I reserve the right to suspend any player found to be incompetent." By late January 1937, Huber and the union still had not come to an agreement on accepting Feldman and Conn into the orchestra. Huber said, "Unless the orchestra management has a right to replace a member with a far better one, provided it is a city musician, I can see no other recourse for the organization than to fold up." Local 40 said it would let Feldman and Conn attend only rehearsals until the situation was resolved. Huber disagreed: "The union's attitude against women musicians shows nothing to me as much as a confession of weakness or inability to cope musically with the fairer sex." The women reportedly would not agree to refrain from working with the orchestra until the matter was settled, so the union blocked their membership. Many local women's organizations, such as the Business and Professional Women's Council, the National Women's Party, and the Interprofessional Association, said the women were suffering from "unjust discrimination" and called for a boycott of the Baltimore Symphony.

SYMPHONY PLAYERS THREATEN TO QUIT

Will Walk Out Today If Non-Union Women Take Places With Orchestra

Huber Orders Two Others To Appear For Rehearsal To Meet Emergency

ORCHESTRA CHANGE ASSAILED BY APPLE

Head Of Musical Union Criticizes Replacement Of Two Men By Women

Declares Question Of Sex Does Not Enter Into Controversy

On Feb. 12, Musical Union Local 40 of the American Federation of Musicians called a strike. Several performances were immediately canceled, and Mayor Jackson summoned Huber and union officials to his office. The union agreed to accept Huber and Schelling's demands while the male musicians who had been dismissed to make room for the women were reinstated. The canceled concerts were restored and resumed within the week. And from this point forward, women could be members of the Baltimore Symphony as long as they were also members of Local 40. "My mother did not talk about it that much to us at the time," says Maurice Feldman, a present symphony supporter. "It was her job and she didn't bring it home." Sara Feldman remained a member of the Baltimore Symphony until the 1970s. At the time of her retirement, she recalled, "There was no unpleasantness to me personally [at the time]. Many of the men were just not ready for the change." Feldman helped pave the way for Baltimore's women in the orchestra. Within 10 years, 21 of the Baltimore Symphony's 85 members were women.

Female musicians first appeared on the symphony roster in early 1937.

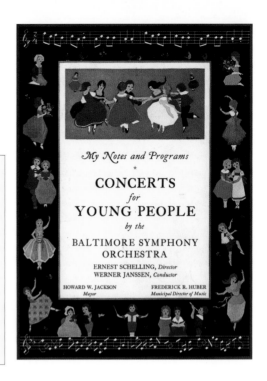

More Rehearsals For The Symphony

An Added $5,000 Is Requested From The City To Improve Performances Of Orchestra—Slice In Brass Band Expenditures Proposed As Substitute

The union continued to play an active role with various ensembles throughout the city. Local 40 worked at organizing the newly created 40-member Women's String Symphony, while Local 543, which represented the city's black musicians, sought to organize the City Colored Orchestra and refused to let any of its members work in that ensemble. Local 40 pressed that all musicians in the city "who play for profit" should join the union, and insisted that all musicians be naturalized citizens. While these demands let the Baltimore Symphony continue its work, they greatly strained relations between Huber and the union. Since the first concert in 1916, Huber, as municipal director of music, had been the sole decision-maker for the symphony. His struggles with the union threatened his power and control.

After plans were set in place for the 1937-38 season, Huber received a message from Ernest Schelling, who was at his home in Geneva, Switzerland. Schelling was suffering from a detached retina and could not travel. To accommodate Schelling, the symphony delayed its opening until Jan. 9, 1938. But the situation was further complicated when Schelling's wife's health suddenly deteriorated, and doctors told Schelling that his need for an eye operation would prohibit travel for at least three months. As Schelling canceled his American engagements, Huber scrambled to find a replacement. He selected Werner Janssen as the orchestra's guest conductor for the 1938 concerts. A former musician in a "Boston Honky

Tonk," Janssen had made his mark conducting symphony orchestras on stage and in Hollywood recording studios. His wife, Ann Harding, was a popular Hollywood actress. Janssen was well-versed in the Baltimore Symphony's structure as a municipally-funded orchestra. "I think the Baltimore Symphony is supported the way it should be, through ticket sales and municipal subsides. I'm not Socialist, but I believe this slightly Socialistic idea is the answer to the orchestra question," he said. After his January debut, Janssen was hailed as "an imaginative colorist, an earnest and persuasive interpreter, and a virtuoso conductor." The Sun labeled Janssen "the conductor of tomorrow."

Schelling officially resigned from the Baltimore Symphony in March 1938, and the musicians urged Huber to hire Janssen as the permanent conductor. Huber wanted that to be his decision and told the musicians they were "hired to play, not pick a leader." But within a few weeks, Janssen accepted the position as the symphony's fourth conductor. He promised that the 1938-39 season would include "musical surprises," such as music by Buxtehude, Marcel Poot, and Walter Piston, alongside performances of solo Chopin études. In anticipation of increased demand for seats, Huber persuaded Mayor Jackson to test a repeat performance of each subscription concert. If successful, attendance could reach 6,000, double its normal sold-out performances. Thus, Sunday evening concerts were repeated on Thursday nights. But, the

A symphony is a municipal cultural undertaking just like a library or a museum. It should be paid for by the city.

WERNER JANSSEN

experiment failed, as only about 1,000 people attended the second night of performances.

Janssen quickly became part of the long list of conductors who grew frustrated by the symphony's municipal structure. Like his predecessors, he wanted to improve quality. He wanted a longer season and a livable wage for the musicians, which would draw better talent to Baltimore. He saw great potential in the Baltimore Symphony, since "symphony management was actually blamed by the public and press for making the symphony so successful" and its tickets thus hard to obtain. The annual budget had reached $30,000, but Janssen would incur an additional $2,000 to the city allocation. After the 1939 season concluded, Janssen was vague about his return for the following season. In an editorial, the Sun feared his potential loss and put out a call for increasing the symphony's budget, artistry, and visibility: "We are hanging on the edge, as it were, of achieving something rather remarkable with our local band. It would be a pity, from every point of view, were we to fail to find the means wherewith to capitalize our hopes."

This time, Huber was "surprised and shocked" when his latest conductor resigned, in October 1939. Janssen said that he regretted the decision but that "there was no justification for my driving the orchestra so fiercely toward a goal which cannot be attained under the present limitations." Janssen's demands and disappointments were nothing new to city leaders, but his resignation forced them to look for solutions. Some called on Peabody to become a partner with the symphony and others thought that the municipal structure was no longer working.

Huber's immediate task, however, was to find a replacement for Janssen. Once again, he turned to Ernest Schelling. But Schelling was unavailable and seemingly uninterested. Schelling had returned to Baltimore earlier in 1939 but as a guest conductor of the National Symphony Orchestra, not the Baltimore Symphony. So Huber next settled on Howard Barlow. In May 1939, Barlow had served as a guest conductor for a special Baltimore Symphony concert for a Baltimore gathering of the National Federation of Music Clubs conference. Following that appearance, Barlow wrote

a flattering letter to Huber that praised the director's "whole-hearted cooperation [along with] the unbounded willingness and the priceless ingredient of emotional expression which your orchestra gave me. ... It is something that I will never forget." His letter made a strong impression and Barlow was hired just one month after Janssen's resignation.

In announcing his decision, Huber called Barlow a man who was "an authority in this field of musical endeavor and is regarded by musicians and laymen alike as one of the outstanding celebrities of our day. ... I know that the orchestra will gain immeasurably in its musical standard and in national prestige under his conductorship." Barlow called himself "a plain American from Plain City, Ohio." In 1923, he had founded the American National Orchestra, which consisted of 75 American-born and American-trained musicians, building on post-World War patriotism. Also, Barlow specialized in American composers, which appealed to audiences and municipal officials as the clouds of war were again gathering around the United States. And unlike many of the previous conductors, Barlow agreed to make Baltimore his permanent home.

Like the conductors before him, Barlow did not shy away from his desire to improve the orchestra's quality and lengthen its season. Even before his official debut, he held open auditions. He pledged to make the Baltimore Symphony the "best orchestra in the country," but acknowledged that it was a long-term goal. His agenda included increasing the season length to 26 weeks and touring. Barlow thought that "a full-length season would improve the orchestra as well as give Baltimore music lovers more for their own musical organization. It would mean better incomes for Baltimore musicians and the orchestra would benefit by the longer association of the artists with each other. This last is essential to a good symphony." Barlow also believed that the community had to remain interested in the orchestra. Tours not only fostered prestige and visibility elsewhere, they encouraged local pride and interest. His initial list of cities for possible tours included Washington, Philadelphia, Reading, Pa., and Richmond, Va.

Top. Kranz Music's store window on Charles Street celebrates the arrival of conductor Howard Barlow and his initial concert on January 7, 1940.

Bottom Left. In 1940, concerts during the holiday season had a 'Season's Greetings' stamp on the program covers.

Bottom Right. Children's concerts, under conductor Howard Barlow, often came with activity booklets for audience members.

The beautiful enthusiasm,
the whole-hearted cooperation,
the unbounded willingness
and the priceless ingredient of
emotional expression which
the orchestra gave me in our
all too brief association was
something that I will never forget.

HOWARD BARLOW

In 1941, Huber helped commission a 25th anniversary booklet called "Baltimore, Cradle of Municipal Music." Written by Kenneth S. Clark, the booklet celebrated Baltimore's accomplishments in its municipally-run musical programs. All city-funded musical organizations, from the Baltimore Symphony Orchestra to the Municipal Band and the City Colored Orchestra and Chorus, had their histories detailed. The booklet documented every work that the symphony had performed and when the performances occurred. The works that had received the most attention since the orchestra's 1916 inception included Beethoven's Symphonies No. 5 and No. 8, Brahms' Symphony No. 2, Debussy's *Prelude to the Afternoon of a Faun*, Franck's Symphony in D minor, Lalo's Overture to *Le roi d'Ys*, Rossini's *William Tell* Overture, and many overtures and selections from Wagner. Noticeably absent were Brahms' Symphony No. 4, Debussy's *La mer*, Dvořák's Symphonies No. 7 and No. 8, Mendelssohn's Symphony No. 4, Schubert's Symphony No. 9, and any works by Copland and Prokofiev. Printed with silver lining, "Baltimore, Cradle of Municipal Music" was highly criticized. Production exceeded the allocated budget and many people thought that the booklet was unnecessary. A booklet from 1932 already existed and was well-known by those interested in the municipal structure. Some thought that this booklet, overseen and approved solely by Huber, was a self-gratifying publication.

MUSIC UNION FIRM, NEXT CONCERTS OFF

Players Cold To Mayor's Plea For New Delay In Black Listing Of Huber

---

Jackson Set To Ask Council To Create Board To Control City Music

---

The Baltimore Symphony began the 1941-42 season on Jan. 11, 1942, with Barlow on the podium in a concert that featured an all-Russian program. But tensions were already escalating between Huber and the Musical Union of Baltimore. On Oct. 1, 1941, the union had raised its pay scale from $5 a performance to $6 for organizations that employed its members for fewer than six performances a week. Huber refused to abide by the pay raise, and called the move discriminatory toward the city. He also accused Local 40 of providing underqualified musicians and using the city as an "employment agency." The letters, which passed through Mayor Jackson's hands, led to the union's pressing charges against Huber and calling for his ouster as municipal director of music. On Feb. 1, 1942, the American Federation of Musicians officially "blackballed" Huber and stated that he must sever all ties with the orchestra, resign from his management position at the Lyric, and leave the board of the local Metropolitan Opera support group. The union also called for "the immediate cancellation of the symphony orchestra's current season."

The third Baltimore Symphony Orchestra concert of the 1941-42 season was performed on Feb. 8, again with Barlow on the podium. Featured was Beethoven's Symphony No. 8, the very first piece ever performed by the Baltimore Symphony, from its 1916 inaugural concert. But ironically, Beethoven's Eighth Symphony would mark the final concert of the municipally-run symphony. The union and Jackson agreed that all future concerts were canceled until further notice.

The battle between Huber and the union played out in the press during the next few months. Many decried the union's demand for Huber's removal and cited his quarter-century commitment to municipal music. The union blamed Huber as tainting the public's view and perception of it. Jackson quickly established a new Municipal Department of Music, and studied Huber's actions and job description. The new music board discovered that Huber's contract with the city had expired in 1939. His position then was essentially eliminated. The board also believed the structure established and governed solely by Huber had become archaic. At this point, the municipally-funded "experiment," the Baltimore Symphony Orchestra, was officially disbanded.

In September 1941, Reginald Stewart moved from Toronto to Baltimore and became the new director of the Peabody Conservatory.

On his first day at work he told reporters, "My first job will be to learn the musical situation in Baltimore." Stewart was charged with strengthening Peabody's role in the community. He thought that Peabody should be "the center of all musical activity in the city and that all the musical forces should be coordinated as much as possible." Peabody had an excellent foundation in the community, he said, but he wanted to build on it.

His first collaboration with the Baltimore Symphony Orchestra was as the piano soloist for the symphony's opening concert on Jan. 11, 1942. Stewart, a concert pianist, performed Tchaikovsky's Concerto No. 1 in B-flat minor. But the opening concert of the 1942 season was the only formal evening concert of the 1942 season. The once seemingly ideal concept of municipal music had run its course. As the musicians' union and Frederick Huber reached a final impasse, the Baltimore Symphony ended its 25-year history as the prime example of an orchestra's surviving as a strictly municipally-funded entity. By summer 1942, Stewart was involved in a new project that addressed his desire to strengthen Baltimore's musical community. He was helping to lay the groundwork for a rebuilt and restructured Baltimore Symphony.

In July 1942, Stewart presented the Musical Board of Baltimore with a plan to revive the orchestra. It included income from a combination of subscription sales, private support groups, and municipal subsidies. Stewart thought that this plan could secure the symphony's finances and help raise the artistic product. The board received Stewart's plan enthusiastically, calling it "so constructive and promising with reference to the future of symphonic music in Baltimore that it meets in general the approval of the board." Mayor Jackson threw his support behind Stewart and the plan, stating, "If music is good in peacetime, it is more than ever needed in dark days such as these. This is the beginning of a new era in municipal music." The city promised to purchase tickets, for prices between 35 cents and a dollar, as part of its subsidy.

Reginald Stewart knew that Peabody could receive considerable attention and benefits from a rejuvenated hometown orchestra. Stewart's daughter Ursula Koerber saw her father's passion for the new symphony firsthand. "He loved having an orchestra and he thought that Baltimore should have an orchestra of its own," says Koerber. His grand plan would benefit both Peabody and the new Baltimore Symphony. "He offered many of the [BSO] musicians teaching positions at Peabody, and he felt it was important to expose the new orchestra on tour. It was all part of the scheme of things," recalls Koerber.

The restructured Baltimore Symphony Orchestra was incorporated on Sept. 9, 1942. Formally named the Baltimore Symphony Orchestra Association Inc., the organization's

Top. The "New" Baltimore Symphony with conductor Reginald Stewart, advertised outside the Lyric in November 1942.

Bottom. A Hochschild, Kohn & Co. department store display window promotes the Baltimore Symphony Sustaining Fund in 1943. The fund's slogan was "Symphony Music Maintains Morale on the Home Front."

budget was set at $185,000. Its incorporation allowed for the acceptance of both public and private money in addition to ticket sales. The City of Baltimore pledged $50,000, and about $73,000 was budgeted as earned income through admission fees. The balance was dependent on support groups. This led to the formation of the Baltimore Symphony Women's Association, renamed in 1977 as the Baltimore Symphony Associates.

Stewart, with the assistance of new symphony president R.E. Lee Taylor and Mayor Jackson, said the plan called for an orchestra of 90 "skilled" musicians employed for a minimum of 15 weeks. To address issues of quality and prestige, the announcement promised an "adequate rehearsal schedule that will provide sufficient time for the proper preparation and presentation of each program to be given." The 1942-43 season was to include 14 Thursday evening subscription concerts, five Saturday morning student concerts, and six city-subsidized Sunday night concerts. Stewart told the city that such a structure was "minimal for Baltimore, and … should lend itself to a healthy growth that will make the orchestra more and more valuable to the city from season to season." He then quickly assembled an orchestra that included out-of-town temporary hires and long-serving veteran members of the previous orchestra.

Baltimore Symphony Associates

When Mrs. Richard N. Jackson agreed to assemble a group of influential Baltimore women for tea, she had little idea that the gathering would pave the way for the Baltimore Symphony's most influential and generous support organization. This tea party, hosted by conductor Reginald Stewart on Oct. 7, 1942, was a necessary step in the orchestra's new status as an incorporated organization. As of September 1942, the symphony was able to accept public and private donations for the first time. According to an interview in the Sun, Catherine Jackson had "never organized anything before" and "did not know quite what she was getting into" when she became the first president of the Women's Association of the Baltimore Symphony.

The initial purpose of the association was to enlist Baltimore women in selling tickets for the 1942-43 season. Over the years, the group has evolved, and so has its mission: "To provide an organization for volunteers which offers the challenge and opportunity to become involved supporters of the Baltimore Symphony Orchestra through financial activities."

The group has accomplished its goal through numerous programs: Symphony Balls, the symphony store, Youth Concert sponsorships, and the popular springtime Decorators' Show House. In 1977, the Women's Association accepted men into its membership and was renamed the Baltimore Symphony Associates. From 1977 to 2007, the show houses raised over $4 million for the Baltimore Symphony, and the figure has continued to grow.

"The most important mission of the Associates is the only mission, to fund and support the orchestra's educational programs," says past president Marge Penhallegon. "I joined the Associates because I heard what they did, and I felt that it was important. Through my experience with the Associates, I've learned so much about the organization, and I've enjoyed getting to meet the orchestra, staff, and board members."

Maurice Feldman has enjoyed a long relationship with the orchestra. His mother, Sara, was the symphony's first female musician. Feldman says, "I began volunteering with the Associates in the 1970s as an usher for the mid-week Youth Concerts. As I learned more about the goals of the Associates, I became more involved as a member of the organization. One thing led to another, and in 1999 I became the first male president of the BSA. This was an honor and a challenge, one that I enjoyed and I hope was a benefit to the BSA and the BSO." In 2014, Maurice's wife, Sandy, assumed the organization's presidency. Sandy Feldman says, "Being a part of the Baltimore Symphony Associates has brought a new kind of music to my life. I've been a BSO subscriber for many years, but not until I became involved with the BSA did I have a true understanding and appreciation of what it takes to support an orchestra. I am honored to be a part of an organization that truly makes a difference."

The entire Baltimore Symphony organization relies on the Associates' advocacy and fund-raising. Generations of Baltimore-area schoolchildren have benefited from its Youth Concert sponsorships. In addition to the annual Decorators' Show Houses and Youth Concerts, the Associates sponsor Family Concert Luncheons, Holiday Photo Projects, a 'Music Adventures' education and music appreciation programs, 'Parties of Note' private music gatherings, and 'Tea and Conversation' guest speaker events. The success of the Baltimore Symphony Associates is proof that a group of die-hard music lovers and "a pound of tea" can achieve anything.

THE BALTIMORE SYMPHONY ASSOCIATES

You know how you start
a symphony orchestra?
Buy a pound of tea.

REGINALD STEWART

Opp. Left. C.C. Cappel became
the symphony's first manager as
a non-profit institution in 1943.

Opp. Right. The Baltimore
Symphony on stage at the Lyric
during the 1940s.

On Nov. 19, 1942, Stewart and the newly-incorporated Baltimore Symphony Orchestra made their debut performance at the Lyric Theatre. Taxing the Lyric staff, the capacity audience represented a cross-section of Baltimore. As the Sun reported, "Society matrons elbowed with shop girls; top-hatted, white-tied men mingled with defense workers; professional people, soldiers, sailors, marines, all were out to hear" Stewart and the new orchestra. The concert was delayed by 40 minutes before the orchestra's new manager, C.C. Cappel, welcomed the enthusiastic audience. The ambitious program included Dvořák's *Carnival* Overture, Ravel's *Alborado del gracioso*, Enescu's Romanian Rhapsody No. 1 in A major, Brahms' Symphony No. 1 in C minor, and several arias sung by the Metropolitan Opera soloist Risë Stevens. Peabody professor and historian Lubov Keefer called the event "phenomenal," and praised Stewart's "unflagging energy and resourcefulness."

After its rousing debut, the Baltimore Symphony Orchestra Association was charged to plan and prepare for financial soundness. In April 1943, the organization announced a $150,000 capital campaign that was championed by community leaders and the newly formed Women's Association. Seventy-five teams of women, headed by Mrs. Howard M. Kern, embarked on a door-to-door campaign to raise awareness of the orchestra and solicit donations. But an ambitious three-week campaign timeline challenged the lofty goal. At the end of May, the campaign had raised $100,000, $50,000 short of its goal. Nevertheless, the effort was praised and provided for the symphony's future for the next two years.

After his initial year, Stewart recruited some of the country's best young talent to come to Baltimore and join the orchestra. During Stewart's tenure, now-legendary orchestral musicians such as oboists Ray Still and Alfred Genovese, and clarinetist Stanley Hasty joined the roster. In 1945, Britton Johnson joined the symphony as its principal flutist and remained in that prominent position for the next three decades.

Touring remained a priority for Stewart throughout his tenure. "He felt that it was important to expose the orchestra and take it on tour," says Koerber. He thought that the exposure was not only good for the Baltimore Symphony, but that it also brought attention to the Peabody Conservatory, where he continued to serve as director. However, the first planned tour was canceled due to war restrictions. In February 1945, the Baltimore Symphony made its first commercial out-of-town appearances with concerts at the U.S. Naval Academy in Annapolis and at Washington's Constitution Hall with the violinist Jascha Heifetz. These performances were immediately followed by five concerts in Georgia, South Carolina, and Virginia.

The symphony's exposure continued after it returned home, as it developed a relationship with the National Broadcasting

Co. radio network. And in December 1945, with wartime restrictions ended, the orchestra embarked on a 12-city tour of New York, New England, and Canada. Over the next five years, the Baltimore Symphony performed bi-annual concert tours that alternated between the North and the South, usually for three to four weeks at a time.

The orchestra traveled by railroad, which sometimes meant cramped accommodations and frequent delays. During one tour of Florida, the train was stopped in the middle of an orange grove for hours. The musicians left the train and began picking oranges. Before the train eventually began to move, authorities boarded in search of stolen fruit. No charges were filed, since the officials could not find any illegally picked oranges. About 10 female musicians had stored the stolen fruit in their sleeping berths. The long railroad tours paved the way for the long-standing tradition of poker-playing among the musicians. The Sun reported, "During the ten-hour trip from Elmira to Baltimore, the international [musicians] spent the day playing poker. Russians lost money to Americans; Americans lost to Germans; an Austrian lost money to everyone. But there were no signs of an East-West split."

Top. Symphony musicians take a break during a Florida tour in 1947.

Bottom. Under the management of C.C. Cappel, the Baltimore Symphony actively sought out-of-town engagements. By 1945, the orchestra appeared regularly on the National Broadcasting Company's "Orchestras of the Nation" series.

1833   1897

JOHANNES BRAHMS

During the season 1946-1947 the Baltimore Symphony Orchestra and the Peabody Conservatory of Music will sponsor the performance of all the works of Brahms with the following assisting artists and organizations:

ARTISTS	
ROSE BAMPTON, *Soprano*	November 15 - 4 p. m.
ROBERT CASADESUS, *Pianist*	January 8 - 8:30 p. m. (with Baltimore Symphony Orchestra) Lyric Theatre
AUSTIN CONRADI, *Pianist*	February 28 - 4 p. m. April 12 - 8:30 p. m. (with Stanley Hasty)
ALICE GERSTL-DUSCHAK, *Soprano*	March 7 - 4 p. m.
LEROY F. EVANS, *Pianist*	April 12 - 8:30 p. m. (with Stanley Hasty and George Neikrug)
CECIL FIGELSKI, *Violist*	January 7 - 8:30 p. m. (with Albeneri Trio) January 21 - 8:30 p. m. (with Kroll String Quartet) January 24 - 4 p. m. (with Anna Kaskas) February 4 - 8:30 p. m. (with Gordon String Quartet)

Top Left. A window at the downtown Pratt Library promotes the citywide Brahms Festival in 1947.

Top Right. During its 1947 Brahms' Festival, the symphony advertised its instrumental soloists during the citywide celebration. During the festival, under the direction of Reginald Stewart, every work, symphonic and chamber, was performed at venues throughout the city.

A traditional musicians' poker game takes place on a train ride through New York State during 1946.

The symphony reached a significant milestone in February 1946 when it marked its 30th anniversary. A celebration concert on Feb. 10 paid tribute to three musicians who had been with the orchestra since its initial concert, cellist Bart Wirtz, clarinetist Gilbert Strange, and bass player Edwin Moffit. It also featured an appearance by founding conductor Gustav Strube, and accolades from Mayor Theodore McKeldin and the City Council. The orchestra and Stewart were praised for "carrying the musical message to far-off places – a message that Baltimore is a music center." The 1946-47 season was one of the most ambitious to date, as Stewart announced that the Baltimore Symphony, with the help of Peabody and other Baltimore music groups, would perform the entire orchestral repertoire of Brahms. During the season, nearly 700 compositions by Brahms marked the 50th anniversary of the composer's death. The New York Times reported, "A few alarmed [Baltimore] concertgoers spoke seriously of fleeing into the hills of western Maryland until the whole thing blew over." But the effort was a rousing success, and Stewart received high praise for securing and locating many lost manuscripts, which he had recorded on 35mm film. After the scores were hand-copied by Peabody students, these lesser-known works of Brahms were donated to the Library of Congress.

In October 1946, clarinetist Gordon "Gordy" Miller began his now-legendary five-decade tenure with the orchestra. His first rehearsal was on the day he was married. "We were rehearsing and somebody said, 'You've got to go, you're going to get married!'" Miller recalls Stewart as a nice guy who was "never nasty. He was a big, tall, lanky guy and was a good musician. [Stewart] was interested in increasing the talent of the orchestra." When Miller joined the Baltimore Symphony he performed second clarinet to Stanley Hasty, who later became one of the most prominent faculty members at the Eastman School of Music. "Hasty was an interesting guy to play with and was very cooperative," Miller says. "When he left [the BSO] he wanted me to audition for principal, but I just didn't have it. I was much too humble. I was a schmuck."

On Feb. 5, 1947, the Baltimore Symphony joined the ranks of other major symphony orchestras by making its debut performance in Carnegie Hall. The BSO appeared in Salisbury, Md., the night before and traveled by railroad to Manhattan. But when the musicians arrived in New York for their only rehearsal in the hall, they found that the larger instruments were delayed on a separate train, so the rehearsal was shortened. The Carnegie Hall premiere opened with two Bach transcriptions, followed by Brahms' Symphony No. 3, the New York premiere of *Pantomime* by Lukas Foss, and George Enescu performing the Brahms Violin Concerto in D major. The Times called the "rehabilitated and municipally-supported" Baltimore Symphony "a highly deserving ensemble of musicians who fully carried out the leader's wishes and who neglected not a strand of polyphony or a note in the score." But the review also stated, "That this orchestra cannot expect to match the foremost symphonic bodies of the land is self-evident." The New York Herald Tribune awkwardly called the BSO "a reasonably efficient machine for making music." Despite the critical comments, the Baltimore Symphony returned to Carnegie Hall the following year. On Feb. 9, 1948, under the continued direction of Stewart, it presented Hindemith's Symphony in E-flat, several arias by the Italian tenor Ferruccio Tagliavini, and Ravel's *Daphnis et Chloé*. The reviews were more favorable for this appearance, and the orchestra was praised for its "well-proportioned sonority and competence." But the Baltimore Symphony did not return to Carnegie Hall until March 1965.

CARNEGIE HALL

REGINALD STEWART
Conductor

GEORGES ENESCO
Soloist

Opposite. The Baltimore Symphony with Reginald Stewart perform make their Carnegie Hall debut on February 5, 1947.

Top and Bottom.
Two pages are displayed from the Baltimore Symphony's Carnegie Hall debut on February 5, 1947.

ALFRED SCOTT • PUBLISHER • 156 FIFTH AVENUE, NEW YORK

CARNEGIE HALL PROGRAM 5

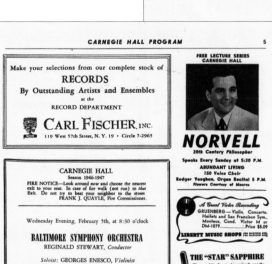

Make your selections from our complete stock of
RECORDS
By Outstanding Artists and Ensembles
at the
RECORD DEPARTMENT

CARL FISCHER, INC.
119 West 57th Street, N. Y. 19 • Circle 7-2965

CARNEGIE HALL
Season 1946-1947
FIRE NOTICE—Look around *now* and choose the nearest exit to your seat. In case of fire walk (not run) to *that* Exit. Do not try to beat your neighbor to the street
FRANK J. QUAYLE, Fire Commissioner.

Wednesday Evening, February 5th, at 8:30 o'clock

BALTIMORE SYMPHONY ORCHESTRA
REGINALD STEWART, *Conductor*

Soloist: GEORGES ENESCO, *Violinist*

•

PROGRAM

Fugue in C major . . . . *Bach-Weiner*

"Komm, Süsser Tod" . . . . *Bach-Stewart*

Program Continued on Second Page Following

FREE LECTURE SERIES
CARNEGIE HALL

NORVELL
20th Century Philosopher
Speaks Every Sunday at 5:30 P.M.
ABUNDANT LIVING
150 Voice Choir
Rodger Vaughan, Organ Recital 5 P.M.
Flowers Courtesy of Macres

A Great Victor Recording
GRUENBERG — Violin Concerto.
Heifetz and San Francisco Sym.,
Monteux, Cond. Victor M or
DM-1079 . . . . Price $5.09
LIBERTY MUSIC SHOPS

THE "STAR" SAPPHIRE
The world's finest phonograph needle tipped with a genuine hand polished sapphire.

DUOTONE
799 BROADWAY
NEW YORK 3, N. Y.
*Unconditionally guaranteed.
Five dollars.*

BALDWIN . . . . TODAY'S GREAT PIANO
Played by today's great Pianists—The favorite companion of Stars of the Opera and Concert Stage.

BALDWIN PIANOS
20 East 54th Street • New York, N. Y.
Serge Koussevitzky and the Boston Symphony Orchestra use the Baldwin Piano exclusively

Pops

It may be surprising these days to realize that the nation's first full-time orchestra was a "Pops" orchestra. In 1867, the Theodore Thomas Orchestra began presenting concerts that featured classical works along with popular music. Thomas and his 80-piece orchestra traveled throughout the country but returned every summer to New York City for Central Park garden concerts. According to the book *Theodore Thomas, an Autobiography*, Thomas performed "compositions of the great classical and contemporary composers to an audience that was drinking, smoking, and often chatting." The Theodore Thomas Orchestra membership eventually merged into the New York Philharmonic, and in 1891 Thomas left to become the Chicago Symphony's first permanent conductor. But in 1885 the Boston Symphony Orchestra had established its own series of concerts of "light classics and popular music of the day." The Boston Symphony "Popular Concerts" moniker was shortened to "Boston Pops" in 1900, and Arthur Fiedler made the series his own in 1930. Fiedler and the Boston Pops gave this concert format an accepted identity.

The Baltimore Symphony performed its first "Pop" concert on Nov. 20, 1949, featuring "popular music and popular prices." Conducted by Reginald Stewart, the orchestra performed "lighter" compositions by Mendelssohn, Enescu, Liszt, and Stamitz. The series was originally performed on Sunday nights, but switched to Saturday nights after just a few years. When Massimo Freccia arrived as music director, he embraced the Pops format and "insisted that good music need not be long-haired." He also frequently presented Pops concerts with repertoire that was audience-selected. "I want to find out the audience's taste," said Freccia. But it wasn't until the end of the 1950s that Baltimore Symphony Pop concerts expanded from classical works to show tunes and movie scores.

"*Pops* means popular music, period," says the Baltimore Symphony's current principal Pops conductor, Jack Everly. "It used to mean light classics, but they evolved over the years because American popular music has evolved." Everly thinks that the current meaning of "Pops" was the result of summer gazebo concerts and artists' recording contracts with labels like RCA Victor that had their own orchestras. "Recording artists had budgets, and musicians like Artie Shaw and

Benny Goodman often recorded with string accompaniment. By the end of the 1950s and 1960s, instrumental versions were often arranged for popular songs. Hollywood music was easily transferable to the concert stage," says Everly.

By the early 1960s, the Baltimore Pop concerts were in transition. Associate conductor Elyakum Shapira preferred to use the expression "music in the lighter vein," and Fiedler hired the Baltimore Symphony to tour the South in 1965 as the Boston Pops Tour Orchestra. But the concerts also proved problematic for the Baltimore Symphony. On March 30, 1963, the orchestra celebrated the grand opening of the Baltimore Civic Center as part of the city's Star-Spangled Festival. Over 5,000 people attended the concert, which featured three Civil War Navy howitzers and dozens of high school trumpeters. Spurred by this success, the following year the symphony tried its own series at the Civic Center. Ticket sales were dreadful and concerts were frequently canceled. A June 1964 concert went on as scheduled with about 3,000 people in attendance. Most had complimentary tickets. The series was a financial disaster for the organization.

Everly was not drawn to the music of the Beatles until he heard Fiedler's recording of their music with the Boston Pops. "I was a classical music snob at the age of 10. I loved show music and classical music," he says, "and I didn't know from the Beatles and I didn't care for the Beatles." The album *Arthur Fiedler and the Boston Pops Play the Beatles* changed everything. He thought, "Good heavens, there's melody here, and I'm sensing the orchestrational possibilities of what a good melody, along with rhythm and harmony, means to a successful orchestral piece. It was a turning point for me."

 BALTIMORE SYMPHONY
POP CONCERT

ELYAKUM SHAPIRA, *Conductor*

LYRIC THEATRE
An American Gala
AN ALL-CITY HIGH SCHOOL CHORUS
DONALD REGIER, *Director*   DOMINIC DeGANGI, *Trumpet*
February 22nd, 1964—8:30 P.M.

Everly believes in the power of song. "I think that people are hungry for a melody. It has always been the case," he says. "Singing a tune is very fulfilling for the soul."

About 1966, the Baltimore Symphony Pop concerts became the Baltimore Symphony Pops. It was a means to capitalize on the Boston Pops' identity and acknowledge the orchestra's long-term relationship with Fiedler. He remained a frequent conductor of the Baltimore Symphony Pops into the 1970s. By the end of the decade, arranger Eric Knight was appointed the orchestra's first principal Pops conductor. Knight conducted the Baltimore Symphony's final appearance at the Lyric Theatre in May 1982, which featured the show music of Kern and Hammerstein.

Pops concerts in Baltimore never fully escaped controversy. In 1980, Sun critic Stephen Cera referred to Pops performances as "a form of cancer which strikes at the musical marrow of our major orchestras." In 1987, a "serio-comic organization" named the Anti-Pops League protested the large numbers of Pops concerts performed by the Baltimore Symphony. League sympathizers wore round buttons that read "Pops" with a red slash through it. The Anti-Pops League also called for the "prohibition of a performance of any piece [of music] that lacked a key signature on each stave of music." But attendance at Baltimore Symphony Pops concerts was already in decline. A name change to "SuperPops" did little to change that.

The decline was only reversed when Marvin Hamlisch joined the Baltimore Symphony as principal Pops conductor in 1996. Hamlisch was already famous for his Broadway and movie scores, including *A Chorus Line* and *The Sting*. In every one of

his four years, attendance percentages increased by double digits. Hamlisch left the position in 2000 for one at the National Symphony. In 2003, Everly became the next principal Pops conductor. Everly had extensive experience as a conductor on Broadway with the American Ballet Theatre, and with the Indianapolis Symphony Orchestra, famous for its Yuletide Celebration.

Everly and Hamlisch worked together on many occasions, usually with Hamlisch at the piano and Everly on the podium. "I saw first-hand how Marvin envisioned Pops concerts, and I learned so much," he says. "I always envied Marvin's spontaneity and humor, needless to say his artistry as a composer." One of Everly's earliest successes in Baltimore was a Celtic celebration that featured the late addition of Mayor Martin O'Malley and his band. Even though the concert became somewhat of a "three-ring circus," Everly kept things moving and flowing: "In the end, it all made sense and we got it done."

Though Everly has spent much time developing programs through his Pops Consortium, he feels that conductors are not interested in studying Pops concerts: "Everybody thinks that they can do it, but only through experience do they find out if they can or can't." For him, it's about having fun and performing good melodies. Pops audiences are starved for melodies, and Everly's love of the genre, especially from early exposure to albums like Fiedler's *Jalousie* with the Boston Pops, comes through in his programs. But he stresses one feeling above all others when it comes to a successful Pops program: "It's always in how you do it. It's all in how you present it." That's show business.

Top. Reginald Stewart greets composer Igor Stravinsky in an undated photo.

Bottom. The Pratt Library advertised an all-Mendelssohn program by the Baltimore Symphony in 1947, which celebrated the centenary of the composer's death.

Opposite. After establishing itself as a private entity in 1942, the Baltimore Symphony made frequent urgent appeals for funds by the mid 1940s.

After the two successful Carnegie Hall appearances, and touring programs that brought the orchestra to at least 30 cities annually, the Baltimore Symphony began to suffer from deteriorating financial conditions. A $100,000 fundraising campaign in early 1948 only raised $70,000. Mayor Thomas D'Alesandro, Jr. pleaded to the public for support, saying, "Surely, there must be many Baltimoreans, many Marylanders, who for one reason or another have not been approached concerning the financial needs of the Baltimore Symphony Orchestra. Now is the time for them to come forward." To address the financial challenges, symphony manager C.C. Cappel and Mayor D'Alesandro amended an agreement in April 1948 with the Musical Union and shortened the 1948-49 season by three weeks. These turnaround efforts were further complicated when Cappel died suddenly just days after the amended agreement was signed. In December 1948, the Baltimore Symphony launched its "Save the Symphony" campaign. The $150,000 emergency fundraising drive was necessary to guarantee a 1949-50 season. But by early February, only $14,000 had been raised and management discussed disbanding the organization.

On Feb. 14, 1949, the board of directors unanimously approved a resolution calling for the establishment of a civic committee that would operate the organization, in exchange for the board members' resignations. The members felt that they had become ineffective in fundraising, and urged business and civic leaders to come forward. Charles S. Garland, president of Baltimore's Association of Commerce, and Robert O. Bonnell, vice president of Fidelity Trust Co., did come forward to lead a new board. Under this new board, the past debt was erased and a new commitment from the Baltimore business community was established.

The year 1949 also saw the second of two tragedies that occurred while the orchestra was on the Lyric stage. Benjamin Sosner, a first violinist, took ill during a performance of Brahms' Symphony No. 1 on Nov. 2, 1949. During the third movement, he left his chair, walked offstage, and collapsed. He was declared dead at Mercy Hospital. Earlier, on March 14, 1946, clarinetist Georges Grisez collapsed during a performance of Gershwin's *Rhapsody in Blue*. He died as he reached the dressing room. Both Sosner and Grisez were helped offstage by violinist Walter DeLillo, and Stewart was the conductor at both performances. After the performance, Stewart said of Sosner's death, "It was awful. I had seen that same pallor before [with Grisez], and I tried not to look." In both instances, the music never stopped despite the onstage illnesses.

By the early 1950s, relations between Stewart and symphony leaders had become strained. In November 1951, Alan P. Hoblitzell, a senior official at the United States Fidelity and Guaranty Co., was appointed as the new president of the Baltimore Symphony Orchestra Association. On his first day, Hoblitzell reportedly pointed to Stewart's name on a piece of stationery and quipped, "We won't be seeing that name around here much longer." Hoblitzell felt that it was time for new artistic leadership. Concert attendance had dropped and people had grown openly critical of Stewart's demeanor. "Some people may have been put off [by my father]," says Stewart's daughter Ursula Koerber. "He spoke with a British accent and acted very reserved." Maurice Feldman recalls one incident that his mother, symphony violist Sara Feldman, had with Stewart at Peabody. "My mother and sister were in an elevator at Peabody and Reginald Stewart came in. Stewart asked my sister, 'Now, young lady, what instrument do you play?' In a straight face, my sister said, 'I play the radio.' My mother was certainly embarrassed but my sister couldn't care less," says Feldman. But some city leaders and board members had grown frustrated with Stewart. Newspapers reported that Stewart earned a salary of $34,000 through his duties at the Baltimore Symphony and Peabody Conservatory. People complained that he earned more than the mayor and the superintendent of schools, and some members of City Council ordered that he put half of his salary back into the symphony budget.

Reginald Stewart resigned on Jan. 18, 1952. In a letter to Hoblitzell, he said "he was unwilling to continue under existing conditions." Some of the reasons he gave involved the reduction of the season by two weeks, a noncompetitive compensation package that had led to the recent departure of 30 musicians, disagreements with management, and frustration over the continued appearances of visiting orchestras. Though he retained his post as director of Peabody until 1958, Stewart did not make another symphony appearance for almost a decade. In later years, through an article in the Sun, Stewart described the symphony's

situation when he arrived in Baltimore in 1941. "It was a civic orchestra when I arrived, entirely supported by city funds, a 'catch-as-catch-can' orchestra that gave about 10 concerts a year. … It was a community orchestra, but we changed things. There's nothing like daily rehearsals." Part of the change was the result of quiet financial contributions by Stewart himself. He had become the orchestra's second-highest donor. His support helped pay guest artist fees, support players' salaries, and underwrite Carnegie Hall expenses.

In his resignation letter, Stewart had stated, "It is quite possible another conductor with a fresh approach might have greater success." In February 1952, the leadership of the Baltimore Symphony Orchestra Association sought that fresh approach by putting the organization's artistic future in the hands of Massimo Freccia.

FIVE

1950s

In February 1952, the Baltimore Symphony Orchestra Association announced the appointment of Massimo Freccia (clarified as "MAHS-ee-moh Fretcha" in a Sun announcement).

Born in Florence, Italy, Freccia had studied in Vienna, and formerly conducted the Havana Philharmonic and the New Orleans Symphony. In most social and media appearances, his wife, Maria Luisa Azpiazu, accompanied her husband and was almost exclusively mentioned as just "Mrs. Freccia." This Mrs. Freccia was a Cuban heiress and former cheerleader. While the Baltimore News American referred to Massimo Freccia as "the Master of Music," Mrs. Freccia was "the Master of Grooming." After his first rehearsal with the orchestra, a female violinist told the Sun that the conductor was "very sharp," referring to his attire. After rehearsals, Freccia stated that he enjoyed spending his evenings with Mrs. Freccia, who recited Shakespeare, Proust, and Balzac.

Freccia made demands on his players and the management. "I don't cue in the players," he said. "I just look at them and they know they have to come in." Violinist Raffaele Faraco recalls that Freccia would come off the podium during rehearsals and stand by musicians who he thought were making mistakes. "He wanted to know where it was coming from, " says Faraco. Clarinetist Gordy Miller remembers Freccia's often-used comment, "You must get it, you must get it!" After Freccia's debut performance on Nov. 5, 1952, Sun critic Weldon Wallace stated, "The Baltimore Symphony has never sounded like this before. The strings were radiant, the brasses were clear. … All sections were united in the creation of expressive sound." To meet Freccia's wishes, management increased the season to 20 weeks, including 13 Wednesday evening performances, 10 Sunday afternoon popularly-priced performances, and 12 children's concerts.

The following year, he urged the management to move the Sunday afternoon concerts to a Saturday evening series. But following a successful start, interest fell dramatically after the initial two performances. The Baltimore Symphony Women's Association took charge of helping Saturday evening concert sales. Groups of women went throughout their neighborhoods and to community organizations with stacks of tickets. Other members of the association acted as concert hostesses for the Saturday evening series. Stationed at the Lyric's doors, these hostesses helped "introduce people, answer questions, and make everybody feel welcome." Through their coordinated efforts, the Women's Association helped raise Saturday evening single-ticket sales from 434 individual seats sold per concert in 1953 to 1,888 in 1954.

Because of his international profile, Freccia was able to attract a consistently higher caliber of soloist compared with Reginald Stewart's tenure. In the 1953-54 season, Freccia engaged soloists such as the singer Eleanor Steber, the pianist Rudolf Serkin, the violinist Joseph Szigeti, and a young pianist named Leon Fleisher. Mistakenly advertised as a violinist, Fleisher made his Baltimore Symphony debut in March 1954. It marked the beginning of a relationship of

I will give all my energy and knowledge as an artist to make it a success. But I cannot do it alone. I need your full enthusiasm and love for music which I know you have.

MASSIMO FRECCIA

more than six decades between the pianist and the orchestra. Fleisher performed the Brahms Piano Concerto in B-flat major with Freccia as the conductor. Sun critic Wallace stated that Fleisher "met the requirements [of the concerto] admirably. In toto, however, this was a presentation one would expect from a player twice his age."

"Twice his age'? What was I, 10? I was just a kid, a teenager," Fleisher says in reflection. "Wallace was the editor of the religion page and they put him on music. I don't remember any of his reviews on Jesus or anything." But Fleisher recalls Freccia quite clearly. "Freccia was the essence of Italian, with an explosive personality. He was all spirit, *con spirito*, but not too profound. I was fascinated by him. I was quite young at the time and he seemed in a certain sense the embodiment of a certain type of conductor with his personality." Former principal oboist Wayne Rapier felt differently about Freccia, even when compared with Stewart. Rapier left the orchestra after Freccia's tenure for positions in the Philadelphia Orchestra and Boston Symphony. He had told the Sun, "Most of the players had the feeling that the board hired Freccia because he was flashier. But Freccia knew only about three programs and was over his head once he got beyond that. Stewart was always well-prepared and the repertory was large. Freccia was just passing through; Stewart really cared."

By 1954, the Baltimore Symphony was again experiencing hardship. An attempt to form a 200-voice Baltimore Symphony Chorus, under the direction of James Allen Dash, took away time and resources. The chorus failed to become "an integral part of the entire community" and disbanded after its initial performance in 1954. In its 1954-55 annual report, the symphony board stated that it could not continue operations unless its finances dramatically improved. The report stated, "With its existing deficit the credit of the Association is in jeopardy and its creditors risk loss of monies due. This is a situation to be deplored. It reflects adversely upon our entire community. Should the orchestra have to disband, that fact would be at once publicized across the entire United States. The city will have lost one of its fine assets and the loss will not likely be recouped in many years to come."

In addition, the orchestra was facing challenges from new technologies. Television and advanced radio systems competed for entertainment time and dollars. One board member threatened to solve the orchestra's money woes by reducing the number of musicians by one-third, scheduling works of smaller size such as those by Mozart, Beethoven, and possibly Brahms, and amplifying the orchestra to boost its sound. But technology also helped the orchestra. A seven-hour radio-thon on WWIL hosted by Gov. Theodore McKeldin helped raise awareness of the symphony and much-needed funding. The orchestra even invested in a shortwave tuning receiver. One symphony manager stated, "As long as the tuner is in working order, the orchestra will always have absolute pitch, even if all of the oboe players fail to show up for the concert."

You are cordially invited
to attend the
Fortieth Birthday Celebration
of the
Baltimore Symphony Orchestra

Sunday, the nineteenth of February
Nineteen hundred and fifty six
at three o'clock in the afternoon

Baltimore Museum of Art
Wyman Drive
Baltimore 18, Maryland

Musicians show off their new concert attire. From left to right: Remo Bolognini, Dean Farnham, Charlene Hecker, Evelina Martini, Sylvia Shor, Dorothy Gennusa, Stanley Petrulis, and Ignatius Gennusa.

Members of the Baltimore Symphony Woodwind Quintet pose for the camera in the late 1950s.

But perhaps one of the greatest benefits from technology was achieved through the assistance of Freccia. He helped devise a plan between the Baltimore Symphony and various boards of education, along with WITH-FM, that brought taped concerts into classrooms. More than 300,000 schoolchildren would benefit from the symphony's educational programs at no cost to the schools. All funding was secured through sponsorships that preserved the orchestra's bottom line. The plan did not solve the revenue shortfalls, but it did bring in needed resources – and much-needed attention throughout the entire state. The orchestra's "Adventures in Learning" series became a fixture in Maryland classrooms.

In a surprise announcement, Freccia announced his intention to retire at the end of the 1955-56 season. He declined to state his reasons and said only that he was not going to make any more "permanent plans" in Baltimore. Behind the scenes, the symphony's board learned that Freccia had struggled with management. His relationship with orchestra manager Robert MacIntyre had grown toxic. Freccia also had grown tired of the orchestra's financial concerns amid his own desire for a raise. The Sun acknowledged this issue through an editorial that asked, "[One] must wonder from time to time whether the struggle to maintain the orchestra is worth it. … This new crisis is only one of a series that stretches back a long way."

To appease Freccia, the symphony board removed MacIntyre, one of a long line of managers who only stayed for about a year at a time throughout the 1950s. The Sun celebrated this decision and noted, "The orchestra is a lot more durable than its chronic financial ill health seems to indicate."

On Jan. 27, 1956, Mayor Thomas L. J. D'Alesandro Jr. invited more than 200 businessmen to an emergency breakfast meeting. He wanted to "avoid civic disgrace" should the orchestra disband. By the end of the meeting, the mayor had sold $60,700 in $100-a-plate dinner tickets. Gov. McKeldin approached legislators in Annapolis, who reluctantly gave an added $50,000 appropriation to the symphony. These measures encouraged Freccia to reconsider. On Feb. 19, 1956, Freccia helped celebrate the Baltimore Symphony's 40th birthday at the Baltimore Museum of Art. The two-and-a-half-hour event featured dignitaries and personalities from the organization's past, such as Frederick Huber, Mabel Garrison, Werner Janssen, and members of the families of Gustav Strube and Mayor James H. Preston. Instead of a large concert, the celebration included a short recital that featured works by the composers from the orchestra's debut concert: Beethoven, Saint-Saëns, and Wagner. The Women's Association played a large role in the event's planning.

For most of his tenure, Freccia programmed works that he deemed "salable." He once said, "I have to think of my symphony board. They give me a free hand but I don't want to bankrupt them." The symphony frequently performed works by Tchaikovsky, Beethoven, Strauss, and Gershwin, and rarely presented any "modern" works or premieres. Freccia said that he was baffled by Baltimore audiences and shrugged that the city would not support concert opera "to any great extent." He said in a 1957 Sun interview, "From the broad point of view, the temperature of success is the box office. Therefore, the opera [*Cavalleria rusticana*] was a fiasco." He quipped that Mascagni should not be a difficult composer to enjoy, but noted that "his music requires a little mental effort, but so does a serious book. You can't read only magazines." Freccia wanted to schedule Mahler's Symphony No. 2, but believed that it would be a financial disaster. The Mahler, he said, "is not something you might want to hear often. It is not our daily bread. It is not important enough. But it should be heard once in a while."

In October 1957, Freccia decided not to renew his contract. In a letter to board president Dr. C. Bernard Brack, Freccia wrote, "In view of the many offers which I am receiving for guest conducting engagements throughout the year, I am afraid it would be impossible for me to commit myself to accept the position of music director and conductor of the Baltimore Symphony Orchestra next year. … I feel that the time has come when I should broaden my scope of activities and take advantage of the many opportunities I have been receiving to conduct the major orchestras of Europe." His decision was accepted "with regret," and Freccia accepted the title of musical adviser to the Baltimore Symphony's 1958-59 season. He agreed to conduct the first six weeks, and line up guest conductors and soloists. This gave the orchestra board time to find the next music director.

That director would be Peter Herman Adler, the symphony announced in October 1958. Adler was a conductor with the NBC *Opera Theatre* television program and had appeared several times with the Baltimore Symphony. Sun critic

Massimo Freccia

On behalf of the Baltimore Symphony Orchestra Association, I wish to express to MR. MASSIMO FRECCIA the sincere appreciation of the Symphony Association for his fine accomplishments as Music Director and Conductor of the Baltimore Symphony Orchestra.

Under Mr. Freccia's leadership the Baltimore Symphony Orchestra has grown in artistic stature and is now recognized as one of the major symphonic organizations in the United States. We are proud of the acclaim our Orchestra has received both at home in Baltimore and on tour, and we are grateful to Mr. Freccia for the splendid contribution he has made to the musical life of our City and State.

The Symphony Association cordially extends to Mr. Freccia its sincere best wishes for continued success in his distinguished musical career.

C. Bernard Brack, M.D.
President

Left. After Massimo Freccia announced his departure in 1958, the Baltimore Symphony Association publicly thanked him for his musical contributions and wished him continued success.

Opp. Left. The Baltimore Symphony performed an all-Gershwin program on December 14, 1958. The event was free to all those who purchased Israel Bonds from November 1 to December 14, 1958.

Opp. Right. Throughout the 1950s, the Women's Association of the Baltimore Symphony Orchestra presented a series of free chamber music concerts at the Enoch Pratt Free Library. Those concerts were funded in part by the Music Performance Trust Fund in cooperation with the Baltimore Music Union, Local 40.

Wallace called Adler "musicianly, suave, and sympathetic." For his part, Adler stated that the Baltimore orchestra was "remarkable" and "growing in quality and spirit." Pianist Leon Fleisher remembers Freccia as "explosive" and Adler as "energetic." He recalls, "Adler was an opera conductor and that was his great credit. He was always looking for big singers. He discovered Mario Lanza." Freccia said Adler "will be a wonderful acquisition for the musical life in Baltimore." But first it was time for Baltimore to say goodbye to Freccia. His final scheduled appearance was a performance of Richard Strauss' *Elektra*. The two-hour concert opera was seen as a gift from the board to Freccia, who frequently grew frustrated over his limited choices for repertoire. The performance on Nov. 26, 1958, took months to plan, but was a "triumphant" success and a fitting end to Freccia's tenure. Freccia planned to stay in Europe for the next three years and would not return to America for some time. When asked what he would miss most about Baltimore, he said, "Maryland shad roe and terrapin."

Before he arrived in Baltimore, Adler announced that the symphony had been guaranteed a three-week concert tour in spring of 1960. "This development is important for the prestige of the symphony," he said. "This is the first national publicity received by the local orchestra since the days, three years ago, when its financial crisis received wide notice and its future looked shaky." He believed that touring would tell national audiences and followers that the Baltimore Symphony was flourishing. His debut as music director was on Oct. 14, 1959. A capacity audience at the Lyric gave Adler a "warm" response. Wallace wrote in the Sun, "There is a certain rugged simplicity about his manner. He is a grandfatherly kind of figure and he applies himself to the music without concern for personal aggrandizement and with the kind of respect for the music that any fine craftsman shows for his material. The audience seemed to be with him." That review conveyed more than perhaps even Wallace knew. Adler was committed to building and promoting the Baltimore Symphony, but over the next several years his baton technique tended to get in the way.

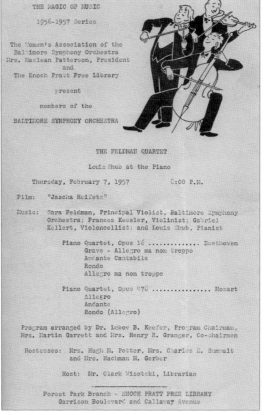

SIX
1960s

Peter Herman Adler brought a wealth of experience in conducting opera to the Baltimore Symphony.

He had spent 10 years as artistic director of the NBC Opera Symphony Orchestra, working at the network on artistic matters alongside the famed Arturo Toscanini, conductor of the NBC Symphony. Though he was "recognized as an international authority in the field of televised opera," Adler's success in that field overshadowed his work as a symphony orchestra conductor. Some musicians recalled his conducting style as "spastic," "strange," and "inept," while others saw him as a "nice, likable guy."

In April 1960, Ralph Black was hired as the new manager of the Baltimore Symphony after Betty Danneman resigned. A former manager of the National Symphony in Washington, Black brought a wealth of experience and knowledge to the post. He had worked on President Dwight D. Eisenhower's music committee and was an active leader with the American Symphony Orchestra League. "I'm an absolutely firm believer that if you get enough people coming to hear concerts, you will get support for an orchestra," he said. "They will help not because it's a chore but because they really want to. The emphasis should be on people before dollars." Black's enthusiasm helped offset any concerns regarding Adler's artistic leadership. Within one year of his arrival, Black, along with symphony board members and an emergency committee headed by Theodore Wolfe, had raised over $154,000 and erased the orchestra's debt. Black commented that due to the committee's efforts, "the orchestra would never again have to cry Wolfe."

Adler relied on the symphony's principal players to help him prepare for rehearsals and concerts. "He invited principal winds and string players to come to his apartment and rehearse with him," says Bonnie Lake, a flutist who served from 1957 to 2005. "Adler was really an opera conductor, and he was learning [the repertoire] with their help." Clarinetist Chris Wolfe states, "Adler made a big deal over the principal players. He gave them parties. He was a nice guy. But he couldn't conduct." Former principal oboist Joseph Turner recalls, "The principal woodwind players had an addendum in their contracts that they would contribute a certain amount of their services for youth concerts. But it also gave Adler the chance to go over their parts before every subscription concert. The principal strings met with him and went over bowings, but he just practiced conducting with the woodwinds. I remember one time meeting with [Adler] before a Bach *Brandenburg No. 1* performance, and it was just myself and [principal horn] Bob Pierce!" Turner also recalls one out-of-town concert when Adler accidentally stepped off the podium during a Brahms symphony and lunged into the orchestra. "Most people were so oblivious [to his conducting] that they didn't even notice."

Two musicians whom Adler particularly depended on were flutist Britton Johnson and clarinetist Ignatius Gennusa. Both had studied at Philadelphia's Curtis Institute of Music and served long tenures with the orchestra. "Adler gave Brit Johnson the chore of running the wind section," says clarinetist

Peter Herman Adler
conducts the BSO.

Wolfe. Joe Turner, an oboist and Johnson's stepson, says Johnson became the leader of the woodwinds "by virtue of his seniority, ability, and personality. He came within a whisper of William Kincaid's job" in the Philadelphia Orchestra. But Wolfe adds, "Brit was a good player, but he was very difficult to get along with. There was always conflict between Iggy and Brit. We had to stop a couple rehearsals because they were fighting about intonation or something. [Brit] was like this all the time. It used to drive us nuts."

"Iggy" Gennusa was widely admired as principal clarinetist. He belonged to the same legendary group of clarinets as Anthony Gigliotti, Mitchell Lurie, and Harold Wright, and was the Baltimore Symphony's principal clarinet from 1951 to 1970. After leaving the orchestra, he kept his teaching position at Peabody until 1993. Gennusa's reputation was well-known throughout the musical world. His longtime second clarinet colleague at the Baltimore Symphony, Gordy Miller, states, "Iggy was a great guy. If he had a brain, he'd be dangerous!"

In January 1961, Leopold Stokowski was scheduled to make his debut as a guest conductor with the Baltimore Symphony. Stokowski had appeared in Baltimore on numerous occasions as conductor of the Philadelphia Orchestra. In the early 1960s, the Philadelphia Orchestra maintained a 10-concert series at the Lyric. "It's amazing that we even existed with [the Philadelphia Orchestra] in town," says Wolfe. "But the only time we had toilet paper in the Lyric was when Philly was in

Trombonist John Melick, violinist Zoltán Szabó, and English horn player George Aranow warm up backstage at the Lyric in October 1960.

town." Stokowski canceled his January 1961 appearance due to illness and was replaced at the last minute by former music director Reginald Stewart. It was Stewart's first appearance with the orchestra since he left in 1952, and also his last. His "sweeping arms" and "long-stretched fingers," never again returned to the Lyric stage. But Stokowski did return, to conduct the symphony in February 1962 for a series of performances. The board and management were taken by Stokowski's presence. After his initial rehearsal, Stokowski said there was a need for seven additional string players to achieve a better balance among instruments. Critics praised Stokowski's appearances for "rich vibrant sounds and subtle shades of golden sonorities," and an "elegance of rhythm and subtle immediacy of response to Stokowski's slightest desire."

These statements were in sharp contrast to the sentiment about Adler's characteristically pedantic performances. One letter to the editor in the Sun read, "The Baltimore Symphony is a third-rate ensemble which is generally heard in a poor acoustical environment while playing under a man adequately equipped with neither conductorial technique nor musical sensitivity." When Adler's three-year contract expired in 1962, the board of directors hesitated. Adler wanted a raise, but the board wanted Stokowski. "There was talk that Stokowski might come to replace Adler," says flutist Bonnie Lake. "Adler signed his contract just minutes before a midnight deadline." He got an undisclosed pay raise, but the one-year contract put him on notice, and the board and management made certain that Stokowski remained on the guest-conductor roster. Wolfe recalls, "Stokowski was a man of very few words. He'd conduct with his finger and just say, 'Do better, do better.' That's all he would say." Over the next 10 years, Stokowski was a frequent guest conductor at Baltimore Symphony concerts. The one casualty from the Adler contract was symphony manager Black. Adler convinced some of his loyal board members that they had to choose between the men. He had the votes, and Black moved on to become a celebrated author and leader in the orchestral world.

While the relationship with Stokowski helped address some artistic concerns, the Baltimore Symphony remained plagued by continual financial challenges. A board advisory committee

Audience-favorite and assistant conductor Elyakum Shapira appears shortly after his hiring in 1962.

Popular principal clarinetist Ignatius N. "Iggy" Gennusa was a driving artistic force in the orchestra from 1951 to 1970.

produced a document titled, "Do We Want a Major Symphony Orchestra in Baltimore?" It saw no immediate doomsday scenario, but said Baltimore needed to make a better financial commitment to the orchestra to improve its quality and reputation. It stressed the need to improve public and private contributions and endowment size. "There are some who say it can't be done in Baltimore," said the board report. "'We're a branch-plant town,' they say, 'we don't have the resources they have in Detroit, Cleveland, or Pittsburgh.'" At $625,000, the Baltimore Symphony had the 12th highest budget of American orchestras. But that was only about one-fourth the size of the Boston Symphony's budget. In the end, the document helped develop a strengthened donor program.

In 1962, the Peabody Conservatory hosted the Peabody Ford Foundation American Conductors Project. The Baltimore Symphony served as the resident orchestra for the workshop. A young conductor named Elyakum Shapira, "a heavy-set and gregarious" native of Tel Aviv, Israel, captured the attention of Peter Herman Adler. Shapira was named the symphony's new associate conductor in July 1962. Shapira had studied with George Szell, Eugene Ormandy, Leonard Bernstein, Max Rudolph, and Alfred Wallenstein, director of the Ford Foundation workshop. Symphony leadership took notice of Shapira. The symphony still supported Adler as its "permanent conductor"; Shapira was assigned to the youth and pops concerts, also known as the "Saturday Series." At his introductory news conference, Shapira said, "I think students are able to understand any piece of music. [The youth concerts] are shorter, so you must use shorter words to explain it, but with the right preparation, they will understand." However, Shapira was not known for accessible youth concerts. "He just wanted to learn the repertoire. The kids just fell asleep," says clarinetist Miller. Shapira "thought too much of himself," says Wolfe. "We'd do the whole *Daphnis et Chloé* for kids. It was horrible." Shapira continued as associate conductor until 1967, when he left to pursue guest-conducting opportunities – and relieve himself of conducting youth concert programs.

Principal flutist Britton Johnson speaks to a colleague during a rehearsal.

	Exhibit III	
	COMPARISON OF	
	BALTIMORE SYMPHONY ORCHESTRA'S BUDGET	
	FOR 1961-62 SEASON WITH ACTUAL 1960-61 DATA	
	FOR EIGHTEEN MAJOR ORCHESTRAS	

(In Thousands of Dollars)			Income from Contributions, Benefits, Endowments, etc.*
In Order of Budget Totals	*Total Budget*	*"Earned Income" as % of Total*	
Boston	$2,178.	84%	$375.
Philadelphia	1,464.	78%	258.
New York	2,009.	65%	706.
Chicago	1,268.	59%	525.
Cleveland	1,120.	45%	618.
National (Washington)	928.	70%	275.
Pittsburgh	812.	55%	339.
Detroit	796.	51%	361.
San Francisco	740.	57%	262.
Cincinnati	683.	49%	350.
Minneapolis	683.	54%	313.
St. Louis	593.	56%	235.
Houston	503.	47%	238.
Dallas	493.	45%	157.
San Antonio	480.	56%	186.
New Orleans	410.	40%	228.
Indianapolis	391.	55%	156.
Kansas City	317.	54%	150.
Average of 18 Major Orchestras	$ 881.5	57%	$318.
Average of 15 Major Orchestras other than Boston, Philadelphia, and New York	$ 681.	53%	$293.
Baltimore (1961-62 Budget)	$ 625.	61%	$244.

* Where figures in last column are less than the reciprocal of earned income percentage, deficits are indicated.

In 1961, the Baltimore Symphony presented this budget comparison chart of 18 American orchestras to a gathering of Baltimore's top businessmen.

Interestingly, the Baltimore Symphony chose to celebrate its 50th anniversary during the 1964-65 season. On Oct. 7, 1964, amid "festive excitement and sartorial elegance," Adler led a repeat performance of the initial concert from February 1916. Numerous dignitaries, such as Mayor McKeldin, praised Adler and the orchestra for its accomplishments over the years. After the anniversary concert, the symphony opened a three-day auction at Mount Royal Station. A black tie reception was held on the night of the concert, at which attendees viewed unusual auction items, such as a rare leopard coat valued at $50,000, frozen ducks, caviar, and celebrity memorabilia. The sale also featured livestock, such as a Guernsey bull and heifer; two trained jumping horses; and a Welsh pony. Organizers were initially disappointed by many low bids, and the auction raised only $25,000, half its goal.

Guest musicians during the Golden Jubilee season included pianists Glenn Gould, Leon Fleisher, and Rudolf Serkin; violinist James Buswell; baritone William Warfield; and conductor Erich Leinsdorf. One of the season's final performances was a concert of 20th century music at Carnegie Hall on March 19, 1965, the symphony's first date there since 1948. Conducted by Adler, the concert featured Theodor Berger's *Rondo Ostinato*, Schoenberg's Chamber Symphony No. 1 in E major ("Kammersymphonie"), and the premiere of Gottfried von Einem's *Das Stundenlied*, based on a text by Bertolt Brecht. The Rutgers University Choir assisted the von Einem work. The New York Times praised Adler for bringing "plenty of zest" to the performance, and gave accolades to the Baltimore Symphony and the Rutgers choir for "matching enthusiasm." However, the Times called the von Einem premiere "wandering" and "indignant but obvious."

This page. Various pieces of ephemera celebrated the Baltimore Symphony's Golden Jubilee Season, 1964-1965.

Opposite. In February 1965, the Baltimore Symphony, traveling as the Boston Pops Tour Orchestra, readies to board a plane in Florida.

By the 1960s, the Baltimore Symphony was spending a significant amount of each season as a touring orchestra. The winter and spring tours had been established under Stewart's tenure. In 1955, the Eastern Shore Symphony Society was formed in Salisbury, Md., under Freccia's direction of the orchestra. Within the next 15 years, numerous "Symphony Societies" were formed throughout the state. Each sponsored a series and had its own board of directors. The Harford County Symphony Society was formed in 1962, followed by Howard County in 1964 and Catonsville in 1966. Other societies were established for Dulaney Valley, Carroll County, Frederick, Northeast Maryland, Mid-Shore, Severna Park, and Prince George's County. The Salisbury series was among the most loyal and successful, but it was the farthest from Baltimore. The Eastern Shore concerts were traditionally held at Salisbury State College's Holloway Hall. On performance days, symphony musicians left Baltimore at 8:45 a.m. for a 1 p.m. youth concert in Salisbury. After the youth concerts, the musicians were spread among four motels, where they could rest and eat before the evening concert. The musicians returned to Baltimore after the performance, well after midnight. "We were always on the road. We lived on the bus," says clarinetist Wolfe. "We all smoked like fiends. You'd get on the bus and, 'Ugh.'" Gordy Miller's wife, Roz, recalls, "They took the top of my sewing machine and used it as a poker table." Both Wolfe and Gordy Miller recall the bus

rides with some fondness, though. "Brit [Johnson] and Gordy shared the same travel trunk," says Wolfe. "Brit must have weighed 400 pounds. Brit wasn't on this one tour, and Gordy grabbed one of Brit's pairs of pants out of the trunk. Gordy crawled inside the pants and held the suspenders up and walked around. We couldn't even get the concert started, because it was so funny."

One of the more unusual tours occurred in February 1965. For three weeks, the symphony toured the South with Arthur Fiedler as the "Boston Pops Tour Orchestra." The trip included stops in Norfolk, Va.; Birmingham, Ala.; Charleston, S.C.; Atlanta; and other locations throughout Florida, Tennessee, Virginia, and the Carolinas. The tour began on Feb. 21, after a performance on the regular Baltimore Symphony Pop Concert Series with Fiedler conducting. Announcement of the Boston and Baltimore collaboration was not all positive, as some Baltimoreans thought that the symphony was selling itself out. "It seems to me a shame that the Baltimore orchestra, which receives very little, if any, national recognition, will receive none for its forthcoming efforts. … To say the least, our city is not nationally known for its cultural offerings. … We deserve some recognition in this area, we should demand and exploit it, rather than abdicate it to a city already rich in cultural fame," read one letter to the Sun. Flutist Lake also recalls the situation in the South at the height of civil rights protests: "We left Birmingham and the state troopers

Far Left. The Baltimore Symphony, conducted by Arthur Fiedler, performed an "A La Boston Pops Night" on February 20, 1965. The orchestra immediately embarked on a southern tour under the name 'Boston Pops Tour Orchestra.'

Left. The Baltimore Symphony had a strong commitment to educational programs throughout its lifetime. This flyer promoted a 1964 collaborative program with the Baltimore Zoo.

followed us. They thought that we were northern activists. We always played four or five encores, and the last was always 'Dixie.' It wasn't until Miami that we finally played 'Stars and Stripes,' thank God."

In 1965, Wilmer Wise joined the orchestra as assistant principal trumpet, becoming the first African-American member of the Baltimore Symphony. A native of Philadelphia, he was a student of Sigmund Hering of the Philadelphia Orchestra. In addition to numerous jazz and Broadway appearances in New York, Philadelphia, and Atlantic City, Wise had also performed with Pablo Casals on the first "Musicians from Marlboro" concert tour. "I almost didn't take the job because I was too busy," says Wise. "But I was offered a job as an adjunct professor at Morgan State. That put it over the top." Wise also is credited with being the first African-American faculty member at Peabody. He does not recall any ill sentiment from his colleagues in the orchestra, but remembers that his greatest challenge was trying to find housing near the Lyric. Also, he says, "after rehearsals, a number of orchestra musicians used to hang out at a bar across from the Lyric. But the bar wouldn't serve me, so the musicians boycotted the place."

Wise served as the "urban consultant" for the orchestra. "I would escort people like Benny Goodman into different parts of the city. It was a front-office job that lasted for a

'hot minute.' I needed the extra money." He left the orchestra in 1970 and was proud that Langston Fitzgerald, another African American, won his vacated position: "Fitz got the job after I left, so there was never a gap between the black trumpeters!" Wise became a member of the American Symphony Orchestra and a successful Broadway musician. He performed in the orchestra for five of Stephen Sondheim's biggest hits and played lead trumpet when Bernstein conducted a recording of *West Side Story* in 1984. He died after a long illness on Jan. 30, 2015.

In July 1965, the Baltimore Symphony Orchestra Association quietly announced what would be one of the most important events in its history: that home builder and shopping center developer Joseph Meyerhoff had been elected to a two-year term as president of the board of directors. In 1964, Meyerhoff reportedly was approached by a delegation from the orchestra that asked him to "help rescue" the financially-strapped symphony. In a Sun interview, Meyerhoff recalled that he told his wife about the request. "I laughed and said, 'Can you imagine that? I wouldn't have that headache for anything in the world.' But she looked at me and said, 'Why not? Somebody's got to help.'" Meyerhoff immediately put his expertise and influence to work. He was known as a talented businessman who made firm decisions and stood by them. Oboist Joe Turner says, "Without Joe Meyerhoff, I'm not sure where the orchestra would be today."

Joseph Meyerhoff

The name Joseph Meyerhoff is practically synonymous with the Baltimore Symphony Orchestra. Thousands annually attend concerts at the Joseph Meyerhoff Symphony Hall, but many may not know who Meyerhoff was. Joe Meyerhoff was not just a commercial and residential real estate developer, he was, according to friend Eugene Schreiber, "the most philanthropic person that I've ever met or heard of." Meyerhoff personally gave over $10 million of his own money to build one of the country's finest concert halls. He didn't want his name on it, but the Maryland State Legislature felt otherwise since his share of the cost was equal to that of the State and Baltimore City. They decided to name the Maryland Concert Center project as the Joseph Meyerhoff Symphony Hall.

Meyerhoff was born in 1899 in Ukraine, the fifth of six children. His family came to America in 1906 and started a new life. After initially living in East Baltimore, the Meyerhoffs eventually settled on Druid Hill Avenue. Part of Joe's earliest education took place just across from the stage door of the hall that bears his name. He attended Public School 49, a select junior high school that was "reserved for smart kids," says his son Harvey M. "Bud" Meyerhoff. Joe Meyerhoff graduated from the University of Maryland Law School, practiced law and then joined his brother Morris in the real estate business. The firm eventually experienced financial troubles and was dissolved in the Depression. Despite a bankruptcy filing, Joe Meyerhoff felt morally obligated to repay his debts in full as soon

JOSEPH MEYERHOFF, Baltimore builder-developer, has been elected president of the Baltimore Symphony Orchestra Association. Mr. Meyerhoff, who "cannot even carry a tune," said that he will try during his two-year term to bring financial stability to the orchestra.

as he could which he did. "After he and his brother went broke, Joe made sure that every creditor got paid," says Schreiber.

Meyerhoff, along with his family, found success in commercial and residential real estate. By the early 1980s, he had built and developed over 15,000 homes, 17,000 apartments, and 19 shopping centers, in Maryland, Florida, New York, and other locations. Prominent Baltimore neighborhoods such as Guilford, Stoneleigh, Homeland, and Roland Park contain homes built by the firm. "I built damned good houses, solid houses, and I always took great pride with them," he told the Sun.

As his wealth increased, so did Meyerhoff's commitment to the city. His chairmanship of the symphony board was not the only mark he made on Baltimore. The Meyerhoff name can be found on colleges, hospitals, and numerous other institutions. Meyerhoff also supported numerous projects in Israel and served as a president of The Associated Jewish Charities, now known as the Associated: Jewish Community Federation of Baltimore.

"My grandfather was a leader, a leader's leader," says Terry Meyerhoff Rubenstein. "He wanted to set an example. He wanted to give more than anybody else, and he wanted to do more than anybody else. He was just one of those kinds of people." The Baltimore Symphony is fortunate that Meyerhoff answered its call for leadership in 1964.

Joe Meyerhoff teamed up with world renowned architect Pietro Belluschi to build one of the great symphony halls in the country and was pleased that Sergiu Comissiona would build one of the country's finest orchestras. "Sergiu brought a new presence to the Baltimore Symphony ," says Bud Meyerhoff. Joe knew that Comissiona wanted a new concert hall for the Baltimore Symphony to achieve its major-league goals. "Dad felt that the Lyric was too old. It was a traditional European style theater," Bud Meyerhoff says. As the new hall began to take shape, Joe kept his eye on construction. "Dad stopped off at the site every day as he was on the way to the office," says his son. Schreiber notes, "Joe was very detail-oriented. He wanted to make sure that the hall was being built the way it should be."

However, Meyerhoff did not want the cost of construction to compete with the orchestra's capital or endowment campaigns, or pose a financial burden to the community. In September 1982, Meyerhoff and Baltimore witnessed the opening of the city's new cultural centerpiece. At the opening gala, he told the Sun, "I don't want a lot of nonsense about what a great hero I am." The Joseph Meyerhoff Symphony Hall was a gift to the community and the symphony, and it also pleased Comissiona. But Meyerhoff was devastated when Comissiona announced his departure three months after the hall opened. "Joe felt that Comissiona turned his back on Baltimore," says Schrieber. Comissiona later openly regretted the decision.

After Comissiona's departure, Meyerhoff remained committed to the symphony. He actively participated in the selection of David Zinman and continued as board chairman until his death in 1985. And the Meyerhoff legacy did not end then. Members of his family continue to play active roles with the Baltimore Symphony, and through the Joseph and Harvey Meyerhoff Family Charitable Funds. "I'm enormously proud to be a Meyerhoff," says granddaughter Terry Rubenstein. "I'm proud of what our family has accomplished and I'm glad that we made a difference." Son Bud Meyerhoff says his father "did something remarkable and great for the city." He also states that though his father paid for half of the hall's construction, he never accepted complimentary seating and always paid for his seats, "and so do I," says son Bud. The family tradition continues.

Joseph Meyerhoff once told the Sun, "My parents felt – and instilled in us – a belief that you should endeavor to leave things a little better than you found them – I've always tried to practice that." His practice paid off, and the Baltimore Symphony, along with the entire community, is grateful for the generous leadership set forth by Joe Meyerhoff and his family.

Meyerhoff and symphony manager Oleg Lobanov applied for a grant from the Ford Foundation. Ford had pledged to award up to $85 million to symphony orchestras through a matching challenge toward endowment funds. It hoped "that orchestra seasons can be extended and that more people can attend concerts, because of the longer seasons and added tours. The quality should be improved with salaries of musicians to be raised." In 1965, the Baltimore Symphony had a budget of approximately $800,000 a year, with about 50 percent coming from ticket sales. It had a deficit of $100,000. The 88 musicians earned a base salary of $138 a week. Principal players got an extra $20. The 30-week season included 24 "adult" concerts, 18 youth concerts, 10 pops concerts, and 10 Civic Opera performances. It also performed 14 "adult" concerts and 30 youth programs throughout the state, and 24 out-of-state concerts from Michigan to Virginia. While European orchestras were mostly fully funded by their governments or state radio corporations, the Baltimore Symphony received just $200,000 in state and local grants, along with $150,000 in private contributions.

Only six months after Meyerhoff assumed the organization's leadership, the Baltimore Symphony became the recipient of a $1.75 million grant from the Ford Foundation. Of that,

$1 million came in the form of an endowment fund that needed to be matched over the next five years. The remaining $750,000 was earmarked for salary increases and lengthening the season. Meyerhoff said, "If we had endowment income like that, we wouldn't be in financial difficulties all the time. This provides a real stimulus to help us establish such an endowment fund for the future." One of the first gifts to the campaign came from Maryland National Bank. Chairman Robert D.H. Harvey noted the symphony's role in the "cultural renaissance of Baltimore," and urged Baltimoreans to "recognize that without a successful symphony we are only part of a city." Meyerhoff easily was elected to another two-year term as board president. He cited increased season ticket sales and annual fund contributions as the hallmarks of his second term.

While Meyerhoff continued his work on improving the orchestra's finances, he also began addressing artistic concerns. Adler's relationship with the musicians had been stormy from the first. By 1966, Adler had already fired two concertmasters, Michael Rosenker and Hugo Kolberg, because of artistic differences. Rosenker complained to the Sun that Adler was "becoming too friendly with some members of the symphony board" and added, "They'll never have a good orchestra with the man." In January 1967,

Left. Assistant Principal Trumpet Wilmer Wise and Principal Trombone Douglas Edelman practice outdoors in a city park.

Opposite. Members of the horn and bass sections appear during a casual moment at a 1960s rehearsal.

Meyerhoff announced that Adler would leave his post as music director after the 1967-68 season. Adler agreed to conduct the first two concerts of the season as well as the final performance. "My experience in Baltimore, although at times beset with challenges and crises, has been one of the most rewarding in my career," Adler said. He praised Meyerhoff as "the best president the orchestra ever had," and Meyerhoff returned the favor by saying that "Adler's leadership [had] greatly enhanced not only the orchestra but also the cultural atmosphere, where his work was deeply appreciated." But Meyerhoff had been working to get rid of Adler for months. And with the help of a committee, he had compiled a list of 271 possible successors – which had now been narrowed to 15.

The Baltimore Symphony announced five guest conductors for its 1967-68 season who were under consideration to be the next music director: Gerhard Samuel, Werner Torkanowsky, Antonio Janigro, Pierino Gamba, and Sergiu Comissiona. The list was further narrowed when two of the candidates canceled their appearances. Many Baltimoreans, especially in the Jewish community, urged the symphony to consider Shapira for the position. But on April 24, 1968, Meyerhoff announced that Comissiona would be the symphony's next music director. His three-year contract would begin with the 1969-70 season.

To fill the one-year gap, Meyerhoff also announced that Brian Priestman, who had ties to orchestras in England and Canada, would be resident conductor for the 1968-69 season. Board members, especially Meyerhoff, were eager to be rid of Adler. "Comissiona owed Adler his career" in Baltimore, says clarinetist Wolfe. Musicians' spokesman Keith Kummer, an oboist, praised Comissiona's hiring. "The musicians were consulted at every stage, and we are delighted to hear that the committee's choice is the man who was the overwhelming choice of the orchestra," he said.

Comissiona's decision to come to Baltimore was not an easy one. According to *A Romanian Rhapsody*: *The Life of Conductor Sergiu Comissona*, a biography by Cecilia Burcescu, Comissiona was also under consideration for the directorship of the Denver Symphony. Comissiona thought that Denver was a "better orchestra," and found the surroundings there "more appealing." He described the 70-member Baltimore Symphony as displaying "a modest professional level" and believed the city to be "rather provincial and depressing." But according to Burcescu, Comissiona's confidante, John Edwards, a former Baltimore manager in the late 1940s and recently appointed head of the Chicago Symphony, felt that an appointment in Denver could be a "dead-end road." Edwards thought that "the Baltimore Symphony, if substantially improved, would make

Sergiu a name." Comissiona announced that his plan for Baltimore would be to increase the number of musicians, develop a tour strategy, commission new works, and reach out to audiences, especially in Philadelphia and Washington.

Because of Comissiona's music directorship of the Gothenburg Symphony Orchestra in Sweden and numerous previously scheduled guest conductor appearances, Brian Priestman would help to set the tone before the new conductor's arrival. As a first-time conductor of an American orchestra, Priestman "wanted to come and see how a potentially great American symphony in the seventh-largest city in the United States operates, how well it is backed by the local population, and what sort of support it receives." Of serving as an acting music director, Priestman stated, "Any decision requiring the artistic judgment is referred to me. I take full responsibility for it. Naturally, I keep Mr. Comissiona informed of what I am doing." But unbeknownst to the musicians, Priestman had a list with about a quarter of their names – the ones Comissiona wanted to be replaced. Priestman earned the reputation of being Comissiona's "hatchet man." Trumpet player Wise recalls, "Priestman had to clean house so that Comissiona didn't seem like the bad guy."

...our future Music Director

Sergiu Comissiona

...our brand new Resident Conductor

Brian Priestman

these famous guest conductors...

Leopold Stokowski   Aaron Copland   Gunther Schuller   Lukas Foss   Hugo Weisgall   Antonio Janigro

this exciting roster of guest artists...

Pianists

Van Cliburn
Jeanne-Marie Darre
Philippe Entremont
Eugene Istomin
William Masselos

Violinists

Yehudi Menuhin
Masuko Ushioda
Stanley Weiner
Kalman Banyak

Bass-Baritone

Simon Estes

Soprano

Veronica Tyler

Cellists

Mstislav Rostropovich
Mihaly Virizlay

Guitarist

Andres Segovia

Double Bassist

Gary Karr

Right. Violist Sara Feldman takes a picket line break during an early work stoppage.

Far Right. After the departure of Peter Herman Adler and before the arrival of Sergiu Comissiona, British conductor Brian Priestman served as the orchestra's resident conductor.

The 1968-69 season was delayed by the first labor unrest since five musicians walked out of a rehearsal in 1921. Negotiations began in December 1967, and disagreements centered on higher pay and creation of a pension plan. The Baltimore Symphony had become the last major orchestra in the country without a pension contribution fund. On Sept. 26, 1968, the musicians went on strike. Picket lines were formed around the Lyric and battle lines were drawn. One musician representative told the Sun that the strike was necessary because the musicians wanted the Baltimore Symphony to become the next great American orchestra: "[We] have faith in the abilities of the membership; we are convinced of the orchestra's artistic potential. [We] want it to be the kind of musical product which will impress people." Management insisted that the orchestra "may fold" if the musicians did not return to work. William Boucher III, executive director of the Greater Baltimore Alliance, told the press, "Management cannot be asked to commit money they don't have a reasonable prospect of giving." He complained, "It is another negative controversial chapter in the history of the Baltimore Symphony and comes at a time when everything, including the symphony fundraising capacity, was on the upbeat." Meyerhoff wrote a letter to the musicians titled "Doing My Best." It said, "If they [musicians] feel they have to strike, there is nothing more I can do than I've already done." The

work stoppage lasted about four weeks and was settled through the assistance of Mayor D'Alesandro, III. Musician pay was raised from $150 a week to $175 immediately, and $200 and $210 in years two and three. Additionally, a pension fund was developed to provide a $17,000 benefit and the season was increased from 34 to 38 weeks. Both sides praised D'Alesandro's assistance. With the three-year agreement in place, the Baltimore Symphony was able to start its 1968-69 season, though labor strife would recur many times in the next several decades.

In 1968, to continue its commitment to education, the orchestra hired Allan Miller as its first full-time director of education. Miller was placed in charge of youth concerts and instrumental competitions. While the organization acknowledged the importance of education, it realized it was more of a mission than a revenue generator. Miller believed that concerts needed to be affordable to encourage a younger audience. "We are no longer a service organization if we price ourselves as an orchestra for the rich only," he said. "The image of 'exclusivity' has long since disappeared from the symphony. No more could we afford to eliminate the musical opportunity the orchestra provides for students by dollar tickets and low-cost concert series. Or the low-cost admissions to the Saturday night 'pop' concerts, which are snapped up by hundreds of grateful teenagers. This is

Brian Priestman addresses the orchestra in October 1968 after the settlement of the musicians' strike.

money-losing, of course, but again, it is the Baltimore Symphony's educational and cultural obligation to encourage as many youth audiences as we can. ...We are definitely an educational institution – indeed, our tax-exempt status is based on the orchestra's educational, rather than cultural, service."

As resident conductor, Priestman wanted to bring a new level of artistic integrity and energy to the orchestra. He always made a grand entrance and jumped onto the podium with excitement. Once, at a concert in Northeast Maryland, this energy got the better of him. Stage managers had warned him that the podium was on casters. He chose to ignore their advice. As he made his signature leap, Priestman slid into the viola section and landed flat on his back.

Priestman quickly grew frustrated with Baltimore audiences. He preferred touring over local performances, as some found his concerts, often in excess of two and a half hours, to be too long. In March 1969, Priestman was front and center in a Sun article titled, "A Symphony Without a City That Cares." He complained about a broad lack of support in the community. In regard to the orchestra's traditional touring circuit, he said, "We're playing to an awful lot of people, taking the fame of Baltimore up and down the coast – but Baltimore couldn't care less about that, could they, really? Do you think, because they don't see the orchestra here, we're selling vegetables or something else?" Ultimately, the native of Birmingham, England, simply did not like the place. "The last thing you could call Baltimore is cosmopolitan," he said. "It's an industrial city, a functional city. It doesn't have polish, a sophistication which you would expect a large, long-established American city to have."

Priestman also was resentful that the Philadelphia Orchestra had since 1907 been a consistent presence at the Lyric: "The Philadelphia is a great orchestra, but I don't know whether it really gives its best concerts here; we're deluding ourselves if we think that Philadelphia thinks highly of Baltimore." He urged that the local group's name be changed to the Maryland Symphony, saying, "Don't let us forget that the impact of the Baltimore Symphony upon the world at large is not enormous at the moment, nor is it great inside the city of Baltimore – but it is very good in the state of Maryland. So why not foster that angle?" He was pessimistic about the future of classical culture in Baltimore. "I think the arts in this city are going to have a great struggle. I'm sorry I am not going to be here to help," he said. "It's not only going to be a hard struggle; I really wonder whether it is ever going to work. Unless things change, it's going to be very difficult to find anybody to stay and build the symphony." Brian Priestman came and went quickly, but he did not go quietly.

What I owe this orchestra
and this city is everything.
It's my musical love story.

SERGIU COMISSIONA

On Oct. 1, 1969, Comissiona made his official debut. His opening concert featured a performance of Mahler's Symphony No. 2 ("Resurrection"). "I want to resurrect this orchestra," he said, adding that this concert was only the beginning of his work. He told the Sun, "You cannot judge the orchestra today, only in a few years." On March 21, 1970, the orchestra appeared at Carnegie Hall as part of the Carnegie Festival of Orchestras, culminating a six-state tour. The performance featured Shostakovich's Symphony No. 9, Ravel's *La valse*, Roger Sessions' Rhapsody for Orchestra (a Baltimore Symphony commission), and Benjamin Britten's Diversions for Piano Left Hand and Orchestra, with Fleisher as soloist. "The Britten is a wonderful piece. It's a theme and 11 variations and is built on ascending fifths and descending fourths. The work is an absolute inspiration and ends in a death-defying tarantella," says Fleisher. The New York Times lauded the entire performance and noted, "With all the symphony orchestras that play in New York regularly, including those of Boston, Philadelphia, Washington, and Cleveland, one would think that other visiting groups would be hard put to come up with fresh program ideas for their appearances. The Baltimore Symphony and its new conductor Sergiu Comissiona seem to have no such trouble."

The Baltimore Symphony had gained artistic momentum and increased visibility, and it looked as if Comissiona was the person that Priestman had thought "would be difficult to find." But his adventurous programming was not as eagerly received at home. As the orchestra entered the 1970s, Maryland Living magazine could express only cautious hope for Comissiona's future. It noted "the disastrous years of Peter Herman Adler, during which the Baltimore Symphony slipped into almost ludicrous oblivion," and asked, "Will Sergiu Comissiona blossom out in his second year as music director or will the orchestra find itself saddled with another unimaginative, if not downright incompetent, leader? Can Sergiu Comissiona lead the Baltimore Symphony out of its dark age, and establish it beside the other great American orchestras? Has he the musical integrity and clarity, the conducting precision and personality?" The magazine's doubts proved unfounded. Comissiona was to transform the Baltimore Symphony into one of the country's most visible and influential orchestras.

Assistant Principal Clarinetist Christopher Wolfe rehearses the premier of Howard Thatcher's Clarinet Concerto in April 1969. Paul Freeman conducts the orchestra with the composer in attendance.

CHAPTER
THE

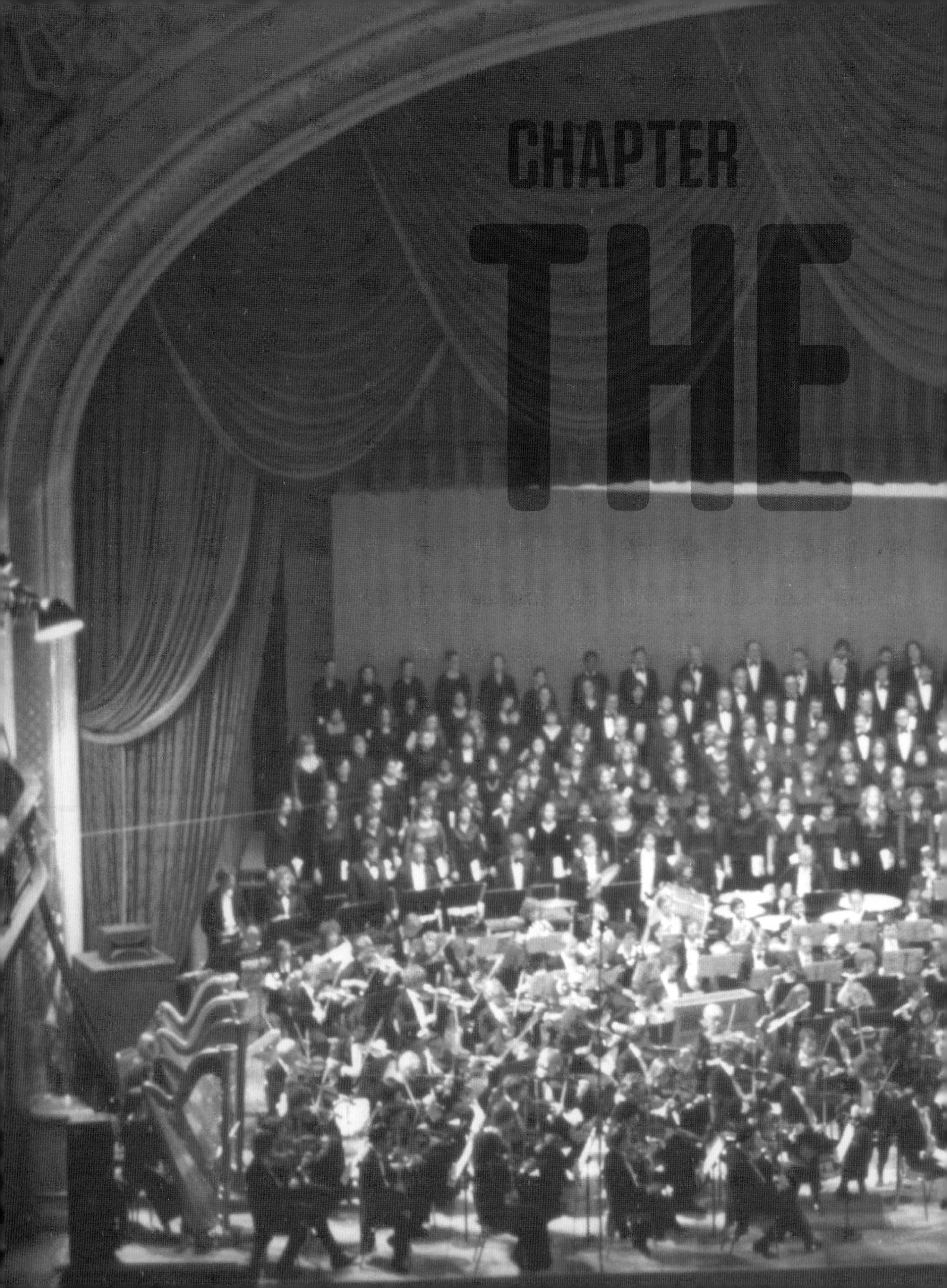

SEVEN

1970s

The Baltimore Symphony entered an entirely new era under Sergiu Comissiona's tenure.

Comissiona was now the new face of the Baltimore Symphony Orchestra and had the full backing of symphony president Joseph Meyerhoff. When he was initially engaged as music director, Comissiona presented a list of needs to Meyerhoff. To improve the symphony's artistic imprint, Comissiona wanted musician salary and benefit increases, a 52-week season, a recording contract, annual Carnegie Hall appearances, international tours, and, eventually, a new concert hall. Comissiona thought that these improvements would make the Baltimore Symphony more attractive to better musicians, and encourage them to make Baltimore their long-term home. Meyerhoff encouraged the board and community to champion Comissiona's wishes. He wanted one musician in particular to make Baltimore his long-term home – Comissiona.

"I loved Comissiona," says the violinist Pinchas Zukerman. The musicians first met in Haifa, Israel, when Comissiona was conducting the orchestra there. "We had a symbiotic relationship. He had a way of conducting and I could never understand how his hands worked!" Comissiona was very popular in Europe, and because of his international reputation he engaged many high-profile soloists for Baltimore. He was determined to improve the orchestra, but learned early that that would not come easily. During his first year, Comissiona tried to fire nine musicians and quickly found that the union contract prevented such swift actions. He was unfamiliar with the contractual dismissal process, and the union and

musicians assured him that a mass firing would hurt his engagements with other orchestras. Comissiona backed down but learned how strongly the musicians felt about the issues surroundings their jobs.

In fall 1971, the musicians threatened to call a strike unless a new contract was signed. The organization had experienced its first major work stoppage four years earlier, and the musicians were frustrated and wanted more growth in salary and orchestra size. The annual base salary in 1971 amounted to $7,980 for 42 weeks. Comissiona feared a work stoppage, and decided to personally address the musicians in early December. The meeting grew tense, as Comissiona told the musicians that their demands for better pay and working conditions were absurd and unrealistic. After the adversarial meeting, Meyerhoff called Comissiona and criticized him for getting involved. "I always felt bad about that meeting," says piccolo player Laurie Sokoloff. "It was terrible, and I knew that he was working behind the scenes to acquiesce in the musicians' needs."

On Dec. 28, the musicians began a strike that would last 10 weeks and put Comissiona's second season at risk. After 22 days, mediator Leon Sachs tried to engage both sides in dialogue. He grew frustrated and told the Sun, "This is an hour of decision in the community, and that decision ought to be made by the people of the community. I'm not sure the

Top. Sergiu Comissiona with the orchestra.

Center. Rebecca and Joe Meyerhoff pose with Robinne Comissiona at the October 1973 opening concert.

Bottom. Symphony musicians on the picket line, December 29, 1971 outside the orchestra's Mount Royal Avenue offices.

board ought to assume the sole responsibility. I think it needs a wider forum." The work stoppage ended on March 10, 1972, when Mayor William Donald Schaefer established a blue ribbon panel to address the orchestra's struggles and needs. On it were more than 100 Baltimoreans, who expressed their views on every aspect of the orchestra. Schaefer declared that the panel's findings would be "morally binding." The two questions posed by the panel's chair, Dr. Otto Kraushaar, were, "Where do we want to go?", and, "How to get there?" Where they ended up was a $10-a-week wage increase every year for the next three years, and a 44-week season for 1974-75. The 1972-73 season started with a new contract and without incident. And once the dust had settled, a number of Comissiona's wishes for artistic and organization growth had been accomplished.

The symphony's board had felt attacked during the strike by the musicians and the community. In an article in the Sun, the board discussed its role and structure. The typical board member was described as a "white male businessman with a locally based firm" who was chosen for one of three attributes: fund-raising, musical knowledge, or political connections. The board called Baltimore "a tough community to raise money in" and "without the extreme wealth of other cities." It outlined its contributions to the orchestra, such as legal assistance, fund-raising, marketing, and even medical treatment for musicians.

Baltimore Symphony Chorus

What began as a series of "sing-alongs" in May 1969 paved the way for a Baltimore Symphony institution of over 30 years. The Baltimore Symphony Chorus was the brainchild of Sergiu Comissiona. Upon his arrival as music director, Comissiona wanted to expand the symphony's choral offerings. He ordered Allan Miller, the symphony's educational and Youth Concert director, to hold "no experience necessary" readings of selections from Handel's *Messiah*, Mozart's Requiem, and Haydn's *Creation*. These informal sessions were held in the Gilman School auditorium. After five ambitious months, the newly organized Baltimore Symphony Chorus made its debut on Oct. 1, 1969, in a performance of Mahler's Symphony No. 2 ("Resurrection").

For its initial season, the chorus had only 35 members. Early on, the small ensemble was often supplemented by the Peabody Conservatory Chorus, and its quality was cited as "uneven" and "weak." After a few years, Comissiona called in chorus manager Felice Homann, pounded his fist on the table, and told her, "Do something!" Homann spread the word, notifying area choral groups about the symphony chorus' potential. During subsequent seasons, the Baltimore Symphony invested more resources into its chorus. The group became stronger every year and blossomed under BSO associate conductor Andrew Schenck. Schenck left Baltimore in 1980 to become resident conductor of the San Antonio Symphony. He "was very brilliant and very professional," recalls Homann. After his departure, the Baltimore Symphony turned to the chorus's accompanist as its new director. The partnership between Edward Polochick and the chorus thrived for two decades. "Ed was relentless, and he tightened up the group's discipline," says Homann.

As Polochick began his tenure with the chorus in 1980, Comissiona had programmed incredibly ambitious works. In his first season as director, Polochick had to prepare the chorus in such difficult repertoire as Walton's *Belshazzar's Feast*, Berlioz's *L'enfance du Christ*, and Schoenberg's *Gurre-Lieder*. Polochick says he told Comissiona, "That is not possible!" Comissiona wouldn't hear it. "Make it happen," he replied. So Polochick and the chorus made it happen. Over the following years, the chorus performed twice in Carnegie

Hall, recorded twice with the Baltimore Symphony, and participated in the September 1995 concert with the symphony in honor of Pope John Paul II's visit to Baltimore. The performance received national attention and was sponsored by leaders in the Catholic and Jewish communities.

The chorus also worked closely with such notable choral conductors as Margaret Hillis of the Chicago Symphony Chorus and Robert Shaw, director of the Atlanta Symphony Orchestra Chorus and the Robert Shaw Chorale. "Hillis said that she felt the BSO Chorus was just a notch below the Chicago Symphony Chorus in quality," states Polochick. "And one time, the chorus was in a piano dress rehearsal with Robert Shaw, and [Shaw] stopped and stepped off of the podium. Shaw said, 'How do you get them to sound like that? They just sound fantastic, and they are only one-half to two-thirds of the size of my chorus in Atlanta!'" To maintain the group's quality, chorus members had to audition every year. After receiving a special National Endowment of the Arts grant, the chorus hired ringers as paid section leaders. These members had to take mandatory workshops in voice, ear-training, and sight-reading. Other members often joined in these classes, which were also partially funded by the Baltimore Symphony organization.

While Comissiona had championed the chorus' formation, it was his successor, David Zinman, who developed a deep relationship with it. "David loved the chorus," says Polochick. Zinman conducted the chorus in about 50 works. But Polochick says Zinman's feeling was not reflected by the symphony's management. When Zinman announced his departure in 1996, Polochick says he knew that "the writing was on the wall for the chorus." Without Zinman's advocacy, the management, including executive director John Gidwitz, began to tell Polochick that the orchestra couldn't program so many choral works and that audience members were switching their tickets. "That was absolutely not true," says Polochick. "It was just the opposite." Frustrated, Polochick left the chorus in January 1999. New Yorker Frank Nemhauser of the Mannes School of Music replaced Polochick. But after his final rehearsal with the chorus in 1999, Ed Polochick told some of the members to "watch your backs."

What had once been unthinkable became real on Jan. 12, 2002, when executive director John Gidwitz came to a chorus rehearsal and announced that the group would be disbanded at the end of the 2001-02 season. Some singers expressed shock and grief, and demanded to know who had done this, and why. Others simply remembered Polochick's parting words. The chorus made its final appearance in June 2002 in a performance of Mahler's Symphony No. 3 with Yuri Temirkanov. The work involved only women's voices, but the ensemble had remained committed to finishing out the season. Looking back, Gidwitz says the chorus was a "good, committed group," and the decision to dissolve it was "controversial and unpopular" in the community. "We looked ahead at the challenges that were ahead [for the entire organization] and we decided to put our resources [in others areas]," he says. One of the main reasons management gave was financial, as the annual cost of maintaining a chorus was approximately $150,000. Gidwitz added that it would take an investment of $400,000-$500,000 a year to produce a world-class chorus. At the time, Polochick told the symphony leadership, "Are you out of your mind?" He says the fallout

affected concert attendance, charitable contributions, and community goodwill.

It's unfortunate that the Baltimore Symphony Chorus is often remembered mostly for its demise and not for over 30 years of devoted, quality music-making. The predominantly volunteer group was a crucial member of the Baltimore Symphony family. It's true that a large number of American orchestras do not manage and maintain their own chorus. And since the Baltimore chorus was disbanded, groups such as Concert Artists of Baltimore and the Baltimore Choral Arts Society have brought their artistry to the Baltimore Symphony for choral programs. But the passion for the symphony chorus remains. "I want people to remember that we were very much a family," says Felice Homann. The chorus "helped shape many of our lives. We provided a superior product and it was very important to us." Polochick, who continues as director of Concert Artists of Baltimore, wants people to remember the Baltimore Symphony Chorus for its music: "If you were to ask David Zinman, Christopher Seaman, the late Robert Shaw, the late Margaret Hillis, and others in the choral world, they would want you to know what a great symphony chorus this was."

The year 1973 was important for the Baltimore Symphony, institutionally and artistically. In May, the orchestra made an annual Carnegie Hall appearance as part of the International Festival of Visiting Orchestras. And in June, a new administrative era began with the appointment of Joseph Leavitt as the orchestra's general manager. A percussionist and former director of the Wolf Trap Foundation, Leavitt built a strong relationship with Meyerhoff and Comissiona. Leavitt never forgot his musical roots and brought considerable leadership skills to the orchestra. "Joe Leavitt laid the foundation and roped in the other two," says Carol Bogash, orchestra manager during the 1980s. "It was a terrific team. It was really an exciting time. Joe Leavitt didn't put himself front and center. He knew how to do that with Joe Meyerhoff and Comissiona." In 1981, the symphony board would acknowledge Leavitt's contributions by naming him executive director.

The following month, the famed pianist Leon Fleisher joined the Baltimore Symphony as associate conductor. Fleisher had made his Baltimore Symphony piano debut in March 1954 under Massimo Freccia. He developed a severe cramp in his right hand 10 years later. His affliction, eventually diagnosed as focal dystonia, affected his solo career. Fleisher continued to teach at the Peabody Conservatory and perform piano works for left hand alone. After receiving encouragement,

Fleisher took up conducting and eventually made his Baltimore Symphony conducting debut at a November 1970 youth concert in Annapolis. Upon his announcement as assistant conductor, Fleisher told the Sun, "I have great affection for the city, the orchestra, and the people in it." Fleisher had unanimous support from Comissiona and the musicians, and his new position helped solidify a musical partnership that has endured since the mid 1950s.

The symphony remained committed to its longtime youth concert series at the Lyric. Having done narration work at Peabody, Rheda Becker was asked to narrate *Peter and the Wolf* in May 1974 and jumped at the chance: "It was my dream to do *Peter and the Wolf*, and here was the dream of a lifetime." She planned to volunteer her services for her initial appearance until Leavitt told her, "You're such a pro, you should never volunteer." Becker says, "He offered $50 for back-to-back performances. It was thrilling! It was my first paying musical job and the beginning of my career." Over the next 40 years, Becker estimates, she has narrated over 1,000 youth concerts. Becker also has been one of the orchestra's most ardent supporters and has maintained close ties with its leadership. She influenced other audience members and supporters to become advocates for the orchestra's educational programs. As a teacher, Marge Penhallegon often brought her students to youth concerts.

Over the years, she says, "I was here so often that Rheda and I got to know each other. I would write to her and let her know how the students liked the program. [Rheda] invited me to be on the symphony's education committee." After years of influence and involvement, Penhallegon was elected president of the Baltimore Symphony Associates.

Becker recalls Comissiona as a "very imaginative and community-minded" person. "Sergiu was very interested in making friends for the symphony," she says. Meyerhoff had an affinity for Comissiona and his wife, Robinne. He "helped make sure that they had a wonderful place to live. He made sure that they were happy here," Becker says. "Robinne and Sergiu just finished each other's sentences. They would tell stories and it was just fun to be with them." On one runout concert to Frederick, the conductor arrived without his tuxedo pants, Becker says: "It was very rainy out, and Sergiu realized he only had his tuxedo jacket. He didn't want to ask any of the musicians, because they needed their tux pants. He asked Robinne if he could try on her pants." Comissiona conducted the concert while wearing his wife's pants. After the concert, violinist Sylvia Shur told him that he looked "very sexy" in her trousers. He responded, "Well, Robinne is sitting in my dressing room wearing a raincoat!'"

Meyerhoff trusted Comissiona and wanted to grant his wishes. One of the greatest of those was a new concert hall. In April 1972, Meyerhoff openly discussed the matter. "I don't think there's any question that we need a new concert hall," he said. "I don't mean a remodeled Lyric. The seats are so tight and they're not luxurious. They're just very inadequate. … I've been to some new concert halls, and my mouth just waters. I just wish we could have one like that. I'm liable to build one. A new music hall excites me, and remodeling the Lyric doesn't." Three months later, Meyerhoff purchased the Deutsches Haus, a six-story German restaurant and rathskeller at Cathedral and Preston Streets. The building originally served as the Bryn Mawr School from 1890 until the mid-1930s, when the German-American societies of Baltimore moved to the structure. In the 1960s, the Deutsches Haus had been threatened with demolition by proposed plans for the East-West Expressway, and its popularity had declined, since "the younger generation did not share their parents' enthusiasm for German-language activities." Meyerhoff was all too happy to buy the place. The Sun called the purchase "a move that might be a prelude to a new home for the Baltimore Symphony Orchestra."

Opp. Left. Sergiu Comissiona meets with Girl Scouts during their cookie drive on February 20, 1975.

Opp. Right. In 1974, Rheda Becker began her long tenure as narrator for the Baltimore Symphony's Youth Concerts.

Left. Sergiu Comissiona leading the orchestra during a rehearsal in the early 1970s.

In April 1974, the symphony board approved plans to build a $15 million concert hall on the Deutsches Haus property. The decision was in response to a bill in the Maryland General Assembly to give the Lyric $2.5 million for upgrades to its air-conditioning system and interior renovations. Meyerhoff and the board thought that improvements to the Lyric were not in the best interest of the symphony. For the building's design, Meyerhoff engaged Pietro Belluschi, a former dean of the Massachusetts Institute of Technology School of Engineering, in association with Jung/Brannen Associates of Boston. The elliptical building was designed to seat 2,300 patrons and feature perfect acoustics. Meyerhoff personally paid for the $200,000 design plans and promised significant personal funding, to be matched by public and private grants. Groundbreaking for the new concert hall would occur four years later, once supporters successfully campaigned to obtain state funding for the project.

The move was a turning point for the orchestra and the city. Elliott W. Galkin, the Sun's music critic, stated, "The accomplishments and status of the Baltimore Symphony Orchestra since the appointment of Sergiu Comissiona as its music director five years ago have become particularly impressive. The orchestra has earned new esteem and respect. It is now represented in the international world of phonograph recordings and has recently signed a contract for further recordings, one of a relatively small group of major American symphony orchestras to enjoy such distinction."

In January 1975, the documentary *In Search of a Maestro* was aired nationally on PBS. The hour-long, Emmy-winning special documented the Baltimore Symphony's first Young Conductors Competition. It was narrated by Comissiona and produced by WMFB. Comissiona personally provided the $2,000 first prize. Candidates had to compete in conducting symphonies and concertos, dictation exercises, and identifying score errors. Arthur Fagan, 23, won the 1974 competition, followed by Carl Topilow in 1976, Roger Nierenberg in 1978, and Peter Bay in 1980.

The 1975-76 season began on an ominous note when musicians threatened another work stoppage. They grew frustrated that the advice from the 1972 blue ribbon panel report was not being followed. Though the report had acknowledged the responsibility of "realistically possible growth," musicians' wages were still falling below those of their peers. The Baltimore Symphony was ranked 20th in wages out of the country's 20 top orchestras. And there still was no individual pension plan. The panel had stated, "Unless a players' economic package is forthcoming that moves towards parity with other cities of comparable size and orchestras of equal stature, the BSO is destined to become a third-rate symphonic organization." As negotiations broke down in early October 1975, a federal mediator called a meeting in an attempt to beat an Oct. 5 strike deadline. A strike was averted with agreement on a new three-year contract with a total wage increase of $50 a week spread out over the three years. Despite a $1.1 million

Baltimore Symphony Orchestra

SERGIU COMISSIONA, Music Director

120 West Mount Royal Ave.
Baltimore, Maryland 21201
301 / 727-7300
Cable Address: BALTOSYM

Joseph Leavitt
General Manager

Opp. Left. The 1972 demolition of the former Deutsches Haus at Cathedral and Preston Streets eventually paved the way for the new Meyerhoff Symphony Hall.

Opp. Right. Cellists Paula and Mihály Virizlay are seen in this concert photograph from the 1970s.

Right. A 1974 notice from the BSO Board of Directors stated, "Maestro Comissiona has just signed a long-term contract with the Symphony. So why don't you return the compliment by signing up for a season with us?"

Dear Music-Lover:

For some time now our audiences have been telling us that the Baltimore Symphony Orchestra has a "great new sound." Of course, we've noticed it too. And so have many of the country's top music critics. "The Baltimore Symphony," wrote Harold Schonberg in the New York Times, "can be accounted one of the better American ensembles. Smooth and colorful strings; superior balances; accurate attacks and releases; first class solo playing; the Baltimore Symphony did itself proud....."

In fact, it's not only a new sound -- it's a whole new spirit. The driving force behind the resurgence of the 58-year old B.S.O. is its music director, Sergiu Comissiona. Under his baton the sound and spirit of the orchestra have changed. Not only have we received hard-earned critical acclaim, we are now recording on the Vox, Columbia and other labels and receiving world-wide recognition.

If you haven't yet heard the B.S.O.'s "new sound," you should. And the best and most economical way to do this is to sign up for one of the series of concerts listed in the centerfold. There's something for everyone, from classics to pops, from Isaac Stern to Count Basie!

By subscribing to an entire series now, you can make sure of getting the seats you want at a saving of up to 40% over the regular single ticket prices. But please mail in your order right away -- subscription renewals are running much higher than usual, and we may well be sold out of choice seats before the season opens. Right now, good seats are still available.

Studded with our own Symphony stars and world-famous virtuosi, next season will be our best ever. Come and hear for yourself what the B.S.O.'s "new sound" and new spirit are all about!

Sincerely,

The Officers and Board of Directors
Baltimore Symphony Orchestra

PS. Maestro Comissiona has just signed a long-term contract with the Symphony. So why don't you return the compliment by signing up for a season with us?

OFFICERS: 1974-75

Joseph Meyerhoff, President
Frank Baker, Jr., Vice Pres.
Mrs. Robert H. Levi, Vice Pres.
George D. F. Robinson, Jr., Vice Pres.
L. Patrick Deering, Treasurer
Henry R. Lord, Secretary

Board of Directors:

Mrs. George C. Alderman
G. Cheston Carey, Jr.
Norbert R. Christel
Mrs. Clyde Alvin Clapp
George L. Clarke
Owen Cole

Richard Davison
Mathias J. DeVito
Donald L. DeVries
Luther C. Dilatush
Sidney Friedberg
Dr. Otis D. Free
William F. Gliss, Jr.
Richard Franko Goldman
Louis L. Goldstein

Donald E. Grempler
Willard Hackerman
Harley W. Howell
James J. Jacobs
Lester S. Levy
Robert Hall Lewis
William Martien
Robert E. Michel
Decatur H. Miller

E. Kirkbride Miller
John J. Neubauer, Jr.
Mrs. Roland N. Patterson
Jack H. Pearlstone, Jr.
Mrs. Henry A. Rosenberg, Sr.
Randolph S. Rothschild
Bernard W. Rubenstein
Gerald D. Sarno
Dr. Roy O. Scholz

Dr. Albert Shapiro
Earle K. Shawe
F. Bradford Smith
Mrs. G. Ashton Sutherland, III
H. Mebane Turner
C. E. Utermohle, Jr.
Albert H. Walker
Mrs. Sewell S. Watts, III

accumulated deficit, the season grew to 45 weeks. The board was pleased to have a contract but unsure of its ability to find the additional funding.

The Baltimore Symphony celebrated its 60th anniversary in 1976 with a repeat performance of the 1916 inaugural concert. In a Sun interview the following year, Comissiona reflected on his eight years in Baltimore. "We're starting to have a personality, a Baltimore sound, if you want," he said. "It's a combination of European sound and tradition with the American diversity. Most American orchestras are playing well in one category of work. ... I try to characterize the future of the Baltimore sound as a combination of Viennese schmaltz with a French flexibility with an American

technicity (sic) of brilliance – in a way, to make a large chamber group. This I'm trying, and very often I succeed." Principal trumpet Don Tison recalls Comissiona as a "wonderful musician" who looked like he "painted pictures" when he conducted. "Overall, Comissiona brought the orchestra's level up and up during his time in Baltimore," he says. Comissiona's success in Baltimore captured the attention of other orchestras. Over the next few years, he was approached by the Cincinnati, Kansas City and Indianapolis symphonies as a possible music director candidate. He became the music adviser of the American Symphony Orchestra and was a frequent guest conductor with the Houston Symphony Orchestra.

In 1973, the Baltimore Symphony presented its first summer concert series with four Brahms Festival concerts at Goucher College and three performances at the Morris Mechanic Theater. The following year, the orchestra made its first appearance at the Merriweather Post Pavilion and expanded its presence at Goucher with an open-air Concert Connoisseur series. Though it was intended to be the summer home of the National Symphony, the Merriweather Post Pavilion hosted a Baltimore Symphony summer concert series until 1981. But Baltimore lacked its own summer music venue. As the symphony season grew, so did the demand for a facility. The symphony performed 17 outdoor concerts at Oregon Ridge Park, off Interstate 83 near Hunt Valley. General manager Leavitt was thrilled by the response and supported making Oregon Ridge the orchestra's summer

home "if current facilities can be improved and if a covered pavilion can be eventually constructed there." In 1977, Julianne Alderman, executive director of the Baltimore County Commission on Arts and Sciences, urged the County Council to construct a permanent summer concert venue at the park. A projected $5.5 million, state-of-the-art performance and education center at Oregon Ridge was placed on a November 1978 ballot as a $4 million bond issue. County residents rejected the idea and that center was never built. County officials scaled back their plans and a more modest structure, without permanent covered seating, was eventually constructed. Though the symphony was disappointed that the original Oregon Ridge amphitheater never materialized, the summer season reached thousands of concertgoers who rarely ventured downtown.

Opposite. Crowds gathered to hear a performance at Baltimore County's Oregon Ridge Park, during one of the symphony's earlier concerts at the venue.

Top. From left to right, Baltimore city comptroller Hyman Pressman, board chairman Joseph Meyerhoff, Maryland state comptroller Louis Goldstein, and music director Sergiu Comissiona assist with the hall's official groundbreaking in November 1978.

As the decade progressed, many of Comissiona's designs for the symphony were realized or came closer to fruition. Groundbreaking for the Maryland Concert Center took place on Nov. 10, 1978. Meyerhoff, Mayor Schaefer, State Comptroller Louis Goldstein, Comissiona, and architect Robert Brannen attended the celebration. The following season marked the Baltimore Symphony's first performances outside the United States. In September 1979, the orchestra appeared as part of the Inter-American Music Festival with additional sponsorship by the National Autonomous University of Mexico. Three performances were held in Mexico City's newest hall, the Sala de Conciertos Nezahualcoyotl, and others were performed at the Teatro de la Ciudad in Mexico City and the Auditorio de la Reforma in Puebla. "It was beautiful weather and you had the feeling that you were doing something worthwhile," reflects trumpet player Don Tison. "We played well and it was our first exposure outside America." Unfortunately, the orchestra returned home without one harp, four basses, four cellos, and two timpani. Luckily, the missing instruments arrived on a later flight. The orchestra also returned home to the news that it was planning its first European tour in 1981.

XI FESTIVAL INTERNACIONAL DE MUSICA

INAUGURACION
ORQUESTA SINFONICA
DE BALTIMORE

AUDITORIO DE LA REFORMA
19 DE SEPTIEMBRE 1979
21:00 HORAS

PUEBLA MEXICO

Top. In 1979, Symphony musicians toured Mexico during the orchestra's first international tour.

Left. A tour poster is shown for the orchestra's September 1979 appearance at the Eleventh International Music Festival in Mexico City.

Right. Principal oboist Joseph Turner warms up on stage during the symphony's Mexico tour.

Bottom. The Mexico tour was plagued by occasional problems, such as this bus breakdown in rural Mexico.

For decades, the Baltimore Symphony had competed for concert patrons with the Philadelphia Orchestra series at the Lyric. The Philadelphia Orchestra had established a Baltimore concert series in 1907, nine years before the municipally-funded Baltimore Symphony was founded. As the Baltimore Symphony improved and expanded its artistic imprint, it gained the respect and support of its hometown audiences. By 1980, the Philadelphia series had been reduced to only four concerts a year. The Philadelphia Orchestra, though regarded as one of the world's greatest orchestras, lacked major local benefactors and suffered from dwindling attendance. "A number of musicians liked playing at the Lyric, they liked the acoustics," says one current Philadelphia Orchestra musician. One story goes that the

orchestra's then-new music director, Riccardo Muti, received an unfavorable review in the Sun and refused to return to Baltimore. On Oct. 24, 1979, reviewer Stephen Cera said, "Muti's interpretations frequently sound overblown and lacking in subtlety and refinement. … His overtly dramatic approach also led him to some other questionable touches." According to the Philadelphia musician, Muti said, "What's this 'Baltimore?' We're never going back to Baltimore!" Whatever the cause, the Philadelphia Orchestra ended its more-than-70-year run at the Lyric on April 8, 1980, with a performance of Prokofiev's Symphony No. 3. The Baltimore Symphony finally became Baltimore's orchestra, and it entered the next decade with excitement, and much to look forward to.

Stage personnel John Tivvis and
Bill Seibert prepare the Lyric Stage
in 1980.

CHAPTER

THE

The 1980s were pivotal for the Baltimore Symphony. The orchestra stepped off the decade filled with artistic and institutional growth.

It had embarked on its first international tour, made five commercial recordings, and started construction on a new permanent concert hall, thanks to the generous support of board president and benefactor Joseph Meyerhoff. The orchestra also had experienced growing pains, as each contract negotiation with the musicians resulted in a last-minute settlement or a work stoppage.

In 1975, the orchestra had appeared on public television with a performance of Karel Husa's *Music for Prague 1968*. But it was the opening of Baltimore's new waterfront retail and entertainment complex, Harborplace, that provided the orchestra with increased visibility via television. The brainchild of local developer James W. Rouse, Harborplace transformed downtown Baltimore with its $18 million festival marketplace. Harborplace officially opened on July 2, 1980, and the Baltimore Symphony was front and center, performing on two barges and appearing on national television. The televised documentary, *A City Celebrates*, was aired on over 200 public television stations across the country. It was a thrilling event for the city, the Baltimore Symphony, and the mayor, William Donald Schaefer. "The Harborplace opening was unbelievable," says Lainy Lebow-Sachs, Schaefer's longtime assistant. "It put Baltimore on the map." Lebow-Sachs calls Schaefer "a very driven man" and recalls his sentiments on that day. "I remember going back to [Schaefer's] office and everybody was just exhausted. I said

to him, 'Mayor, you must be so thrilled.' He replied, 'Little girl, [the Harborplace opening] has already happened. What the hell else is going on in this city?'"

Lebow-Sachs says Schaefer knew that the Baltimore Symphony "was so important to the fabric of the city. He didn't know much about classical music, but he enjoyed it." With Schaefer's support and passion for promotion, the Baltimore Symphony, as part of *A City Celebrates*, was broadcast nationwide on public television. Later in 1980, a semi-staged performance of Kodály's *Háry János* Suite appeared on cable television with Vincent Price as the story's narrator.

"One of the turning points of the Baltimore Symphony was our first European tour, under Comissiona," says clarinetist Christopher Wolfe. On May 14, 1981, the orchestra embarked on a 12-concert, 22-day tour of East and West Germany. In addition to numerous appearances throughout the two countries, there were two concerts as part of the Dresden International Festival. The agenda also included an appearance at East Berlin's Metropol-Theater. Sponsored in part by the U.S. International Communications Agency, the "Harmonie 1981" tour marked the first appearance of an American orchestra in East Germany. In the biography *A Romanian Rhapsody*, the conductor is quoted as telling the Evening Sun that the theme of the tour was the "joy of music that transcends national boundaries and political

Harmonie 1981
The Baltimore Symphony's East-West German Tour

BALTIMORE SYMPHONY
ORCHESTRA

Sergiu Comissiona
Music Director

Tour Information & Schedule
May 14 - June 4

differences, bringing together musicians and audiences in a celebration of our common musical heritage." Despite that aim, concert promoters made changes to Comissiona's repertoire. "I wanted very much to conduct a Shostakovich symphony, which the orchestra plays very well, but the German agent says this will be taken hard by Germans," he said.

The performances throughout West Germany received rave reviews in cities such as Cologne, Frankfurt, and Bonn. Despite the tour's success, it did have its share of problems. At the orchestra's final appearance in West Germany, Comissiona slipped on the stage of the Auditorium Maximum at the University of Regensburg one hour before the performance. The resulting injury to a leg called his participation at that evening's concert into question, but he conducted –"though his manner was less animated than it can be," according to the Sun. However, the orchestra's appearances in East Germany received the most attention. Four Russian members of the symphony's musicians refused to cross the border into East Germany. Musicians from Munich and Frankfurt replaced the Russian-born musicians at the East German concerts. Violinist Gregory Kuperstein says, "Comissiona understood why some of us couldn't travel to East Germany. They were very gracious about not making us go." Two other musicians were detained at the East German border because of their immigration status. When the symphony buses finally made it

into East Berlin, the musicians found a drab, quiet ghost city with only a few shops and restaurants. "In East Berlin, we had tons of per diem, but there was nothing to spend it on," recalls flutist Bonnie Lake. "By the time the concert ended, they had run out of food."

Conductor Gunther Herbig attended a Baltimore Symphony concert in East Germany. "I met Sergiu after a concert, and he told me that I had to come to Baltimore," he said. "I was surprised by the orchestra. I knew that Baltimore had an orchestra, but I had never heard them." In Dresden, many orchestra members visited a music store and purchased large quantities of scores that were being sold at only a fraction of the price found in Western music houses. The orchestra's East Berlin performance ended with boisterous applause, along with loud, rhythmic clapping and three encores. A 10-minute ovation followed a performance of Mahler's Symphony No. 4 in G major in Dresden. Principal second violinist George Orner said, "I think they were applauding freedom as much as they were the music." Herbig believed that the orchestra's appearances in East Germany might help better relations with the United States. "There was great hope that things might relax," recalls Herbig.

The orchestra returned to Baltimore on June 4. "We came back to Baltimore, we were treated like rock stars," says clarinetist Wolfe. "We had a police escort all the way back to Baltimore from the airport. People thought the Baltimore Symphony was the greatest thing, next to the Orioles and the Colts," as a result of the tour's success. An hour-long audio documentary on the tour, *Echoes of Harmony 1981: Sounds and Voices of the Baltimore Symphony Orchestra on Tour* aired on WBJC-FM. It was produced by Louis Mills and narrated by Rheda Becker. Parts of the documentary were featured on NPR's *All Things Considered* and the entire program was nominated for a Peabody Award. The historic tour brought worldwide attention to the orchestra and Baltimore. On its editorial page, the Sun wrote, "This is only one – and a very obvious – example of the value of this orchestra to Baltimore and to Maryland. The greatest benefit we reap from it, however, is not advertising or prestige, great as they are, but the music it makes."

The Baltimore Symphony entered the 1981-82 concert season without a contract with the musicians. The orchestra had received worldwide attention from its tour of East and West Germany, and the symphony's newfound acclaim encouraged the musicians to seek further growth in their own situations.

The musicians did not share these concerns in the media attention given to the tour. David Fetter, chairperson of the musicians' Players' Committee, says, "Being on tour is like being in Neverland. You have plenty to think about." With a reported $1.8 million accumulated deficit on a $4.5 million annual budget, the symphony board and management entered negotiations with serious financial concerns. The musicians wanted parity with peer orchestras. The calls for higher pay, a 52-week season, greater pension contributions, and other working-condition improvements were in line with the mandate of Mayor Schaefer's 1972 blue ribbon panel. "The musicians [during these negotiations] were a strong group," states Fetter. "They were tough and focused."

Recognizing that a contract satisfactory to them would not be easy to get, the musicians proposed a play-and-talk scenario. But in mid-September 1981, contract talks broke down. The board did not agree to the play-and-talk proposal and the musicians declared the situation a lockout. Union lawyer Lenny Leibowitz represented the musicians and Frank Baker represented the Baltimore Symphony Association. Baker called the musicians' position "unrealistic" and "out of tune." He said, "Baltimore neither has nor can raise the money to meet their demands. [The musicians] are trying to

Left. Leon Fleisher shakes the hand of newly appointed concertmaster Herbert Greenberg at the lockout benefit concert on December 19, 1981.

Opp. Left. Violinist Sylvia Angel Shor and music director Sergiu Comissiona engage in a private conversation.

Opp. Right. Principal cellist Mihály Virizlay prepares for a concert at the Lyric during the early 1980s.

get blood out of a turnip." As the musicians scheduled their own "lockout concerts," management canceled weeks of the season and threatened to cancel the entire year. Both sides were keenly aware that the new Maryland Concert Center was less than one year away from its grand opening, but neither side engaged in consistent talks. Pianist and former resident conductor Leon Fleisher grew frustrated in the lack of progress. "Comissiona was desperate because of the musicians," recalls Fleisher. "Some of them were thinking in terms of leaving, and he had built the orchestra to an international level." On Dec. 18, 1981, Fleisher and the pianist André Watts performed a benefit concert for the musicians at the Lyric. The concert included music by Rachmaninoff, Beethoven, and Copland. The musicians called the event "the last gasp from an organization on the verge of collapsing into the strictly second-rate." Fleisher continued to work behind the scenes and called arts supporters, Gordy Becker and Julianne Alderman, for help. Becker said, "Let's get Ron Shapiro in here."

Shapiro was a baseball agent who had successfully negotiated many contracts for sports figures. After an 18½-hour negotiating session, Shapiro succeeded where federal mediators had not. According to the Sun, Shapiro asked both sides to review both offers, and to "step back and look at the overall package." A tentative agreement was reached on Jan. 10, 1982. In addition to the financial settlement, Fleisher, along with Becker and Alderman, was responsible for a new "Friends of the Baltimore Symphony" support group. They were charged to raise $664,000, but they could not approach any of the current symphony contributors. "We did it, so we kind of saved the orchestra," says Fleisher. "I'm very proud of that."

Shapiro was praised for his skills. He "was such a positive force and a great, influential person," says the Players' Committee's Fetter. By the end of four years, gains would include base weekly salary increases from $410 to $620, monthly pension increases from $400 to $800, and a 52-week season, "the recognized benchmark of major American symphony orchestras," as described in a musicians' labor history narrative. The board and management were pleased that the increases were spread over four years and not three, and that the new symphony hall would be able to successfully celebrate its grand opening the following September.

By the 1980s, a number of Baltimore Symphony musicians had lengthy tenures with the orchestra and were known for their unique personalities. "The greatest quality of the Baltimore Symphony musicians is their loyalty," says Ruth Aranow, wife of former English hornist and personnel manager George Aranow. "Most of the orchestra goes back for many years. The principals were all very ambitious, but the section players had very long tenures. They've stayed through thick and thin." George Aranow retired as the English horn player in 1976 but remained personnel manager. Ruth Aranow says, "George had a wonderful sense of humor and was always full of a chuckle. He stopped playing because he was tired of making reeds. After he retired, he hired himself to play bass oboe for a performance. He told me that he was so terrible that he would never hire himself again!"

Violinist Evelina Martini joined the orchestra in 1940 and retired in 1967. "Evelina would always complain about the [hotel] rooms on tours," says piccolo player Laurie Sokoloff. "After the orchestra checked into the hotel, the personnel manager would always wait for her in the lobby to return. One time, the stage crew went to her room before she arrived and put goldfish in her toilet bowl. Instead of complaining, she found a pet store, and carried the fish in a glass bowl for the remainder of the tour." Sylvia Angel Shor also joined the violin section in 1940 and remained until 1983. The Sun once referred to her as "a florid platinum-hued Florence Nightingale from Park Heights." "Sylvia capitalized on Comissiona's superstitious side," recalls Sokoloff. "Comissiona always wore French cuffs, and he forgot his cufflinks one day. One of her husband's clients gave him some cufflinks that he didn't like, so she always carried them in her violin case. Comissiona arrived at a concert and was in a panic because he didn't have his cufflinks. Sylvia found out and handed him the cufflinks from her husband, and said she had received a message that morning and put cufflinks in her purse. He thought she was a witch, so she knew he'd never fire her!"

Another longtime musician, one of the orchestra's most popular and visible, was principal cellist Mihály Virizlay, affectionately known as "Misi." Virizlay left Hungary in 1956 to escape Soviet repression after the failure of the revolution. He arrived in the United States and became a member of the symphonies in Dallas and then Pittsburgh. Virizlay joined the Baltimore Symphony as principal cellist in 1962 and remained on its roster until 2005. Associate principal cello Chang Woo Lee became his stand partner in 1978. "When I first joined the orchestra, I didn't know how great he was," says Lee. "He was a great musician and had a big heart. We had a fabulous time together. I'd bump into patrons after the concert and they'd say, 'You two are always smiling and laughing. What's going on between you two!'"

In May 1982, the Maryland Concert Center was nearing completion and the Baltimore Symphony prepared for its final

Top. In early 1982, construction workers prepare to install the Meyerhoff's seats.

Bottom. Garbage collects outside the Lyric Theatre during the 1970s. The Lyric's physical and aesthetic conditions influenced Meyerhoff and symphony supporters to build a new concert hall.

concerts at the Lyric. On the 21st, the Board of Public Works, on behalf of the state, city, and symphony, formally renamed the center the Joseph Meyerhoff Symphony Hall. "My grandfather did not request the naming of the hall," says Meyerhoff's granddaughter Terry Meyerhoff Rubenstein. "But it was my grandmother who liked it. They were very proud of the hall." In addition, Schaefer named Meyerhoff the first recipient of the Mayor's Award for Outstanding Support for the Arts by a Private Citizen. Later that month, the symphony performed its final concert at the Lyric after 65 years. Itzhak Perlman joined Comissiona and the orchestra in a performance of Brahms' Violin Concerto in D major.

Over the years, the symphony musicians had grown frustrated with the Lyric and were anxious to leave. "The Lyric was sorely in need of repair," says Sokoloff. "I had two piccolos crack on me because the temperature inside reached over 90 degrees! [The musicians] didn't like the facility, and we weren't in control of our schedule. We often couldn't rehearse there and would end up rehearsing at places like Eastern High School. We were second-class citizens at the Lyric." Still, the orchestra vacated the Lyric in style. At the end of its final concert, the orchestra performed the final movement of Haydn's Symphony No. 45 ("Farewell"), and as directed by the composer, the musicians left the stage slowly, one after the other. Comissiona had requested that there be no applause for this appropriate end to concerts at the Lyric.

Opened in 1894 as the Music Hall, the Lyric Theatre served as the city's major concert destination. Designed by architect Henry Randall of New York, the Lyric was called shortly after its completion, "an unsightly square brick hall with a decidedly unfinished [exterior] appearance, but with wonderful acoustic properties." Its architect modeled the Lyric after Germany's Leipzig Gewandhaus. During the early part of the century, the Lyric suffered frequent financial troubles. In 1909, new owners who intended to transform the Lyric into a grand opera house purchased the hall but plans were abandoned for financial reasons. By 1910, the Lyric reportedly fell into a "deplorably bad condition" and rumors abounded that the theatre would become a trade hall or a garage. By 1920, a new foundation assumed control of the Lyric and hoped "from now on music has found in Baltimore a permanent as well as a fitting and satisfactory home, but a home not yet perfect." The Baltimore Symphony, along with many visiting orchestras, called the Lyric its home from 1916 to 1982.

On Sept. 16, 1982, the $23 million Joseph Meyerhoff Symphony Hall officially opened for a gala concert. The Meyerhoff was designed to seat 2,467 patrons and provide a sound that had "the perfection of a Stradivarius violin." A total of 52 2,800-pound clouds, along with 18 fiberglass discs, hung from the ceiling, 44 to 62 feet above. Comissiona referred to the evening as "the culmination of a dream," while Joe Meyerhoff noted that "the dream was Sergiu Comissiona's dream." But Meyerhoff continued that Comissiona "had the dream and I had the money, and he worried me so long about that damned dream that I finally parted with some of the money." On opening night, Meyerhoff basked in the glory of his new hall. He told the Sun, "I'll probably be shot for saying this, but I always felt when I went to the Lyric, I was going slumming." The gala opening was broadcast live on PBS with the actor Tony Randall as host.

The opening concert featured many special selections. The program began with the world premiere of Morton Gould's *Housewarming*, with the composer in attendance. Richard Strauss' tone poem *Ein Heldenleben* followed. The Strauss work showcased the symphony's relatively new concertmaster,

Herbert Greenberg. But the evening's showpiece was the return of Fleisher as a "two-handed" pianist. Though he was scheduled to play a Beethoven concerto, Fleisher instead performed Franck's *Symphonic Variations* followed by an encore, Chopin's Nocturne in B-flat major. The audience leapt to its feet when Fleisher finished the Franck, thrilled that one of its favorites had overcome his affliction. But Fleisher thought that his return to two-handed piano was "deceptive." He says, "Everybody thought I was cured, and I wasn't. And I knew I wasn't. That is why I had to change pieces. The audience thought, here's his big return and he's fine! It was a terrible evening for me."

Just as new energy was sweeping through the organization, Sergiu Comissiona dropped a bombshell. On Dec. 9, 1982, he said he would not renew his contract after the 1983-84 season. At the same time, the Houston Symphony announced Comissiona as its new music director. Comissiona had served as Houston's artistic adviser for the previous three seasons, and rumors had abounded that he was considering the move. He told reporters, "It's better to leave when I felt my achievements have been done. As an artist, it's better to leave at the top of the

mountain." Meyerhoff had learned about the decision a week before its announcement, and was infuriated. According to *A Romanian Rhapsody*, Meyerhoff scolded Comissiona: "What more do you want? Haven't I given you everything you wanted? Haven't I reached the end of your list? Make another list! You think I wouldn't have the time? I can have the orchestra included in my will if this is your concern."

Comissiona initially asked for the title "Conductor Laureate" but it was promptly denied. He said, "These [past] 15 years have been the most exciting of my life, but it is time for a new challenge, a change, and the time came for a change." He ended his Baltimore Symphony career in May 1984 with a performance of Mahler's valedictory Symphony No. 9. Yet Comissiona's need for change did not guarantee happiness. When he returned to Baltimore some years later, he confided in longtime personnel manager George Aranow. Aranow's wife, Ruth, recalls Comissiona's telling her husband that leaving Baltimore "was the worst thing he ever did." He was not happy in Houston. "He didn't like the community and the community did not embrace him. He knew he made a mistake," recalls Ruth Aranow.

Opp. Top. The gala opening of the Meyerhoff featured a commemorative poster of Pegasus, commissioned by Crown Petroleum and designed by Toronto artist Heather Cooper.

Opp. Bottom. A portrait of Joseph Meyerhoff is presented to the hall's namesake shortly after its opening. Meyerhoff was unhappy with his likeness

and the portrait was never on display during his lifetime. Pictured from left to right: Principal bassoonist Phillip Kolker, Sergiu Comissiona, Joe and Rebecca Meyerhoff, and oboist Jane Marvine.

Above. Newly appointed music director David Zinman stands before the Baltimore Symphony at the Joseph Meyerhoff Symphony Hall.

The Baltimore Symphony quickly went to work to find Comissiona's successor. Much attention was focused on David Zinman. In 1981, Joseph Silverstein had been named the symphony's first principal guest conductor. Comissiona had been spending more time in Houston and the Baltimore Symphony wanted to establish more long-term relationships with other conductors. As Silverstein made his Baltimore conducting debut, executive director Joe Leavitt publicly acknowledged that the orchestra was also courting Zinman, then the music director of the Rochester Philharmonic. By early 1983, just weeks after Comissiona's departure announcement, Leavitt was able to announce that Silverstein would become music adviser for the 1984-85 season and Zinman would be the new principal guest conductor. Leavitt told the Sun, "You can't go without mentioning Zinman. He is a highly qualified and a very good conductor. Nobody says anything but good things about him. He's a conductor with a track record."

But more bad news was in the offing. In July 1983, Leavitt was diagnosed with a brain tumor. He had been the driving organizational force behind the orchestra and had guided the opening of the Meyerhoff Symphony Hall. "Joe managed

it, got it done, and did it well," says BSO manager Carol Bogash. "The unthinkable happened" with his diagnosis. Leavitt eventually returned to work, but the stress of running the orchestra, especially during leadership changes, proved too much. He retired in the spring of 1984. The trio that had led the symphony's artistic and institutional growth for more than a decade had dissolved.

On Oct. 5, 1983, Meyerhoff, who had headed the search committee, named Zinman as the symphony's 10th music director. Meyerhoff called Comissiona's departure "a real blow" and added, "To get someone to succeed Sergiu and do it successfully was not an easy prospect to contemplate. Fortunately we had someone in our midst." Zinman's tenure would start with the 1985-86 season. At the news conference, Zinman said, "Baltimore is a fine orchestra and one with great potential. In fact, it was a top orchestra in the making, and I am committed to working tirelessly to achieve high standards." In a statement, Comissiona said he was "delighted" by the choice, saying Zinman "is an excellent conductor and a person whom I highly admire and respect." Zinman can recall his earliest memories as the Baltimore Symphony's new artistic leader. "I initially came onto

Opp. Left. David Zinman was named music director of the Baltimore Symphony in October 1983. Meyerhoff finally bestowed the title of "Conductor Laureate" to Comissiona in 1984.

Opp. Right. Oprah Winfrey of WJZ-TV co-hosted the annual WJZ/BSO Musical Marathon on September 11, 1983. Also pictured is Associate Principal Horn Peter Landgren.

Right. Clarinetist Christopher Wolfe also served as the symphony's assistant conductor in the mid 1980s. Wolfe is shown here leading the orchestra in 1983 at a Johns Hopkins Medical Center holiday concert for children.

the scene because they needed a principal guest conductor. When Sergiu left, it was a great shock for Joe Meyerhoff, who was very unhappy. But I started off with a very good set of cards. The orchestra was at a high level and the young players were very good. Sergiu had done a very good job with the orchestra." Zinman quickly took over where Comissiona had left off.

A few months after Zinman was named music director, Catherine Comet was named associate conductor. Zinman called Comet "one of the highest-ranking female conductors in the United States." Between 1984 and 1986, she conducted several subscription and educational concerts, and helped advise on artistic matters. "She was a good musician with a lot of integrity," recalls English horn player Jane Marvine. "She was a high-quality assistant and tried to elevate the Youth Concerts to another level." After two seasons in Baltimore, Comet was appointed music director of the Grand Rapids Symphony, becoming the first woman to be named music director of a professional American symphony orchestra.

In April 1984, John Gidwitz began his tenure as executive director. "When I came, everybody was in mourning because Comissiona was leaving," recalls Gidwitz. The new Meyerhoff hall had increased the organization's visibility and respect in the community, but the orchestra still faced institutional challenges. The Friends of the Symphony, a product of the 1981 lockout, produced an annual, nine-hour *Musical Marathon* fund-raiser program on WJZ-TV. From 1982 to 1984, the annual telethon was hosted by local personalities such as Jerry Turner, Donna Hamilton, and Oprah Winfrey, who at that time was a WJZ news anchor. The Friends of the Symphony had committed to raising $750,000 by the end of 1985. Though the telethons raised significant amounts, the group fell short of its goal. Gidwitz also faced continued resentment among the musicians as a result of the 1981 lockout. Former general manager Mark Volpe referred to it in the Sun as "part of the Baltimore Symphony experience. A 16-week work stoppage is not easily forgotten, the musicians remember leaner times."

Baltimore is a very unique place. It has a very down-home quality to it. There is wonderful countryside along with urban blight. But people there are very proud of themselves. Many people were really good to the orchestra in the time I was there. There were people who really put their money where their mouths were. The mayor was very much involved in the orchestra and so was the governor.

When I came to Baltimore, there was this enormous feeling of going forward with Sergiu. I was very lucky to come at a time when Sergiu had taken the orchestra to a high level. I was very happy to be able to continue from that level. Sergiu was a very inspiring conductor who was always after colors. But I felt that for the orchestra to go forward, there had to be rhythm. I worked on that very consciously. We did a lot of Beethoven and we did a lot of difficult modern music which hadn't been done before and that made the orchestra very steady on its feet.

We made a lot of progress with the orchestra. We experimented and we did a lot of things that were really exciting. The recordings are a testament to that time. There are 13 years of broadcasts and if you listen to some of them, they're quite good. I think broadcasting is very important because it allows the orchestra to hear themselves and they're surprised at how good it is. It brings them up to another level.

I don't miss Baltimore. My sister lives in Baltimore so we see it quite often. I still follow what goes on in Baltimore and I still root for the Orioles. I lived for 12 years in Rochester and I don't miss Rochester. I think that it was just one part of my life. You move on. Conductors leave but orchestras go on. I'd probably not return to Baltimore. I'm almost 80 now and I'm trying to slow down as much as I can. Sometimes you just can't go back again.

There are some people in the Baltimore Symphony that I dearly miss. I had a good time with the orchestra. The good things are the ones that I like to remember.

Happy birthday, Baltimore Symphony.

–David Zinman

And then, on Feb. 2, 1985, Joe Meyerhoff – board chairman, philanthropist, and community advocate – died from heart failure, age 85. Frank Baker, the board president, announced Meyerhoff's death to a surprised audience at a Sunday Favorites program. "We have lost a very, very dear friend," he said from the stage. "I could say a great deal about my friend Joseph Meyerhoff… [Before Meyerhoff was board chairman] we were more well-known as a regional company, and we played less than 40 weeks a year. Under Meyerhoff's leadership, our symphony just kept on growing and growing, until now we have a symphony of international repute." Mayor Schaefer simply told the Sun that Meyerhoff "was one of the great men I've met in my lifetime."

"John Gidwitz and I came together at the same time, and things looked like they were going to be terrible," recalls Zinman. "We didn't know exactly what had happened, but very fortunately, people wanted to continue. They had this new hall, and they wanted to continue having the orchestra ascend." Zinman says his early relationship with Gidwitz helped rejuvenate the orchestra and let it take some risks. "John and I were both young, and we sat around and would try something new. We were innovating, and it was a great period of enthusiasm and accomplishment," he says. "We started going to Carnegie Hall, we were recording with Telarc and Sony, and we had a wonderful radio series. We were a very good team together." During his time as music director, Zinman made more than two dozen recordings

with the Baltimore Symphony. "The recordings were hard because you only had a small amount of time to do things. You had to be totally efficient, and thankfully I had a lot of experience making recordings," he says. Flutist Bonnie Lake agrees, saying Zinman "was always prepared to the nth degree. He had a good psychology with recording. He was very competent and kept things calm." Lake calls Zinman "organized, unusual, and innovative. He had clever ideas, his precision was beyond belief, and his ego never got in the way." Fleisher says, "David came along and cleaned things out like Hercules washing the stables. He gives vitality, energy, life, momentum, and direction to the music. I think David is something else. Why he isn't a conductor of one of the top five orchestras, I'll never understand it."

When the musicians' contract expired in 1985, the symphony board took a fresh approach. With a new chairman in place – Calman "Buddy" Zamoiski Jr., head of a large appliance distribution firm – musicians and management tried a less confrontational style and did not use lawyers at the table. The organization had accumulated a $2.5 million deficit and the musicians agreed to lessen the financial stress. The musicians accepted an immediate $10 a week pay cut, in return for improved touring conditions, increased vacation time, and a stronger pension plan. Zamoiski built a coalition that persuaded state legislators to allocate $2 million a year to the orchestra as part of a deficit-reduction plan. The grant consisted of six installments that totaled $10 million to help the orchestra stabilize its finances and grow its endowment. In addition, Leslie B. Disharoon, then president and chairman of Monumental Corp., began a $36 million campaign, designed to increase the endowment from $7.7 million to $35.9 million and also to provide much-needed funds to cover deficits. In weeks, Disharoon had secured $10.7 million in pledges, and within one year the goal had been revised to $40 million. A $2 million gift from USF&G became the largest single corporate donation to an American orchestra, and the total was the largest raised by an orchestra at that time. "Les worked hard to understand the BSO's true needs and raise enough funds to stabilize the orchestra financially for the present and into the future." says Gidwitz. But English horn player Marvine also gives much credit to Zamoiski: "Buddy was the real mover and shaker behind the campaigns. He did it all."

In addition to increased touring and recording, Zinman developed new concert formats. To add to the midweek "Celebrity" concerts and the "Favorites" Saturday evening performances established by Comissiona, Zinman began Saturday morning "Casual" concerts. Starting at 11 a.m., the Casual concerts were light in format and lasted no more than an hour. The concerts were often broadcast live over public radio. Of all the series he developed during his Baltimore tenure, Zinman recalls the Casual concerts as a highlight. "The orchestra had a personality in the Casual concerts," he says. "I wanted to create a series where people could come to the orchestra and feel comfortable. I wanted to bring in the audience, and we did that through the Casual concerts. They were fun concerts and we did amazingly silly things. We had a fake sponsor, the Tapioca Growers' Association of South America. 'When was the last time you had some?' Casual concerts were modeled after *Prairie Home Companion*. We had soloists doing piano tricks, we had skits like Brahms being psychoanalyzed, and one live radio program where the audience was stuck on the JFX in a large traffic mess. [During that live program] I told the drivers, 'OK, you all out there, do the wave!' It was a fun period and it made a difference for the orchestra. It gave them an outside audience because we were broadcast on NPR."

Top. The Baltimore Symphony Woodwind Quintet performs a private chamber music recital during the mid 1980s. Pictured from left to right are: Flutist Timothy Day, oboist Joseph Turner, hornist David Bakkegard, bassoonist Phillip Kolker, and clarinetist Steven Barta.

Opposite. Music director David Zinman and Rebecca Meyerhoff have their photo taken at a symphony gala.

Right Top and Bottom. In April 1987, Zinman inaugurated the Saturday morning Casual Concert series. These innovative audience-interaction programs were broadcast nationwide on American Public Radio and produced by WJHU radio. Lisa Simeone (top) served as a co-host and helped write the radio scripts. Judith Schonbach (bottom) was the series' producer. Based on the Prairie Home Companion format, the broadcast always acknowledged its fictitious sponsor, Tapgasa, the Tapioca Growers' Association of South America.

The Casual series began in November 1987 and lasted for more than two decades. During his first season as music director, Zinman also inaugurated the Discovery series. "Designed only for interested concert-goers and requiring a relatively small number of musicians," the Discovery series was held at Westminster Hall and featured music by the latest composers. The Sun praised the Discovery concerts: "What Zinman appears to be doing is easing Baltimore audiences into the 20th century, breaking down the ingrained myths that modern music is a stark, humorless collection of random noises." Principal trumpet Don Tison remembers the Discovery series as a "tour de force" for the ensemble. "I practiced 20 times longer for these programs than for the others." The orchestra also established a Classically Black series in 1990. The series was designed to reach new audiences, and featured African-American soloists and composers.

Opp. Top. The Baltimore Symphony rehearses at Vienna's Schauspielhaus during its 1987 European tour.

Opp. Bottom. A program booklet for a Baltimore Symphony appearance in the Soviet Union is entirely written and printed in Russian.

Right. Cellist Yo-Yo Ma and conductor David Zinman rehearse in 1988 for an upcoming recording session.

With a successful $40 million campaign and a new, energized music director, the orchestra embarked on its second overseas tour on May 1, 1987. Over four weeks, the Baltimore Symphony performed in several large European cities, returning to East Germany but also becoming the first American orchestra to perform in the Soviet Union since 1976. At a monthly meeting before the tour, Gidwitz mentioned to the symphony board that the Philadelphia Orchestra had recently declined an invitation to perform in Russia. Gidwitz says, "I heard a voice on my right say, 'Why don't we go?' I didn't pay much attention to it, but again I heard, 'Why don't we go?' It was Lyn Meyerhoff, Joseph Meyerhoff's daughter-in-law, and you don't ignore Lyn twice. Two days later, Lyn had an invitation for us to come to Russia during the upcoming tour. The tour was like the Super Bowl for us. We had dramatic success." Zinman recalls, "Not only did we go to England, [the orchestra] went [back] to East Germany. At that time, it was just gray and foggy and smoggy. And then we went to Moscow and Leningrad. We played for such monstrously appreciative audiences. It was a very exciting tour, because it brought the orchestra together." Violist Sharon Myer recalls

the orchestra's final performance in Russia. "At the end of the concert, people from the audience came up to the stage with flowers. The entire street outside the hall was filled with thousands of people. They treated us like rock stars and just wanted to touch us! We played *Candide* [Overture] as an encore, and people just wanted to know what that piece was. We also played [Copland's] *'Tis the gift to be simple, 'tis the gift to be free*. I was just so moved, because I was coming from a country where we are free, and people wanted to talk to you, but could only do so outside of our hotel."

After the successful tour, Zinman, along with the board and management, continued promoting the Baltimore Symphony with out-of-town performances. After a March 1988 Carnegie Hall appearance, the symphony immediately traveled to the West Coast. The orchestra performed in six cities, including San Francisco, Los Angeles, and Tucson, with cellist Yo-Yo Ma. The management developed plans for future touring throughout the East Coast and the Far East. When he arrived in Baltimore in 1985, Zinman had told the symphony board that "a major orchestra plays subscription concerts, it broadcasts, it makes records, and it tours."

But once again, the symphony faced contract talks. The contract would expire in September 1988 and the players thought that it was time to address their needs. They had gone through the lengthy lockout in 1981 and accepted a concessionary agreement in 1985. They had accepted the cuts to facilitate the success of the endowment campaign. By 1988, the musicians wanted parity with other major orchestras, to reclaim lost pay and attract a strong pool of audition candidates. Talks quickly broke down. Musicians complained that they received "a shocking laundry list of 47 givebacks," including "the onerous weakening of the demotion and dismissal procedures." On Sept. 23, 1988, the musicians unanimously authorized a strike. The players held firm to the directives of the 1972 blue ribbon panel. The strike dragged on for weeks without much in the way of productive talks. "There was nothing to talk about," said one musician negotiator. Musicians frequently picketed the Meyerhoff, and the actor Edward Asner, in town for a performance of *Born Yesterday* at the Morris Mechanic Theatre, joined the picket line one October morning.

Top. Concertmaster Herbert Greenberg and Principal Flutist Emily Skala walk a picket line during the 1988 musicians' strike.

Center. Symphony management and musician representatives meet across the table during negotiations on November 17, 1988.

Bottom. Governor William Donald Schaefer announces the end of the symphony strike in February 1989.

Opposite. Flutist James Galway rehearses Corigliano's Pied Piper Fantasy in 1989.

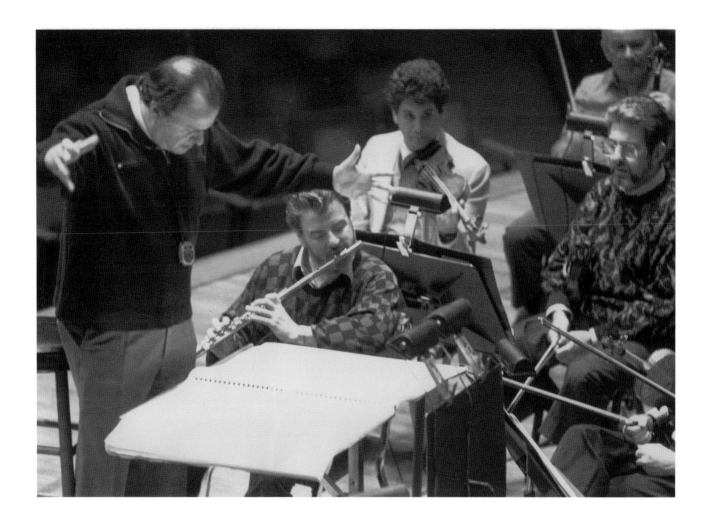

In January 1989, outside mediation proved unsuccessful and the entire season was threatened with cancellation. William Donald Schaefer, now Maryland's governor, grew frustrated with the lack of progress. "When the orchestra was on strike, he was beside himself," says Schaefer aide Lainy Lebow-Sachs. Schaefer contacted Willard Hackerman, president of Whiting-Turner Contracting Co. and a symphony board member, and, according to Lebow-Sachs, told him, "'We can't let this happen.' He told Willard that he had to get involved. He felt that Willard could fix anything." On Feb. 16, 1989, a tentative agreement was reached. The 22-week strike at the time was the longest work stoppage for a major American orchestra. Hackerman personally contributed $180,000 to help settle the dispute. The musicians received some financial gains, along with increased pension and seniority payments. And the primary motivation of the strike, the proposed demotion and dismissal clauses, disappeared.

Still, the strike once again left deep wounds. Piccolo player Laurie Sokoloff says, "In the end, we never came out ahead. We never recouped the money that cost us. We were fighting more for just having a better orchestra." Gidwitz remembers it as "tremendous strife." Zinman thought that "all of the progress that the orchestra made just came to a stop and we had to start over again." In December 1989, a Committee for the Future was formed. It was composed of players, board members, and management. The group worked to instill and improve trust and communication within the organization. The committee agreed to debate and discuss all issues and share "previously sequestered important information." The committee had its work cut out. The strike was hard for all sides, and affected morale and institutional progress in coming years. And yet the orchestra continued on its successful artistic path.

The Baltimore Symphony entered 1990 on a celebratory note.

In February, it won its first Grammy award for a Sony Classical recording of Barber's Concerto for Violoncello and Orchestra and Britten's Symphony for Cello and Orchestra. The recording, with cellist Yo-Yo Ma, won in the category of Best Classical Performer–Instrumental Soloist With Orchestra. The orchestra was enjoying its new relationship with Christopher Seaman, the first resident conductor appointed under David Zinman's tenure as music director. The Sun called Seaman a "tasteful interpreter" and stated that his "capacity to inspire affection among his players has made Seaman – in his way – as respected and as valued a figure" as Zinman. And the work of the Committee for the Future was continuing. Board, staff, and musicians worked to improve the organization's morale and searched for answers to its problems.

But the 1988-89 strike had lasting effects. The work stoppage seemed especially hard on Zinman. "I couldn't understand why [the strike] came to that," he says. "Both sides were so entrenched and not listening to each other. Both sides were just lying to each other, and it really turned me off. All of the progress that we made just came to a stop, and we had to start all over again." Zinman praises the musicians for their attitude after the strike ended. "I have to say that the orchestra was just fantastic, and they went ahead and we moved forward. The minute we came back, the musicians seemed very excited about doing what they came back to do."

But relationships among the board, staff, and musicians didn't improve overnight. When a strike is over and work resumes, he says, "suddenly it's not a pleasant atmosphere, and it takes a while for that to dissipate, because everyone blames everyone else." Through better communication and transparency, the Baltimore Symphony wanted to avoid labor strife when the hard-fought contract itself expired in 1992.

"When David was on the podium, it was easy to engage soloists like Alfred Brendel, Isaac Stern, Emanuel Ax, Yo-Yo Ma, and many others," says artistic administrator Miryam Yardumian. "Everybody wanted to work with David." The symphony musicians benefitted and enjoyed Zinman's relationship with many big-name soloists. "David was such a great musical partner," says Yardumian. "He inspired and elevated the BSO musicians' ability to accompany. They listened to the soloist's phrasing and dynamics, and imitated it in their parts." Performances by a young violinist, Pamela Frank, and the pianist Malcolm Frager helped round out the season. In summer 1990, Frager performed four piano concertos with Zinman and the symphony. They turned out to be his final public appearances. Between concertos, Frager spent most of his time in bed. "We could tell he was in pain. He passed away the following June. It was particularly difficult for David as he and Malcolm were good friends," recalls Yardumian.

Top. Governor William Donald Schaefer presents David Zinman with the Governor's Award for the orchestra's 1990 Grammy win. The pair is joined by management and musician representatives.

Bottom. David Zinman leads a Baltimore Symphony performance during the mid 1990s

Violin virtuoso Hilary Hahn, who was raised in Baltimore says, "the BSO was the first orchestra I saw, in a concert at the Meyerhoff when I was 5." As she prepared for her first full recital in 1990 at age 10, Hahn's Peabody teacher Klara Berkovich, mother of BSO violinist Leonid Berkovich, arranged a test run of the recital on the Meyerhoff stage for a few BSO musicians. "Principal cellist Misi Virizlay had heard me rehearsing the program at some point. Right before I began my play-through at the Meyerhoff, Misi stopped me, ran backstage, and grabbed David Zinman, insisting that he listen to at least some of it. Maestro Zinman wound up staying for the whole thing! Afterwards, he offered to mentor me: to give advice and musical coachings from his perspective, and to help in general with whatever music-related issues might come up for me," recalls Hahn. "When David Zinman took me under his wing, I got to know Miryam Yardumian; she helped me manage my developing career and also introduced me to visiting soloists and conductors when I attended concerts. By being around backstage, I became familiar with more of the orchestra. When it came time to make my first orchestral recording, Beethoven's Violin Concerto and Bernstein's Serenade for SONY, I asked the BSO and Maestro Zinman to join me; it was the only collaboration I could imagine for that record."

The Baltimore Symphony celebrated its 75th anniversary during the 1990-91 season. Many subscription concerts opened with 75-second-long musical birthday greetings from various composers. One of the season's highlights was yet another repeat of the original Feb. 11, 1916, program. "It wasn't too good a program," recalls Zinman. The Sun felt otherwise: "The orchestra of 75 years ago could not have played with such … accuracy, fire, and weight. The Baltimore Symphony looked back 75 years with the clarity and freshness that are characteristic of the current orchestra and its music director." But Zinman wanted to be sure that the anniversary was celebrated in grand form. For the preceding three years, he had urged management to program Mahler's Symphony No. 8 in E flat major, known as "Symphony of a Thousand," as the centerpiece of the celebratory season. "Nothing else would do, because nothing else brings so many things to life," Zinman

said of Mahler's Eighth Symphony. It was a work he had always dreamed of conducting. When it was presented in June 1991, 35 extra musicians, over 300 chorus members, and numerous soloists were led by Zinman from a podium that was two feet higher than usual. Backstage facilities were taxed, and performance costs exceeded a standard subscription program by $90,000. In celebration of the symphony's anniversary, the Saturday night performance was broadcast live on WJHU radio.

But the evening before the broadcast, the scheduled soprano soloist canceled due to an injury. "I had a total of five hours to find someone ready to do Mahler 8 who was near the Baltimore area," remembers Yardumian. As it turned out, Kaaren Erickson, a soprano with the Metropolitan Opera, had sung the work and was planning to drive near the area en route from New York to Tennessee that day.

Above. Music director David Zinman helps celebrate the orchestra's 75th anniversary in 1991.

Right. A souvenir pennant commemorates the symphony's 75th anniversary in 1991. Coupons for a free ticket during the 100th

anniversary season often accompanied the pennants.

Opposite. The Baltimore Symphony performed Mahler's mammoth Eighth Symphony in June 1991, as a culmination of the 75th anniversary season.

Erickson could not leave New York until 4:30 p.m. and the live performance was scheduled to begin at 8:15. "Kaaren arrived at the stage door at 8:20 p.m., and she ran into the dressing room to change into her formal dress," says Yardumian. "She had already done her hair and makeup in the car. David went into the dressing room to give her some notes, and five minutes later they went onstage. It was one of the most incredible and compelling performances that I have ever heard."

Still recovering from the strike and coming up on more negotiations, the symphony worked to mend fences and restore fiscal stability. It canceled a proposed three-week tour for spring 1992 that was to include visits to "undisclosed European capitals." The cost would exceed $500,000, and management stated that the additional funds needed would compete with the $5.6 million in public grants, especially

from the state arts council. In a statement to the Sun, Zinman said he was "disappointed both for the orchestra and for myself." A feeling of institutional fatigue accompanied the orchestra into its 1992 contract negotiations. After participating in the Committee for the Future and working to avoid a stoppage, the musicians agreed to a pay cut to address annual deficits of $500,000 to $1 million. In exchange, they secured increased seniority pay and more days off. Both sides acknowledged the settlement as concessionary, and executive director Gidwitz thanked the musicians "for their willingness to work under the constraints that all American orchestras are facing." The new contract led to the formation of the Strategic Planning Process, a long-range business plan that reviewed the organization's operations, marketing, and development departments through the assistance of a paid consultant.

In December 1992, the Russian conductor Yuri Temirkanov made his first guest-conducting appearance with the symphony. Temirkanov conducted Rimsky-Korsakov's *Scheherazade* and Prokofiev's Symphony No. 5 in B-flat major. The Sun called his debut with the orchestra "genuinely spectacular," and cited him for "enormous architectural sweep, sumptuous color, heart-piercing tenderness, and juggernaut-like momentum." But it had been work getting him there. "Temirkanov was not so easy to reach," says Yardumian. She relied on the assistance of friend and Associates member Carol O'Connell Minkin, who personally offered him an invitation to Baltimore after he conducted a New York concert. "We wanted him to have a wonderful feeling about everything to do with Baltimore. We just sensed something so special about him, and wanted him to return as a guest conductor," states Yardumian. Temirkanov's guest appearance came on the heels of Zinman's contract renewal. Rumors had abounded that Zinman would not renew. "David became frustrated with the Orchestra's financial limitations and the constraints this created, especially for recording, which required substantial subsidies," recalls Gidwitz. Zinman eventually signed a four-year agreement that took him through the 1997-98 season. The Sun supported the conductor and summed up his contributions to the orchestra: "The BSO's current reputation for excellence, however, is intricately connected to David Zinman's presence, and it would have been unfortunate had he left." Not long after he signed his contract extension, Zinman and Ma recorded *The New York Album*. It featured works by Bartók, Ernest Bloch, and Stephen Albert. In February 1994, *The New York Album* won two Grammy awards; Best Classical Contemporary Composition (for Albert, who had died in a car accident less than three months before the recording session) and Best Instrumental Soloist With Orchestra for Ma. The recording's success helped set the stage for the orchestra's 1994 tour.

Opposite. Photographs by David W. Harp.

On Oct. 25, 1994, the Baltimore Symphony embarked on a four-week concert tour of the Far East. The tour was extremely important to the orchestra and its music director. Zinman had grown frustrated that financial constraints had limited many projects that he thought essential to the orchestra's profile and artistic growth. On this trip, the orchestra performed concerts throughout Japan, in addition to appearances in Taipei and Seoul. Japan had become the country with the largest per-capita sales of commercial classical music recordings. It accounted for more than 30 percent of the world's classical music sales. The Baltimore Symphony was anxious to promote its sizable collection of recordings and expand its international sales market. To promote the tour back home, WBAL-TV followed the orchestra and produced a one-hour program, *The BSO – Beyond Baltimore*. Zinman and concert master Herbert Greenberg were the primary narrators. The orchestra appeared three times at Suntory Hall, the "Carnegie Hall of Japan." Greenberg explained, "It was important to get good reviews on our first concert, in order to start the series at Suntory at a high note." Television cameras followed Zinman, violin soloist Anne Akiko Meyers, and cellist Ma backstage at the Tokyo venue.

Many of the Japan concerts ended with a Japanese folk-song encore composed by Baltimore Symphony bass player Jonathan Jensen. Jensen had reached out to the Japanese embassy in Washington, which helped select the song. Jensen's work was a sensational hit with the audiences. The arrangement also included a solo line for Ma that added to the work's emotional impact. "The encore caused a stir," stated Zinman on the TV program. "We approached the encore as, 'Now we are going to play your song,' and the audiences felt, 'You did this for us?'" Cameras also followed such BSO musicians as horn player Peter Landgren, flutist Emily Skala, violinist Ivan Stefanovic, cellist Gita Roche, and percussionist John Locke as they toured the country. The program also included many of the parties and celebrations throughout the tour. Zinman said, "We hung out and traveled, we hung out and traveled. The concerts were almost a relief from all of the hanging out!" In another instance, principal trumpet Don Tison remembers Zinman and Ma traveling by limo while the orchestra went by bus. On one instance, "the top of the limo opened up, and Zinman and Yo-Yo popped out like a Jack-in-the-Box." The BSO and Zinman had achieved "stardom" through their trip, but Zinman said, "If we're not back within three years, the tour will have been wasted. We made real inroads into the Asian market, but touring is only good if you do it continuously."

Another concert innovation led by Zinman was the Dance Mix series. These concerts were aimed at younger audiences. One contemporary work melted into the next, much like a disc jockey would do. When questioned about the series, Zinman said, "What do we have to lose? Fortunately, Baltimore is a place where we can experiment." The average age at a Dance Mix concert was about 25, whereas the typical ticket subscriber was about 55. Dance Mix produced its own compact disc, but did not last. "Dance Mix was a unique idea," recalls Zinman. "I'm sorry that it didn't go further. It featured music for young people that they could really get into but it cost too much to produce."

David Zinman appears with audience members and supporters of the orchestra's Classically Black series in 1993.

In January 1996, the symphony announced the hiring of Marvin Hamlisch as principal Pops conductor and the violinist Pinchas Zukerman as SummerFest director. Hamlisch was originally hired for just a year, but stayed until 2000. He told the Baltimore Jewish Times, "We need to give young people the idea that this is a place where good music is available to them." He said he hoped to bring "theatrics" to the Pops series, but added, "By the same token, you will not be bombarded by concerts for young people. We don't want to scare off the audience that has been coming to the symphony for years." Zukerman recalls, "David said he wanted me to do a summer festival. 'You'd be a perfect conductor.' I told Miryam Yardumian, 'Let's close [Preston] street and get some food. We had a wonderful time." Zukerman continued in the job until 1999.

But growing pains and financial challenges continued. The Far East tour was a success and the orchestra had made many acclaimed recordings, but the debt load continued to grow. In 1995, the symphony reported a budget of over $17 million and an annual deficit of $2.5 million. Those figures were released as the symphony entered another contract negotiation. Faced with a proposal that included the elimination of 12 orchestral positions, reductions in medical benefits, the elimination of the summer season, and a three-year wage freeze, the musicians agreed to a settlement that preserved the structure of the orchestra. The negotiations lasted for 10 months and the agreement was signed in August 1996. The symphony staff also experienced cuts that included one unpaid week, salary reductions, and the elimination of seven positions, including three senior staff positions. Gidwitz called the agreement "the most concessionary contract ever," one that included "very substantial wage sacrifices from the orchestra, more than we would have wanted to have asked from the musicians, but necessary to stabilize the orchestra."

Only five weeks after the agreement was reached, Zinman announced that he would leave his post at the end of the 1997-98 season. He told the Sun that it was "time to do something else in my life." Those in the organization knew that Zinman was growing more frustrated, and the denial of his plan to record all the Beethoven symphonies helped him make the decision. Beethoven was dear to his heart and central to his time with the symphony, "I got a lot out of Baltimore," he said. "I got a chance to do a lot of really great things, but all things come to an end." Since his first guest-conducting appearance with the BSO in 1977, Zinman had been praised for his interpretations, from Beethoven to Schumann and Christopher Rouse, who Zinman had appointed composer-in-residence from 1986 to 1989. Symphony chorus director Edward Polochick states, "Under Zinman, it was the [Baltimore Symphony's] golden years. The orchestra toured, recorded, and added multiple performances of a single program. He built an international reputation for the orchestra." His relationship with prominent soloists boosted the orchestra's artistic profile. So questions regarding his replacement immediately began to surface.

Many musicians and audience members wondered if any candidate could successfully pick up Zinman's momentum. One possible replacement was Yuri Temirkanov. He was the director of the St. Petersburg Philharmonic in Russia, and had worldwide prominence as a guest conductor. Since his 1992 Baltimore debut, Temirkanov had become a popular interpreter of Russian music and classic warhorses during his subsequent appearances. The symphony leadership grew enamored of bringing Temirkanov to Baltimore. "It was quite a challenging idea," says Gidwitz. "He was one of the great conductors of the world, and the idea of bringing Yuri was a little bit bold." In October 1997, the symphony announced that beginning with the 1999-2000 season, Temirkanov would be the orchestra's 11th music director.

Opp. Top. Marvin Hamlisch was named principal conductor of the BSO SuperPops series in 1996.

Opp. Center Right. Symphony supporters and management announce the appointment of music director Yuri Temirkanov in 1997.

Opp. Center Left and Bottom. Patrons enjoy outdoor food and entertainment at the symphony's SummerFest series in 1993.

Below. Baltimore mayor Kurt Schmoke, David Zinman, Senator Barbara Mikulski, and board chair Buddy Zamoiski celebrate the 1997 Japan tour.

Right. Mayor Schmoke discusses the 1997 tour during a press announcement.

But first, there was one more BSO tour under Zinman. The musicians went back to Japan, site of the popular 1994 visit. After that tour, sales of Baltimore Symphony recordings had increased dramatically in Japan, and all BSO recordings with Zinman ranked among the country's classical best-sellers. Zinman declined many interviews before the orchestra embarked on the two-week tour in November 1997. Some people questioned the timing of the Temirkanov announcement right before Zinman's final tour. Polochick calls the news conference as "so uncomfortable." Still, the Japan tour was a resounding success. The orchestra appeared with Isaac Stern at a number of performances and the Sun said the tour included some of the orchestra's finest playing ever. However, Zinman admitted halfway through the trip that he was tired. And with just two concerts left, he was stricken with a kidney stone. He recalls, "I had to go to the hospital. I conducted that concert, but I knew that I couldn't do the next concert. I had another stone once, when I was in Los Angeles, but I had to conduct that one, because it was a symphony by Corigliano and nobody else knew it. They filled me with Demerol or something like that. I remember being absolutely delighted."

The orchestra's assistant conductor, Daniel Hege, conducted the final two concerts in Japan. Hege declined rehearsing with the orchestra before his first performance. He felt confident in his ability to step in, and the musicians had developed a good working rapport with him. Hege was hailed as a hero. The Sun reported, "Hege went on to lead a brilliant concert. … He brought the Suntory audience, Japan's most sophisticated and knowledgeable, to its feet in the warmest ovation the BSO received in its three weeks of concerts." Eighteen months later, Hege became music director of the Syracuse Symphony Orchestra.

Zinman's tenure as music director came to an end in June 1998. Gov. Parris N. Glendening and Mayor Kurt L. Schmoke proclaimed June 2, 1998, as "David Zinman Day." A performance that paid tribute to Zinman's 13-year tenure and featured as soloists Yo-Yo Ma, Emanuel Ax, and Pamela Frank was broadcast nationwide on NPR's *Performance Today*. His final concert on June 13 featured Bruckner's Symphony No. 8 in C minor. Zinman calls the Bruckner "monumental" and "wonderful," but remembers the encore almost as much as the Bruckner. "As an encore, we played 'Country Gardens' by Percy Grainger," says Zinman. "And you cannot imagine what that sounded like after the Bruckner. It was like some little soap bubble that floated in. It was a little ironic, actually." Zinman says of his career in Baltimore, "I learned a lot, both positive and negative things. It wasn't all a bed of roses, but I kept striving and working. I felt good when I left."

David Zinman receives accolades after his final concert as music director in June 1998. Photograph by Robert Smith.

The Baltimore Symphony historically championed young soloists and many have continued their longtime relationships with the orchestra. 11 year-old Nadja Salerno-Sonnenberg (above) made her Baltimore debut in 1972 and regularly appeared at July 4th concerts for many years. 23-year old violinist Joshua Bell had already become a classical music fixture when he made his Baltimore debut in 1991. At the age of eleven, Baltimore's own Hilary Hahn first appeared with the orchestra in 1991.

As the Baltimore Symphony prepared for life without Zinman, it also prepared to expand its presence outside the city. The symphony's traditional summer home, Oregon Ridge in Baltimore County, had never materialized into the facility that had been hoped for. In the mid-1990s, Gidwitz and other symphony leaders sought a new summer home. "We ended up driving around the state with a member of the Department of Natural Resources," says Gidwitz. Board chairman Buddy Zamoiski called Montgomery County Executive Doug Duncan and asked if the group could tour the county fairgrounds. "Doug said that you'll have to hold your nose, but we have a better idea." He suggested the grounds at the Mansion at Strathmore in North Bethesda. Located on Rockville Pike just north of the Capital Beltway, Strathmore, a neo-Georgian mansion built in 1908, had been acquired by Montgomery County in 1979 in the hope of developing it into an arts destination. "We stood on the steps of the mansion and looked out over the lawn. 'This is too ideal a spot for just a summer home, we should build a year-round concert hall here to serve as a second home for the Baltimore Symphony.' The negotiation lasted about 12 seconds; we were all in agreement!"

In September 1996, the Baltimore Symphony and Montgomery County officials announced a plan to establish a second home for the BSO at Strathmore. The Baltimore Symphony would be a founding partner with the county and perform in a proposed $50 million concert facility. The Baltimore Symphony looked forward to increased visibility, revenue, and donor base in what was by then Maryland's most affluent county. "Strathmore would not have happened if it weren't for the Baltimore Symphony," says oboist Jane Marvine. "The symphony wanted it to happen and made it happen." The initial plan drew initial concerns from Glendening, since the new hall could compete with another concert hall under construction at the University of Maryland at College Park. But within two years, Glendening threw his support to the Montgomery County plan. The state gave almost $2 million for the hall's design and work proceeded. "The symphony did not spend any money on the planning or development of the building of Strathmore. There were no out-of-pocket costs," states Gidwitz. Groundbreaking was in April 2001 with an anticipated completion date of spring 2004. Once again, a decade was ending for the symphony with grand plans for a new beginning.

Top. The Strathmore Music Center in North Bethesda, the Baltimore Symphony's second home, opened on February 5, 2005.

The Baltimore Symphony entered the 21st century with a new spirit of optimism.

It had grown artistically over the previous three decades and achieved major-orchestra status, thanks to the efforts and direction of David Zinman, now music director emeritus, and Sergiu Comissiona, now conductor laureate. SummerFest artistic director Pinchas Zukerman, principal Pops director Marvin Hamlisch, and associate conductor Daniel Hege helped round out the orchestra's impressive conducting roster. But the symphony was nonetheless excited to welcome Yuri Temirkanov as its new music director in January 2000. Artistic administrator Miryam Yardumian recalls Temirkanov's introduction to the entire symphony organization. He was asked, what influenced his decision to come to Baltimore? "He answered that months earlier, when he was considering the position, everywhere he went in the city – to the grocery store, department stores, restaurants, hotels, etc. – he asked the employees what they thought about David Zinman. Everyone responded that he was a wonderful conductor and they loved going to his concerts. Zinman had been with the BSO for over a decade and everywhere Temirkanov asked about him, the answer was still positive," recalls Yardumian.

Temirkanov began with strong support, from board members to musicians. "It was clear that the orchestra wanted him," recalls executive director John Gidwitz. "Temirkanov was a great conductor, and was very different from Zinman in some ways. The orchestra was better for having two very different

conductors." One of Temirkanov's most ardent champions was board chairman Buddy Zamoiski. Zamoiski's roots go deep into Baltimore's past, through the appliance and electronics distributorship founded by his grandfather, Joseph M. Zamoiski Co. on Liberty Street. Zamoiski became chairman of the symphony in 1986 and developed many of the traits Joe Meyerhoff showed during his long tenure with the orchestra. Like Meyerhoff, Zamoiski says, "I thought the city should have a good symphony orchestra, and I got more and more involved. The leaders of the community realized that Baltimore couldn't live without a symphony." Meyerhoff had invited Zamoiski to join the symphony board, especially after Meyerhoff agreed to give the Baltimore Museum of Art $300,000 for a new auditorium at Zamoiski's request. Zamoiski led the board throughout the orchestra's successes and struggles during most of the 1990s, and worked closely with Zinman, whom he called "a wonderful conductor." But Zamoiski was especially impressed by Temirkanov. Along with Gidwitz, Zamoiski often traveled to Temirkanov's American appearances in the 1990s. After much persistence, Temirkanov finally agreed to a three-year contract as music director. The conversation took place at a bar after a Philadelphia Orchestra concert. "I just liked the way he looked when he conducted," Zamoiski said.

Another positive was a new labor agreement, reached in May 2000, four months before its expiration. The organization's finances seemed stable, and the symphony's $21 million

Top. David Zinman and Yuri Temirkanov appear in a rare photograph together during the artistic transition.

Bottom. In 2000, banners throughout downtown Baltimore welcomed the arrival of new music director Yuri Temirkanov. This welcome sign was hung on the former Spike & Charlie's Restaurant opposite the Meyerhoff.

annual budget was reportedly debt-free. The new five-year musicians' contract raised base weekly salaries from $1,250 to $1,715. "The 2000 contract was a fulfillment of our dreams, and gave us a contract comparable to our peers," states oboist and frequent musician committee chair Jane Marvine. "Temirkanov wanted us to have a better contract." The new agreement was made possible by three components: the excitement behind Temirkanov's hiring, a new grant from the Andrew W. Mellon Foundation designed to further creative thinking and innovation, and the anticipated opening of the Strathmore Music Center in Montgomery County. "It all seemed possible," says Marvine.

My decision to come to Baltimore owed a great deal to my discussions with Buddy Zamoiski and John Gidwitz. They had come to my concerts in the US and Italy, and persuaded me to take the position of the orchestra's chief conductor. Of course, my previous experience as guest conductor also influenced me. Indeed, I was not a pioneer in Baltimore. When I arrived, I found a high quality orchestra, which had benefited most recently from the outstanding musicianship of Maestro David Zinman. The whole administrative team was wonderful. I particularly enjoyed working with my "bosses" Buddy Zamoiski and John Gidwitz, who had to put up with my not so very easy personality. And Miryam Yardumian was always ready to solve any problems I had. Greg Tucker looked after the PR in exemplary fashion.

And of course the musicians. It fell to me to appoint a new concertmaster to the orchestra – Jonathan Carney, who remains in post to this day. He is one of the finest of concertmasters with whom I have worked during my career. Other players who were hired during my tenure such as Madeline Adkins, Andrew Balio, and Katherine Needleman, were of great help to me in realizing my ambitions for the orchestra.

I recall my time in Baltimore with the warmest feelings. I realize today that the years I spent with the BSO represent an important phase in my life, both musically and personally. I worked with talented players and I made wonderful friendships. I look back on my time in Baltimore with gratitude for the opportunity it gave me to work with such an outstanding team. I congratulate the orchestra on its centenary. I am confident that its contribution to the musical life of America will be at least as great in the next hundred years.

—Yuri Temirkanov

The conducting staff went through some changes during 2000. Hamlisch left the Pops directorship and Zukerman ended his leadership of the SummerFest series. Both departures were expected, but Hamlisch proved hard to replace, and the series used guest conductors. As for SummerFest, the Swiss conductor Mario Venzago was selected as artistic director. Venzago had conducted the Baltimore Symphony on several occasions and had become an audience favorite. "SummerFest was an incredible good time," recalls Venzago. "We played the best-known, most-loved pieces. We were fabulous, but we were not cheap [with our productions]. We were warned not to be too ambitious, but we learned that the more ambitious we were, the greater the audience was." Venzago says that he "loved what Zinman had done with the orchestra" and that Yardumian "never hesitated to get the best soloists for SummerFest. … There was fun, there was food, but the main thing was the music!" Under Venzago, the series developed a loyal following and helped establish a steady and successful summer presence for the orchestra at the Meyerhoff, in addition to its frequent appearances at Oregon Ridge.

While Temirkanov agreed to not make any personnel changes during his first year, he made several over the next few seasons. One of the most visible involved concertmaster

Top. Jack Everly was named the symphony's Principal Pops Conductor in February 2003.

Opposite. Music director Yuri Temirkanov leads the orchestra during a 2002 performance.

Herbert Greenberg. Temirkanov wanted to choose his own concertmaster. After a severance package had been worked out, Greenberg's departure was announced in May 2001. Later that month, Zinman suddenly canceled his Baltimore Symphony appearances. The Sun said Zinman's cancellation was on doctor's orders. "The conductor has been suffering from exhaustion following a recording session in Switzerland," reported the paper. He had also canceled appearances the previous March. Nevertheless, the inference was clear. "David loved Herbie and never forgave us for letting him go," states Zamoiski. In September, Zinman notified musicians and staff that he was formally removing his title of music director emeritus. He had grown frustrated with the direction of the orchestra and thought that his artistic legacy was not being continued. "I spent all my waking moments trying to do something for American music in Baltimore and suddenly it was just shut down," he says. "For me, that was like a big slap in the face." Zinman never returned to conduct the Baltimore Symphony: "Why should I come back and smile and accept it?" In December, Temirkanov named Jonathan Carney as the orchestra's new concertmaster. Temirkanov called Carney "a great musician and a great leader."

Under Temirkanov, the Baltimore Symphony favored touring over recording. Temirkanov was well-known on the world circuit, and the orchestra, under his directorship, embarked on three international tours. In 2001, Gidwitz told the Sun, "Some orchestras don't attach as much importance to international visibility, but all the orchestras that are recognized as major ones are also the orchestras that tour. If you do not tour, you do not get to the top." The first travel under Temirkanov was in November of that year, a three-week, 12-city tour of Scotland, England, France, the Netherlands, Germany, and Austria. With the tour coming just weeks after the terrorist attacks of Sept. 11, extra security accompanied the orchestra. In September 2002, the orchestra went on an 11-day tour to Japan. After the final Tokyo concert, Temirkanov stated, "I hope, in the future in Baltimore, the orchestra will play as well as we played here." An October 2005 trip took the symphony to Spain, Italy, Slovenia, and Austria. In addition, the Baltimore Symphony made three appearances at Carnegie Hall during Temirkanov's tenure.

In April 2001, the symphony broke ground for the Music Center of Strathmore. William Rawn Associates helped design a 1,976-seat concert hall with the assistance of acousticians Kirkegaard Associates, theater designers Theatre Project Consultants, and associate architects Grimm & Parker. The Baltimore Symphony was a founding partner of Strathmore and shared facilities with the Levine Music School, CityDance, the National Chamber Orchestra

(National Philharmonic), and the Washington Performing Arts Society. The Music Center of Strathmore was targeted for a fall 2004 completion date. Zamoiski credits Montgomery County Executive Douglas Duncan for his unwavering support of Strathmore: "Doug Duncan bought the idea of Strathmore right away, and he was a real catalyst at handling the Montgomery County Council. [The county] had never heard of spending $100 million on a project." Zamoiski thinks that "Strathmore is the future of the Baltimore Symphony." He says, "I don't think that Baltimore is big enough anymore to support a symphony orchestra. I don't think they can afford it."

In January 2002, Gidwitz had informed the Baltimore Symphony Chorus members that the group would be disbanded at the end of the season. The chorus was in disbelief. More than 8,000 signatures in protest were collected and distributed to board members, staff, and Temirkanov. The symphony received letters from across the country, including a stern message from Comissiona: "I urge everyone concerned to reverse this unmusical and uncivil decision." Despite the letters of protest, the full chorus ended its 32-year run in April 2002 with three performances of Orff's *Carmina Burana* conducted by Temirkanov. At each performance, chorus members received extended applause as they entered the stage. Once they were in position on the risers, proclamations from the City of Baltimore, State of Maryland, and Baltimore County that honored the contributions of the chorus were read. The decision had made news around the country, but the hurt and anger were strongest in Baltimore's arts community.

Temirkanov inspired deep affection amongst the musicians. Unlike his predecessor, Temirkanov's programs primarily focused on standard repertoire and the conductor championed Russian and French composers. Concertmaster Carney states, "Yuri is not just a great musician and a great conductor, but he is also a wonderful friend to so many of us in Baltimore.

Top and Bottom. Montgomery County officials, along with conductor Yuri Temirkanov, celebrate the construction of the Strathmore Music Center. Photographs courtesy of the Executive Office of the Governor.

Opposite. In an effort to create musical diversity and enhance community outreach, the Baltimore Symphony entered into a partnership with Soulful Symphony, a 75-member orchestra comprised of African-American musicians. Founded in 2000 by composer/conductor Darin Atwater, Soulful Symphony presented a series of concerts at the Meyerhoff from 2004 until 2009. This collaboration was made possible by a $300,000 grant from the Eddie C. and C. Sylvia Brown Family Foundation.

Photograph by Michael G. Stewart, © 2006.

I always marveled at how he was a master of a wide variety of musical styles and repertoire. He was equally at home with Ravel, Mahler and Brahms as he was with Shostakovich, Prokofiev and Tchaikovsky. He also did English music beautifully. I used to joke with him that he must have had an English grandmother. He was a natural Elgarian!" But it was to his native Russia that he turned for the largest project of his tenure. From Feb. 13 to March 2, 2003, Temirkanov coordinated a celebration titled "Vivat! St. Petersburg." The festival celebrated 300 years of Russian art, music and culture and involved such organizations as the BSO, Baltimore Opera, the Baltimore Museum of Art, Center Stage, and the Walters Art Museum. It was billed as the "largest citywide cultural event ever held in Baltimore." As he brought Russian culture to Baltimore, Temirkanov in return brought the Morgan State University Choir to St. Petersburg in January 2004 for a performance of Gershwin's *Porgy and Bess* with the St. Petersburg Philharmonic.

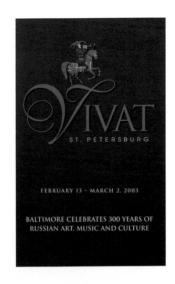

An elaborate brochure accompanied the Vivat! St. Petersburg festival in 2003.

Top and Bottom.
The Strathmore Music Center
begins to take shape in 2002.

Opposite. Concertgoers attend
the Strathmore opening gala on
February 5, 2005.

All photographs on these pages
are courtesy of the Executive
Office of the Governor.

However, by 2003, the impact of reduced ticket sales and contributions following the terrorist attacks of Sept. 11, 2001, was taking its toll. Debts were accumulating and expenses were rapidly growing. Temirkanov's contract expired in 2002, but he agreed to sign one-year agreements for the future. The musicians, for their part, faced a request to reopen the contract and address the once-celebrated pay raises. They "accepted an immediate pay freeze, but we didn't want to end our 'going out' salary in 2006," says Marvine. According to Zamoiski, the board of directors in 2003 expressed a need for turnover in its membership. "After 15 years," he said, "I decided that I would be the first to go. I think I'd served my time." Later in 2003, Gidwitz announced he was leaving after 20 years at the helm. Gidwitz had built a strong and loyal staff during his tenure and felt that they "constituted one of the keys to the institution's success. They worked long hours, possessed great expertise, and frankly were less compensated than their merits deserved." However, the departures of

Zamoiski and Gidwitz did not bode well for Temirkanov. "When the orchestra's financial footing became shaky, Temirkanov had no interest in staying," recalls Marvine. In September 2004, he said he would leave at the end of the 2005-06 season. During his remaining months with the orchestra, Temirkanov frequently canceled appearances for various reasons. But his contributions to the orchestra's artistic growth could not be contested.

With expenses mounting and deficits increasing, the symphony's leaders decided to seek a new administrative executive outside the orchestra field. Recently elected board chairman Philip English championed James Glicker, an Internet executive who had recently been appointed the symphony's head of marketing, as the new president. Marvine says, "The board became enamored with bringing somebody in who would treat this like a business. They felt that somebody from the profit world might help solve our financial problems."

The focus of the symphony's future shifted when the Music Center of Strathmore officially opened on Feb. 5, 2005, making Baltimore the only major American orchestra to have two permanent year-round homes. The opening gala, titled "The Music Begins," featured cellist Yo-Yo Ma and soprano Janice Chandler-Eteme, with the orchestra conducted by Temirkanov. As a founding partner at Strathmore, the Baltimore Symphony initially committed to 40 annual performances, along with assistance in helping the center raise a $30 million endowment. "The BSO could not exist without Strathmore," states Zamoiski, as Montgomery County "has access to much more wealth than Baltimore." Even though no symphony money was spent on the construction of the hall, Strathmore still came at a price. According to Michael Mael, then vice president of the BSO at Strathmore, the startup cost for the symphony at its new hall totaled from $6 million to $7 million, much of which went on an extensive awareness and advertising campaign. This was on top of a projected $12 million organizational deficit by 2008. Every concert in the first season was sold out, and the orchestra continues to build its subscriber and donor base in Montgomery County.

As the organization struggled financially, its different constituencies banded together to discuss life beyond Temirkanov. An Artistic Leadership Task Force gave musicians a greater voice in the selection of the next conductor. The committee studied whether to hire a traditional music director, a principal conductor with more responsibility, or a combination of conductors who worked together in planning and programming. "Glicker seemed able to entertain new ideas about artistic leadership," states Marvine.

The group was initially given a two-year time frame to replace Temirkanov. But with the increasing financial pressures, the timeline was shortened to one year. "We were told that we'd lose money unless a new conductor was chosen," says Marvine. As the situation became more urgent, in July 2005 the musicians asked to speak with the board. "Our opinion was just that we wanted to see three more people," recalls Marvine. The musicians soon learned that the board had thrown its support behind Marin Alsop, the former conductor of the Colorado Symphony and a frequent guest conductor with many of the world's largest orchestras. Hiring

Left. Soprano Janice Chandler-Eteme and Yuri Temirkanov performed Strauss' Four Last Songs at the Strathmore Music Center.

Opposite. Cellist Yo-Yo Ma was a featured soloist at the 2005 opening gala at Strathmore.

her would give Baltimore the first female music director of a major American orchestra. She had also committed to moving to Baltimore, an important factor for the board. But before the musicians could throw support behind Alsop or anyone else, the news was leaked to the Sun, which on July 15 ran a front-page headline: "Top Female Conductor to Take Baton at BSO." The article included a quotation from an anonymous symphony leader: "It's a done deal."

The musicians publicly objected to the way the choice was handled by the symphony leadership. They felt left out of the process and were angry that their involvement with the Artistic Leadership Task Force was largely ignored. The decision came at a cost, with the national media reporting that the musicians unfairly objected to a woman as music director. The misrepresentation angered the musicians. But the controversy also wounded Alsop and her future relationship with the musicians. "I think that it was possibly the worst experience of my life," she says. "It was unfair and devastating, and it manifested in a very hurtful way. I was advised by many people not to take the job. People said that I should 'run as far away from these people as you can.'"

Marvine was chair of the musicians' players' committee at the time and faced the brunt of criticism. "We worked with [Marin], we liked her and knew that she had strong qualities. There was no feeling in the orchestra that there was a problem with having a woman as a music director. We already had some strong female musician leadership, and I'm a woman."

Alsop addressed the musicians directly after the announcement. She outlined her vision and her desire to work closely with the community and expand programming offerings. At the time, she says, "I thought this was a great orchestra, but this is a great orchestra that had the potential to be much better. I felt the fundamentals of the orchestra were so strong. In addition, Baltimore is the last affordable city on the East Coast. There were many attractive things about it." Alsop was conflicted in facing the accolades and dissention that dominated the media. "I had a larger responsibility not just to the symphony or to myself," she says, "but for being the first woman appointed to a major full-time orchestra. There was a certain responsibility to 51 percent of the population. What am I going to do, say no? I was really between a rock and a hard place."

Top female conductor to take baton at BSO

Marin Alsop, often guest leader, known for interpretations of American music

By TIM SMITH
SUN MUSIC CRITIC

Marin Alsop, the New York-born conductor known for dynamic interpretations of American music and for steadily breaking through the glass ceiling in a male-dominated field, is expected to be named music director of the Baltimore Symphony Orchestra, according to sources.

Though the public relations firm representing Alsop stated that a contract has yet to be signed, "everyone knows that the decision has been made," said one symphony insider familiar with the search process, who spoke on condition of anonymity.

"It's a done deal," said another BSO employee.

Alsop, 48, who led the Colorado Symphony for a dozen years and now serves as music director of the Bournemouth Symphony in England, would succeed Yuri Temirkanov, who   [See BSO, 5A]

Musicians urge BSO to keep searching

End 'premature' in music director hunt

By TIM SMITH
SUN MUSIC CRITIC

Baltimore Symphony Orchestra musicians yesterday issued a statement criticizing as "premature" the conclusion of a search for a new music director.

The unusual public protest came a day after news spread that Marin Alsop, the most prominent female conductor on the international music scene, is expected to be appointed next week to the post.

Marin Alsop

Alsop, 48, who led the Colorado Symphony for a dozen years and now serves as music director of the Bournemouth Symphony in England, would succeed Yuri Temirkanov, who announced in September that he will step down at the end of the 2005-2006 season.

"The orchestra members are unanimous in their view that the search process should continue," Jane Marvine, head of the BSO players committee, said yesterday, reading from a prepared text. "The musicians are very troubled by the fact that board members will be asked to make a crucial decision without having a reasonable opportunity to investigate and consider the issues being raised by the musicians."

Anthony Brandon, a BSO board member who served on the music director search committee, said he agreed with the orchestra's stand. "I am disappointed that the committee could not have continued its work in hopes of finding a music director who could be supported by the musicians," said Brandon, president and general manager of the public radio station WYPR.

Meanwhile, Alsop, who is on a cruise off the   [See BSO, 3D]

In an NPR interview on July 22, 2005, she told Fred Child, "The reaction [by the musicians] took me by surprise." She acknowledged the musicians' complaints about the selection process, but stated, "Process is process. Who cares about process? The end result is what's important in life." She knew that her relationship with the musicians would only flourish with mutual respect. But she continued, "I think it's past us. I think we're over it. I definitely would like to put it behind us. I'd like to be able to have a beer with the musicians in a year or two and say, 'God, what happened then? That was wild.' I hope that we can come to that place." Marvine was relieved that Alsop sounded so "nice and gracious." She says she thought, "I looked forward to having that beer one day."

When the dust began to settle, the Baltimore Symphony still faced major challenges. To address the financial crisis, the musicians agreed to salary cuts and furloughs. The staff faced similar cuts, and staff and musician positions remained unfilled. The orchestra accumulated a $3.1 million deficit in 2004 and a further $7.5 million deficit the following year. Morale and trust tumbled. Increasingly desperate measures were investigated to raise much needed funds, including a quickly aborted plan to sell and lease back the Joseph Meyerhoff Symphony Hall. In early 2006, Glicker abruptly resigned, and the board selected recently appointed board member W. Gar Richlin as interim president and CEO. He worked to instill trust and communication within the organization. As a way to extricate the symphony from a burden of debt that was now $16 million (and was to exceed $22 million by the end of June 2006), in March the board approved a decision to transfer the symphony's $90 million endowment into a separate trust. The move let the organization take a draw of nearly 30 percent to pay off debt and build long-time donor trust and fiscal responsibility. Musicians questioned the move, especially as the Joseph Meyerhoff Symphony Hall and adjoining parking garage were also moved into the trust. The move addressed short-term needs but not long-term investment goals. "Gar deserves a lot of credit," says Zamoiski. "He took control of the organization and did it well. It was absolutely essential to move the endowment into a separate institution. The pressure to invade the principal was enormous."

Temirkanov concluded his role as music director in June 2006. He ended with the same piece he started with in January 2000, Mahler's Symphony No. 2 ("Resurrection"). The Sun called it a "soul-stirring program" and applauded Temirkanov's "invaluable gift of artistry." Temirkanov then threw a private party for the musicians, complete with bottles of vodka on every table. In the Sun, principal horn Philip Munds praised Temirkanov for "inspiring players to take musical chances," and violinist Ivan Stefanovic said, "He is the only conductor I know that could lead an orchestra with hands tied behind his back." Sun reviewer Tim Smith stated, "Comissiona gave the orchestra its heart, Zinman gave it intellect, and Temirkanov gave it soul."

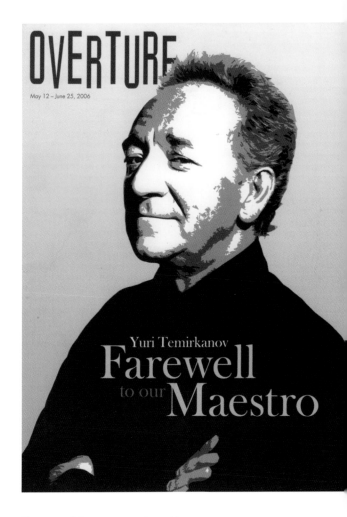

The cover of Overture magazine paid tribute to Maestro Temirkanov during his final month as music director.

Photograph by
Clark Vandergrift

Marin Alsop arrived as the Baltimore Symphony's music director-designate in January 2007 and began her efforts to deliver creative programming and heightened visibility for the orchestra.

Her unofficial debut included a performance of Stravinsky's *The Rite of Spring* and Richard Strauss' *An Alpine Symphony*. Both works were supplemented by students from the Peabody Conservatory as part of the school's 150th anniversary celebration. Emphasizing Alsop's desire to increase the organization's profile through technology, the *Rite of Spring* performance was released on iTunes, where it enjoyed a run as the No. 1 classical download for a time. Alsop was committed to reestablishing the symphony's commercial recording presence. Even before her formal arrival, Alsop and the Baltimore Symphony had recorded John Corigliano's "The Red Violin Concerto" in June 2006 for Sony/BMG, with Joshua Bell as the soloist.

Alsop also had a longtime relationship with the Naxos recording company. Plans quickly formed for projects that featured such composers as Dvořák, Mahler, and Bernstein. A relationship with XM satellite radio was forged that opened up the Baltimore Symphony to over eight million potential listeners. As the organization worked to straighten out and secure its financial status, the orchestra was unable to commit to any immediate touring projects due to funding constraints. "The orchestra had not recorded for a decade," says Alsop. "I think making recordings increases the artistic level of the orchestra because everybody steps up their game. It brings out the best in the orchestra. For an orchestra that can't afford to tour, it's a great marketing tool." Symphony

president and CEO Paul Meecham states, "Alsop's strong recording profile, which had already been established prior to Baltimore, helped to restore the BSO to commercial recording after a drought during the Temirkanov era."

Plans for the 2007-08 season, Alsop's first as music director, were announced in March 2007. As part of the launch, the Baltimore Symphony offered $25 seats for any location in the hall, courtesy of a grant from the PNC Bank Foundation. The $25 ticket price also celebrated the 25th anniversary of the Joseph Meyerhoff Symphony Hall. "The special offer was a much-needed shot in the arm," says Meecham. "Amidst a fanfare of publicity, subscription tickets went on sale [on Mar. 3, 2007] and attracted a line around the building from existing, former, and new subscribers." Alsop recalls, "I was so happy to come to the hall the first day tickets were on sale and see those hundreds of people in line at the box office." At one point, Alsop handed out coffee and doughnuts to the ticket buyers. Meecham adds, "In one bold gesture we had generated excitement for the new season, and by dramatically reducing the cost of a ticket had changed the public perception of the BSO as more accessible." In addition to the reduced cost, the season featured all nine Beethoven symphonies alongside works by "11 Living Beethovens," such as John Adams, Tan Dun, Christopher Rouse, and Thomas Adès. The season also included Alsop's debut at Carnegie Hall. The concert on Feb. 9, 2008, featured works by Stephen

Marin Alsop conducts the Baltimore Symphony during one of her initial performances as music director.

Photograph by Grant Leighton

Mackey, Richard Strauss, Debussy, and Stravinsky. Concert attendees included soprano Jessye Norman, Trey Anastasio of the rock band Phish, Jamie Bernstein, daughter of Leonard, and Gloria Steinem. "To see her leading all that talent on stage was wonderful," said Steinem.

When she arrived in Baltimore, Alsop told the Sun that she had a longtime interest in education and outreach: "I have some big ambitions for the Baltimore Symphony, and they're all achievable." When the symphony obtained non-profit organizational status in 1942, its charter stressed education and outreach. In addition to promoting and developing "the public health, welfare, and happiness by presenting symphonic concerts for public entertainment and recreation," the charter said, the orchestra would "sponsor, hold or promote concerts for the education of children," and "encourage the education and development of skilled musicians or persons having musical talent … and the development and education of artists in related fields." Meecham states, "Accessibility and relevance were constant themes that Marin Alsop espoused. She felt strongly that a 21st century American orchestra could only be successful if deeply connected to its community. Years of budget cuts to the city school system had decimated arts education in public schools. During Alsop's first season, she envisaged an after-school music program for some of Baltimore's most underserved kids."

Concertmaster Jonathan Carney shakes Music Director Marin Alsop's hand during her Carnegie Hall debut in 2008.

Photograph by Grant Leighton

Baltimore is a city that marches to its own drummer. It's made up of people who are the backbone of America. We know how to fend for ourselves; we know who we are and who our neighbors are, and we care about each other. We're not afraid to "roll our sleeves up" and I think the BSO is a reflection of that ethic.

While the orchestra is certainly more connected to the community today than when I first arrived, I wish that the symphony reflected the city's diversity more. When I came to Baltimore, there were certain fundamental challenges that the orchestra faced, regardless of who the next music director was going to be. There was a major disconnect with the community. It was an orchestra that had lost touch and became an island, very isolated and very alone. The two words that I used as soon as I arrived were "access" and "inclusion." We have a lot more work ahead of us to create an orchestra that reflects the community that we inhabit with the same artistic level and standard. I think that the OrchKids program will ultimately impact the make up of the BSO but it's probably going to take a few decades. OrchKids is a program about creating a sense of possibility. The kids learn, as we all learned growing up to be musicians, that anything's possible if you work hard and apply yourself. Now these kids have aspirations.

Today we do things at the Baltimore Symphony because we believe in them and we believe in our responsibility as good citizens of our community. We don't do things solely because others have done them. I think that the musicians are more connected to this city than other musicians in other orchestras, but I hope this connection grows stronger and deeper in the future. I also hope that the musicians will always feel appreciated and respected for who they are and what they do.

While we haven't had the resources to tour internationally recently, I hope the musicians know how proud I am of their achievements. We've made some really great recordings and every time I go to Europe, Brazil, or Japan, I am playing our recordings and promoting the Baltimore Symphony!

Happy 100th birthday, Baltimore Symphony! Here's to the start of a century filled will joy, success, and optimism.

—Marin Alsop

On May 20, 2008, Alsop announced a new after-school music and mentoring project, OrchKids. She pledged $100,000 of her own money to fund the new education initiative. Based on Venezuela's El Sistema program, OrchKids reached out to some of the city's neediest children. "We put a team together and started talking to musicians, community organizations, after-school programs, Baltimore City Schools, and maybe 50 different constituencies. And through the course of a year, we designed a program that addressed every person's concern," says Alsop. The original idea behind OrchKids was for each symphony musician to mentor a child enrolled in the program. The musicians expressed logistical and funding concerns to Alsop and the symphony leadership. "But I'll never forget [former principal second violin] George Orner got the sheriff next door to talk to me. [The sheriff] needed to tell me what a great idea this is because kids happen to get in trouble between 3 p.m. and 6 p.m." Alsop acknowledges that musicians were concerned that OrchKids could draw

funding away from the entire organization. "This is why I started OrchKids with my own money, because I think you have to lead by example." In addition, philanthropists Robert Meyerhoff and Rheda Becker threw financial support to the after-school project. "OrchKids is a program about possibilities, so a kid who never played violin can now play a violin and see the possibilities. It is about how you carry yourself, convey your message, how you listen, and what kind of citizen do you want to be. Many of these kids now have huge aspirations," states Alsop. From its inception in September 2008, OrchKids has grown from 30 students at one elementary school in west Baltimore to over 1,000 students at six schools throughout Baltimore City in 2015.

Through innovative recordings and projects, Alsop brought new excitement and awareness to the Baltimore Symphony and its supporters. "Maestra Alsop has brought so much to Baltimore," states concertmaster Jonathan Carney. "On stage, she has inspired us to harness and focus our natural abilities

Left and above. The BSO's signature inner-city OrchKids program was inaugurated in 2008.

Opposite. In October 2008, the Baltimore Symphony made headlines with its production of Bernstein's Mass at Carnegie Hall

to play together, as a team. She has instilled a renewed sense of rhythmic discipline, concentrating her efforts on stressing the importance of dynamic contrasts, unified phrasing, and a wonderfully blended sound. With Marin as music director, I believe that thinking, rehearsing, and performing as a tight-knit ensemble has been her mantra." Board member and supporter Sandra Levi Gerstung says, "Marin has brought a new image to classical music and our symphony. Her imagination seems boundless."

The spirit of optimism and success was reflected in the first balanced budget since 2001. A hard-working staff increased ticket sales and fund-raising goals. In August 2008, the musicians ratified a new three-year agreement that increased salaries by 17% over its life and restored several unfilled vacancies. The contract was settled almost one month before the expiration date. Sun critic Tim Smith reported, "The fact that a three-year deal, with any raises, could be negotiated at the BSO, well in advance of deadline, is remarkable, given the orchestra's recent history of debt and internal strife." The following October, Alsop led the Baltimore Symphony, soloist Jubilant Sykes, the Morgan State University Choir and Marching Band, and the Peabody Children's Chorus in performances of Bernstein's MASS. The work, whose subtitle, *A Theatre Piece for Singers, Players, and Dancers*, indicates its complexity, had received its premiere on Sept. 8, 1971 for the opening of Washington's Kennedy Center for the Performing Arts. In addition to the Meyerhoff, Alsop and the BSO brought the massive work to the Kennedy Center. MASS was also performed at Carnegie Hall and the United Palace Theater in New York's Washington Heights. Alsop "champions the music of her mentor, Leonard Bernstein, and the performances of the MASS were a true highlight of her second season," says Meecham. Alsop and the symphony received critical acclaim in the New York Times and the Washington Post, and the recording on the Naxos label earned a Grammy nomination.

OrchKids

In the early days of Marin Alsop's tenure at the BSO, she started to cultivate an idea that the Baltimore Symphony Orchestra needed to be more involved with teaching and immersing Baltimore City students in music. After a tremendous amount of mission searching and lobbying and with $100,000 of her own seed money, Marin Alsop started to formulate a plan to inspire and nurture Baltimore City's most at-risk children. She approached Dan Trahey, currently OrchKids Artistic Director, in February of 2008 to design and implement a program inspired by Venezuela's El Sistema that uses music as a vehicle for social change. OrchKids believes that music is preventative medicine and that all humans no matter what race, gender, and ethnicity must have democratic access to music instruction and performance opportunities.

Trahey and current Director of Operations, Nick Skinner, along with the BSO senior staff worked tirelessly with Alsop's direction and encouragement to start in September of 2008, a 3-day per week after-school program at Harriet Tubman Elementary School in West Baltimore for 30 students.

OrchKids is currently starting its 8th year of operation in the fall of 2015 with over 1000 students in 6 elementary and middle schools throughout Baltimore City.

OrchKids is a model and laboratory for programs throughout the country with visitors from major symphony orchestras, universities, city and state governments, school districts, and other socially minded organizations from all over the world spending weeks and months at a time in

Baltimore gathering information and inspiration from the over 65 teachers and staff that maintain a 5-day per week before- and after-school program.

OrchKids is built on a set of guiding principles such as consistency, intensity, early immersion, group music making, and frequent performance all of which ensure a child's safety, development of musical love and skills, and most importantly social mobility.

The program is ensemble based and has String, Wind, and Symphony Orchestras, Jazz Bands, Latin American percussion ensembles, bucket bands, chamber music, creative composition ensembles, choirs, and many more impromptu music-making experiences.

The OrchKids have collaborated multiple times on the stage of the Meyerhoff Symphony Hall with the Baltimore Symphony and Marin Alsop and have performed with Roger Waters, Renee Fleming, Matisyahu, beat boxer Shodekeh,

Pink Martini, Hilary Hahn, Lang Lang, Time for Three, Warren Haynes, and percussionist Colin Currie.

In fulfilling its foremost mission of social change, the OrchKids have performed at Ted X Baltimore, The Kennedy Center, Carnegie Hall, and have toured throughout the East Coast.

OrchKids recently graduated its first class of students into High School and five students attended The Baltimore School for the Arts in the fall of 2015. Ten students have attended the prestigious Interlochen Arts Camp and over 30 OrchKids students attend The Peabody Preparatory.

OrchKids has been recognized for its accomplishments on CBS's 60 Minutes, the New York Times, PBS, Al Jazeera USA, and The Washington Post. In the fall of 2013, student Asia Palmer and Artistic Director Daniel Trahey traveled to the White House to represent the program and receive the 2013 National Arts and Humanities Youth Program Award from First Lady Michelle Obama.

Left. From 2005 to 2010, Jack Everly and the BSO hosted the elaborate Holiday Spectacular concerts. Students from the Baltimore School of the Arts appeared as the audience-favorite Tap Dancing Santas. The concerts ended their run due to increased expense and competition.

Opp Left. The BSO at Strathmore presents popular chamber music concerts called Musical Mondays for its Montgomery County donors and supporters.

Opp. Right. Marin Alsop leads one of the early BSO Academy concerts that features BSO musicians working side by side with amateur participants during the intensive week-long program.

Photograph by Tracey Brown

By the second half of 2008, the American economy was showing signs of distress. A collapse of the mortgage industry and failure of institutions such as Lehman Bros. resulted in sharp stock market declines and staggering unemployment. In November 2008, then-board chair Michael Bronfein addressed the musicians, acknowledging the economic climate but saying he remained committed to upholding the contract. A $10 million fund-raising plan was discussed. But the falling economy was brutal to Baltimore's arts community. After several challenging seasons, having no endowment, and with constant cash flow concerns, the Baltimore Opera Company filed for Chapter 11 bankruptcy protection in December 2008, and subsequently for Chapter 7 liquidation. Once the house orchestra for the Baltimore Opera, the Baltimore Symphony had ended that long affiliation during the 1988 strike. Opera officials established the Baltimore Opera Orchestra after pressure not to hire symphony musicians during the work stoppage. The Baltimore Opera ended its 58-year run in November 2008 with Bellini's *Norma*. In addition, the Baltimore Chamber Orchestra suspended its 2008-09 concert season, and endowment values at the Baltimore Museum of Art and the Baltimore Symphony dropped by over 20 percent in the second half of 2008. Grants issued by the Maryland State Arts Council also declined in value.

In January 2009, the symphony laid off 6 full-time staff positions, 10% of its administration. And by April the symphony endowment had dropped from $62 million to $45 million. To address the economic downturn, the musicians volunteered to give back $1 million in wage increases and benefits. The campaign, named "Music Matters: Play Your Part," challenged supporters and donors to match every $1 given back with $2. Music Matters "put the orchestra front and center," says Marvine. "It was initiated by the musicians and focused on the musicians," who wanted to share the burden that the organization faced. "The board came to us [in November 2008] and told us that things looked dire, but they would go out and raise money," says Marvine. "It really touched us that these leaders were different, and we wanted to help them."

But by 2010, it became clear that the symphony's finances were on the brink. The Music Matters campaign was not enough to make up lost revenue, and the symphony's endowment trust elected not to make its contribution to the orchestra because the fund's value had dropped below the value of the principal corpus. Without the endowment contribution, and with a steep decline in public and private giving, the organization faced potential bankruptcy. That threat ended with a new musicians' contract that included a 17 percent pay cut and an agreement to maintain 16 orchestra positions unfilled. "That contract took us back a full decade," recalls Marvine. After seasons of renewed and rebuilt optimism and financial gains, the

Baltimore Symphony had fallen into another period of institutional hardship.

Since the orchestra now had two homes, educational programs were developed for Montgomery County schools. "From its earliest days at Strathmore, the BSO recognized that in addition to its concert hall performances at the Music Center, education and outreach efforts would be vital both to better establish 'its brand' in Montgomery County and to obtain corporate and financial support for its endeavors in this community," states Richard Spero, community liaison for the BSO at Strathmore. With a combination of corporate and foundation support, along with an allocation from the symphony's own budget, BSO On-the-Go performances in Montgomery County public and private schools began in 2007. The "trick" to making this happen was to find the resources for a sufficient number of BSO musicians to undertake daytime round trips to Montgomery County schools and senior centers so as to establish and sustain a viable outreach program," states Spero. The in-classroom program received many accolades from Montgomery County school officials, and was featured in local newspapers and on television programs.

One of Marin Alsop's initiatives as music director of the Bournemouth Symphony Orchestra in England from 2002 to 2008 invited amateur musicians to perform alongside professionals. So in early 2010, an event for "Rusty Musicians" at Strathmore attracted over 400 amateur instrumentalists.

They were divided into groups and performed side by side with Baltimore Symphony musicians conducted by Alsop in 45-minute segments. Interest exceeded expectations, and the program was later expanded to the Meyerhoff. The concept captured the imagination of the Andrew W. Mellon Foundation, which agreed to fund a summer week-long BSO Academy that was geared toward these musicians in a more intensive and personal setting. Carol Bogash, vice president of education and community development, says, "From a one-evening opportunity to play next to a BSO musician, music-loving amateurs can now participate in an eight-day weeklong "fantasy camp" comprising four separate tracks – orchestral, chamber music and chamber orchestra, music educators, or administrator. Participants come from all over the United States and a few from Europe. BSO musicians serve as faculty, providing lessons, sectionals, coaching, enrichment classes, and general encouragement and bonhomie. The academy has grown to offer instrument clinics, chamber music weekends, Rusty evenings, and Academy 'lite' opportunities throughout the year."

Virginia resident Mary Padilla performed as an oboist in the first 2010 Rusty Musicians event at Strathmore and became a long-time participant in the BSO Academy. Padilla says, "When I first heard about the Rusty Musicians, I had no idea how it would change my life. Excitedly I filled out the application, then I started to worry. … What are they going to think about this software developer sitting next to them professing to be an oboist? If I make a mistake, are they going to laugh? I practiced, but was it enough? We're Rusty Musicians, certainly the maestra will not push us. … All these thoughts and many more were swimming around in my head. I was very nervous and excited when I stepped on that stage. Yes, indeed, the maestra challenged us, thank goodness I practiced! The night was exhilarating – I was hooked and wanted more. When the BSO Academy was announced, I signed up immediately, realizing if 45 minutes could feel like that, imagine what a week would be like – it far exceeded my expectations. For the next five years this was my 'fantasy camp,' in addition to participating in all the Rusty Musician events in between. I have become a better and more confident musician through all of these rehearsals, lessons, classes, master classes, and performances." Padilla says that from the very first day at the academy, "you feel like you are part of something very special. It feels like home." In July 2012, the BSO Academy attracted national attention when an arts reporter from the New York Times participated in the Academy and wrote extensively about his experience in a three-page feature in the Arts & Leisure section.

Between 2008 and 2013, Alsop and the symphony returned to Carnegie Hall on five occasions. In November 2011, she led a staged performance of Honegger's oratorio *Jeanne d'Arc au bûcher*. The New York Times commented, "The work requires an army of musicians, which here included the Peabody Children's Chorus, the Morgan State University Choir, the Peabody-Hopkins Chorus and the Concert Artists of Baltimore. Marin Alsop, the Baltimore Symphony's adventurous music director, who is clearly passionate about the 80-minute piece, marshaled the forces in a tightly wrought performance." The orchestra made several appearances in California and Oregon in 2012. Yearly recording projects remained a part of Alsop's mission. And the OrchKids program continued to grow. Maryland State Assessment tests showed dramatic increases in test scores for OrchKids students. In 2013, OrchKids received the National Arts and Humanities Youth Program Award, presented at the White House by first lady Michelle Obama. Meanwhile, in Montgomery County, the BSO initiated "OrchLab," a multiple-visit performance residency at selected, economically challenged Title I schools in the Montgomery County school system. As of the 2014-15 season, nearly 100 musician OrchLab visits had taken place at 11 elementary, middle, and high schools. Another milestone occurred in 2012, when the Baltimore Symphony acquired the Greater Baltimore Youth Orchestra and created the new Baltimore Symphony Youth

The BSO development staff appears before a 2014 season opening gala performance.

Orchestra. The program consisted of three orchestras: the String Orchestra, the Concert Orchestra, and the high school Youth Orchestra. By 2015, over 240 young musicians from throughout Maryland had successfully auditioned for these three youth orchestras.

The Baltimore Symphony played a visible role in the city's bicentennial celebrations for the War of 1812. On June 17, 2012, Alsop and the symphony performed a "Star Spangled Symphony" concert that featured the premiere of Baltimore native Philip Glass' *Overture for 2012*, Tchaikovsky's *The Year 1812* overture, and a special appearance by Gov. Martin O'Malley and his band. The Maryland War of 1812 Bicentennial Commission sponsored the event. On Sept. 13, 2014, the symphony participated in the city's "Star Spangled Spectacular" event to commemorate the American victory over the British and the penning by Francis Scott Key of the national anthem. Broadcast live on PBS, the Pier Six concert featured such celebrity singers as Kristin Chenoweth, Denyce Graves, and Kenny Rogers alongside Alsop and the orchestra.

In April 2015, demonstrations developed throughout the city following the death of Freddie Gray, an African-American resident who died while in the custody of Baltimore police. On April 27, massive protests broke out. Hundreds of businesses were damaged, and the city was placed under a 10 p.m. curfew and protected by the National Guard. Some of the hardest-hit sections were within a mile of the Meyerhoff. As reporters swarmed into Baltimore, musicians gathered for an impromptu concert outside the Meyerhoff. Organized by oboist Michael Lisicky and supported by colleagues and symphony staff, the concert attracted over 1,000 people and received global coverage. The event was intended to bring a sense of peace and normalcy to the troubled city. Just a few days later, a woodwind quintet from the Baltimore Symphony performed spirituals at Pennsylvania and North Avenues, the epicenter of the unrest. A free "Concert for Peace" was held on May 9 at Mount Lebanon Baptist Church. The program, conducted by Alsop, featured musicians from the Baltimore Symphony, Peabody Institute, Baltimore School for the Arts, OrchKids, Baltimore Symphony Youth Orchestras, Baltimore Choral Arts Society, and several local church choirs. All three performances proved the power and purpose of orchestral music during difficult times.

Top. On April 29, 2015, crowds gathered outside the Meyerhoff for an impromptu performance just 36 hours after the city broke out in unrest.

Center. With numerous worldwide media outlets in attendance, Marin Alsop leads the symphony musicians outside the Meyerhoff.

Bottom. A woodwind quintet of BSO musicians performs at the corner of Pennsylvania and North Avenues only one week after the rioting. The handwritten slogan #ONEBALTIMORE is seen behind the musicians.

Three special events occurred during the latter half of the 2014-15 season; the 10th anniversary of the Music Center of Strathmore, an appearance by principal guest conductor-designate Markus Stenz, and a performance of Bernstein's *Candide*. On Feb. 5, 2015, the symphony officially celebrated its decade at Strathmore. The 2014-15 season introduced a Sunday matinee series at the Montgomery County venue. In May, Stenz led the symphony in performances of Strauss and Beethoven, prior to the start of his three-year appointment as principal guest conductor in October 2015. Stenz, conductor of the Netherlands Radio Philharmonic Orchestra, says, "I felt an enormous amount of trust the orchestra gave to me. This orchestra is full of musical energy and a willingness to explore. A principal guest conductor should give the best that he or she has to offer and must bring something to the party!"

The 99th season ended with a semi-staged production of *Candide*. Because of her personal and professional connection with the family, Alsop has been a champion of Bernstein. The rarely performed complete work was a resounding success. Alsop says, "Sharing my experience as a student of Leonard Bernstein – in terms of communicating with audiences; creating a culture of access and inclusion surrounding the orchestra; and bringing his music to life for our Baltimore audiences has been a great joy. Our production and recording of Bernstein's MASS in 2008 and this season's closing performances of *Candide* were true highlights for the orchestra and for me personally." The Sun concurred, calling it "among the most satisfying BSO ventures of any recent season."

The season end was also marked by the retirement of five long-tenured musicians including assistant principal clarinet Christopher Wolfe after 52 years, the longest tenured musician in the history of the Baltimore Symphony.

After the symphony's February 1916 debut, the Sun reported, "It is not too much to believe that in the course of time, an orchestra that will take its place with the most important organizations in the country will result from the beginning that was made at the Lyric last evening." Over the past 100 years, the Baltimore Symphony has followed a path through hills and valleys as it found its way to civic relevance and artistic excellence. The Baltimore Symphony, from its musicians to its donors and audience members, has been ever more committed to quality. From a municipal orchestra little known outside of Maryland, it has taken its place among the leading orchestras of the nation and has attracted global acclaim. It has done so in a city without the great inherited wealth that backs its larger rivals, and that still trails in economic dynamism. That it has is a testament to its civic and musical commitment. Like the city itself, the Baltimore Symphony is a symbol of pride and resilience to the community, the state, and the world.

Opposite. The 2015-2016 season opening gala featured pianist Lang Lang, former resident conductor Christopher Seaman, along with numerous city and state dignitaries. Members of OrchKids and the Baltimore Symphony Youth Orchestra joined the BSO on its encore selection.

Top. New principal guest conductor Markus Stenz conducts the BSO during a May 2015 rehearsal. September 2015 featured the launch of the BSO's Pulse series, which combined contemporary classical music with indie rock bands, led by assistant conductor Nicholas Hersh.

Epilogue

Where are we going?
How do we get there?

The two questions above formed the nucleus of Mayor William Donald Schaefer's 1972 blue ribbon panel regarding the Baltimore Symphony's future. The symphony was in the midst of another round of growing pains, and the mayor, along with orchestra supporters and civic leaders, wanted to assess the orchestra's role in the community and beyond. Those same questions can be posed today as the Baltimore Symphony enters its second century.

Continual advances in technology are one of the great unknowns in both the nonprofit and for-profit worlds. The violinist Pinchas Zukerman questions the future role of the concert hall, saying its importance "will be diminishing. Technology is everything and the sound is everything. Orchestras need to be 24/7, the way radio used to be." President and CEO Paul Meecham agrees that "through digital distribution, the BSO can be [better accessed] in the classroom and the community." But to him, this does not sound the death knell for the Joseph Meyerhoff Symphony Hall. "The Meyerhoff [can be] the hub of a vibrant neighborhood, and BSO concerts can be perceived as a 'cool' activity by young audiences." The orchestra has been making inroads through younger audiences and continual technological investments, but the path is not easy or cheap. Experts support the notion of cultural institutions, including libraries and museums, becoming "third places," where communities can gather, learn, and work together.

"I think the next big transformative urban development could be around this hall," says music director Marin Alsop. "I think that we can develop this area to be a destination point for tourists, locals, and the community." With the many cultural institutions in the area, such as Maryland Institute College of Art, the Lyric, and Center Stage, Alsop thinks that the Baltimore Symphony "can become more inclusive with the arts in general." The Music Center at Strathmore already houses a host of cultural organizations and continues to strengthen its importance to Montgomery County residents.

Former music director David Zinman says, "Everybody is trying to figure out the future, but it's not so easy. I don't think anybody has the answer." But Zinman believes that the future of symphony orchestras starts in the schools. "There have to be kids playing in orchestras," he says. "Why go to a baseball game? Everybody plays baseball and that's why they go to the games. [As a kid,] if you play music, you're going to have more appreciation for what it is orchestras do." In recent years, the Baltimore Symphony has increased its educational investment, especially through its OrchKids and adult education programs. Alsop also is a strong supporter of educational initiatives. "I want to see if we can't shake up the subscription model a little bit," says Alsop. "I always thought about going more toward mini-festivals, where there is an in-depth educational component. People want to know more."

Frequent BSO guest conductor Gunther Herbig wishes that orchestras could really connect with the next generation, but acknowledges that some ideas "are just simply crazy." During his time in Toronto, one board member suggested that he wear a red jacket on the podium "to liven things up a little. … He also wanted a young girl to come on stage between movements with a poster." Instead, Herbig says, orchestra concerts need to be "so overwhelming in quality." He feels that is something that is "getting completely lost." From its earliest years as a municipal organization, the Baltimore Symphony's growth was practically based on the question of how to improve its quality. As a line item in the city budget, the orchestra could not increase salaries and attract better talent. Investments in quality and programming always come with a price. "Baltimore always had an inferiority complex," states former principal horn and Peabody director Robert Pierce. He believes that Baltimore must change its mindset. "If you have a defeatist attitude and say you can't do something, it isn't going to happen. The town won't support you." Pierce believes that organizations must give "the right message and give the feeling of confidence."

The Baltimore Symphony has come a long way since 1916. Meecham hopes, "The orchestra's second 100 years are financially more secure than the first 100." But the symphony's continued purpose and relevance is dependant on newer audiences and donors, along with the continued support and gratitude of its longtime benefactors. The 1972 Blue Ribbon Panel report acknowledged that Baltimore wanted a creative and community-minded major orchestra that would be competitive with peer orchestras. The questions "Where do we go?" and "How do we get there?" were taken from *Alice in Wonderland*. "Would you tell me, please, which way I ought to go from here?' 'That depends a good deal on where you want to get to,' said the Cat. 'I don't much care where –' said Alice. 'Then it doesn't matter which way you go,' said the Cat. '– so long as I get SOMEWHERE,' Alice added as an explanation. It's not known where the orchestra or the city in 1916 may have seen the Baltimore Symphony being in 100 years. The Sun predicted that the orchestra would "soon develop into a notable feature of our civic life." Looking back at its accomplishments over the past 100 years, it is clear that the Baltimore Symphony has gone "somewhere," and that its future is as hopeful, unknown, and exciting as it was back in February 1916.

Leadership

Presidents and Chairs of the Baltimore Symphony Association, Inc.

R.E. Lee Taylor
1942

Philip B. Perlman
1946

Howard W. Jackson
1947

Robert O. Bonnell
1949

Alan P. Hoblitzell
1951

Francis S. Whitman Jr.
1953

Eugene S. Williams
1954

Dr. C. Bernard Brack
1956

John D. Wright
1961

Clarence W. Miles
1963

Joseph Meyerhoff
1965 (President)
1983 (Chair)

Frank Baker Jr.
1983

Calman J. Zamoiski Jr.
1986

Decatur H. Miller
1990

Calman J. Zamoiski Jr.
1992

Philip D. English
2003

Michael G. Bronfein
2006

Kenneth W. DeFontes, Jr.
2011

Barbara Bozzuto
2014

Presidents, Executive Directors, General Managers

C.C. Cappel
1942

John S. Edwards
1948

John R Woolford
1951

Judith M. Colt
1953

Robert E. MacIntyre
1954

Betty Danneman
1956

Ralph Black
1960

Clinton E. Norton
1962

Oleg Lobanov
1965

Frank Ratka
1969

Joseph Leavitt
1973

John Gidwitz
1984

James Glicker
2004

Paul Meecham
2006

Presidents of the Women's Association of the Baltimore Symphony Orchestra

Mrs. Richard M. (Catherine) Jackson
1942

Mrs. Charles S. (Aurelia) Garland
1944

Mrs. John L. Whitehurst
1946

Mrs. Roy D. Whitlock
1950

Mrs. H. Morris Whitehurst
1952

Mrs. Henry R. (Dorothy) Granger
1953

Mrs. W. McLean Patterson
1956

Mrs. Harry R. (Betty) Christopher
1958

Mrs. Alfred C. (Loretta) Ver Valen
1960

Mrs. Charles J. (Libby) Owens
1962

Mrs. Milton (Henriette) Duke
1966

Mrs. Arthur M. (Peg) Gompf
1968

Mrs. Mark F. (Ollie) Collins
1971

Mrs. William G. (Martha) Hall Jr.
1972

Mrs. G. Ashton (Alice) Sutherland, III
1973

Mrs. Andrew (Eleanor) Braun
1975

Baltimore Symphony Associates

Joan Sadler
1977

Judie Burke
1980

Joyce McCrystle
1983

Bonnie Markell
1985

Nancy Young
1987

Frances E. Angelino
1989

Katie Stevens
1992

Maureen Patton
1995

Carol O'Connell
1997

Maurice Feldman
1999

Carol O'Connell
2001

Susan Hutton
2003

Evart 'Bud' Cornell
2005

Barbara Booth
2007

Winnie Flattery
2009

Marge Penhallegon
2011

Sandy Feldman
2014

Decorators' Show Houses

Cedarwood 1977

Chestnutwood 1978

Leisure Hill 1979

Sherwood Mansion 1980

Zemlyn Porches 1981

Lambeth Green 1982

Guilford House 1983

Oaklands 1984

Laural 1985

Gramercy 1986

Morris House 1987

Historic Hayfields 1988

Oak Hill 1989

Torch Hill 1990

Selsed House 1991

The Lamb Estate 1992

Seven Oaks 1993

Callis-Kennedy House 1994

The Cloisters 1995

Stratford-on-the-Green 1996

Wynddon Estate 1997

Solomon's Corner 1998

Helmore Farm 1999

Loveton Mansion 2000

Foxhall Manor 2001

Rainbow Hill 2002

Legacy House 2003

Guilford House 2004

La Ruche 2005

Villa Vista 2006

Long Crandon 2007

Roland Run 2008

Arden House 2009

Woodholme Estate 2010

Symphonic Suites 2011

Eck House 2012

Legend Hill 2013

Silo Point 2014

Oak Acre 2015

Musician Roster

The roster posted below has been hand compiled from program booklets over the past 100 years. Some information, especially from the organization's first 25 years, is incomplete. Please accept this roster as an informational guide and apologies are offered for any omissions or inaccurate dates.

Violins

Abramovitz, Norman
1927-1945

Adkins, Madeline (AC)
2000-Present

Adler, Leon
1928-1932

Akacos, Alexander
1949-1951

Apreda, Valentine
1926-1941

Alt, Kurt*
1923-1942

Authier, A. Syl.
1919-1920

Baer, Moses
1922-1923

Bangs, Herbert*
1919-1959

Banyak, Kalman
1957-1967

Baron, James
1949-1950

Belfer, Adolph
1953-1960

Berenson, Isadore
1919-1937

Berenson, Morris
1929-1937

Berkovich, Leonid
1984-Present

Bernard, Paul (AC)
1942-1943

Bernstein, Gerald
1969-1977

Berrio, Eduardo
1964-1967

Berul, Wallace
1949-1967

Besrodny, Jack
1952-1956

Black, Arnold (AC)
1945-1946

Black, Eva
1960-1966

Blatt, Jacob
1954-1956

Boehm, James
1970-2015

Bogushevsky, David
1952-1953

Bolognini, Remo E.
1955-1960

Braunstein, Jack
1942-1943

Breslaw, Leon
1942-1943

Briskin, Leonid
1990-Present

Brody, Saul
1956-1957

Browne, Fred
1949-1950

Brusiloff, Leon
1916-1926

Buettner, Emil
1936-1940

Butler, Boris
1983-1984

Butler, Lois
1942-1943

Bykov, Joseph
1976-2003

Cardiff, Kevin
1979-1992

Carlini, Louis (AC)
1949-1956

Carlon, Loyal D.
1920-1937

Carmell, Samuel (CM)
1952-1955

Carney, Jonathan (CM)
2002-Present

Chalfant, Paul
1950-1951

Cheslock, Louis
1916-1937

Choi, Minsun
2013-Present

Chomyak, John
1943-1944

Cianci, Paul
1946-1947

Clarke, Karen
1969-1976

Cohen, Samuel
1975-1979

Colbertson, Robert
1955-1956

Comanda, Enzo
1956-1962

Comanda, Eric
1949-1950

Conn, Vivienne
1937-1946

Conrad, Ruthabeth
1947-1948

Cook, Edmund R.
1921-1929

Corimby, Bertine
1947-1948

Cramer, Ernest
1945-1946

Cusimano, Giuseppe
1949-1950

Davidson, Jane
1968-1970

de Moraes, Nino*
1956-1975

de Pasquale, Robert R.
1955-1956

Deane, Leon
1936-1937

DeLillo, Walter*
1931-1956

DeMaria, Marie
1942-1948

Di Dio, Aurelio
1953-1956

Dore, Carol
1958-1962

Dorman, Israel
1916-1930

Du, Rui
2011-Present

Dubin, Maurice
1932-1935

Dvoskina, Inessa
1979-1982

Dziekonski, Elizabeth
1979-1982

Ehrlich, Paul
1948-1949

Eisenberg, Benj.
1916-1918

Elliott, James C.
1922-1935

Essers, Hendrik A.
1919-1932

Ettari, Fred D.
1945-1946

Eyth, Gerald
1932-1946

Faraco, Raffaele
1954-1989

Farmer, Virginia
1944-1945

Finkelstein, Morris
1916-1920

Fisher, L.H.
1919-1924

Fortunati, Amedeo
1954-1964

Frame, William
1952-1953

Frengut, Leon
1923-1926

Fresco, John E.
1947-1948

Galos, Andrew
1946-1947

Garagusi, Nicholas
1943-1944

Gegner, William
1943-1945

Geidt, W. Albert
1919-1922

Geisinger, Eva
1944-1945

Gelbloom, Gerald (AC)
1949-1953

Gennusa, Dorothy Byrd
1949-1970

Getan, Carmen L.
1962-1987

Getan, Jesus
1962-1977

Ghertovici, Adolph
1973-1974

Gholz, Barbara
1970-1972

Gilbert, Karl V.
1916-1918

Gittelson, Frank (CM)
1937-1941

Godfrey, William H.
1963-1966

Goldfuss, Abraham
1951-1971

Goldscher, Samuel*
1928-1942

Goldstein, Kenneth
1980-Present

Goodman, Harry
1921-1937

Gorin, Edward
1976-1998

Granofsky, Charles
1940-1946

Grau, Gideon (CM)
1953-1954

Greenberg, Herbert (CM)
1981-2001

Grosbayne, Benjamin
1942-1972

Grotsky, Paul
1952-1953

Guile, George
1954-1971

Hahn, Lieselotte
1962-1964

Hecker, David
1919-1923

Heinke, David
1951-1952

Hershow, Russell
1987-1989

Herz, Herbert
1942-1974

Hieger, Nathan
1945-1946

Horvath, Alexander
1958-1960

Hyun, Hai-Eun
1964-1968

Imbrogulio, Joseph
1916-1932

Ippolito, Carmela
1946-1947

Ito, Hiromi
1983-1994

Iula, Ruffino*
1921-1951

Jacobs, Bernard
1943-1944

Jacobs, Jacques*
1942-1943

Top Row. James Olin, Anthony Iovane.

Bottom Row. Gordy Miller, Robert Barney, Mari Matsumoto.

Jakey, Lauren
1962-1964

Jauna, Judith M.
1948-1949

Jia, Hong-Guang
1986-1988

Johnson, Dorothy Cross
1973-1977

Jones, Jeffrey
1973-1975

Jovanovic, Sabina
1970-1972

Judefind, Arlington
1936-1940

Kahn, Eli
1916-1937

Kang, Hyo
1970-1972

Kantorowicz, Lilo
1944-1945

Kaspar, Charles*
1916-1918

Kaufman, Malverne
1962-1966

Kesner, Edouard*
1949-1950

Kessler, Frances
1940-1960

Kim, Wonju
1989-Present

Kimber, Christopher
1963-1966

Kinschner, Raymond
1945-1958

Klasmer, Benjamin
1919-1932

Knudsen, Ronald
1954-1956

Kobler, Raymond (AC)
1973-1974

Kohon, Harold (CM)
1960-1962

Kolberg, Hugo (CM)
1964-1965

Komianos, Polydor (AC)
1934-1960

Kontorowicz, Alex
1949-1950

Koprowski, Boleslav
1944-1945

Kostoff, Karl
1951-1952

Kramer, Charles F.
1916-1935

Krolich, Leah
1944-1945

Kromich, Kurt J.
1946-1947

Kuharetz, John
1951-1953

Kuperstein, Gregory
1980-Present

Landau, Fred
1954-1956

Lanzillotti, Joseph
1942-1948

Leanza, Linda
1989-1990

Lee, Robert C.
1926-1927

Lee, Walter
1926-1935

Lentini, Rosano
1943-1944

Leone, Renato
1942-1943

Li, Qing*
1993-Present

Light, Herbert
1956-1957

Lindbergs, Andre
1951-1952

Lipsch, Bernard*
1926-1943

Llinas, Emilio
1962-1964

London, George
1936-1940

Lyon, Milton H.*
1919-1937

Malizia, Rudolph
1955-1958

Malocsay, Rosemary
1950-1951

Malsh, Carol
1947-1948

Mansfield, Newton
1949-1950

Maratea, Anthony
1942-1943

Martin, Alan
1942-1943

Martin, William Fred*
1950-1980

Martini, Evelina
1940-1967

Matsumoto, Mari
1973-Present

Merrill, Diane
1967-1970

Merrill, John
1971-2013

Miller, Manuel
1922-1930

Mischakoff, Mischa (CM)
1969-1970

Montesi, Louann
1952-1956

Morgan, Arthur
1927-1931

Moses, Abram
1916-1936

Mucci, Victor
1950-1951

Mueller, Andrew
1919-1920

Mulligan, Greg
1980-Present

Mutner, Mildred
1944-1945

Myerovich, Olga
1970-1991

Nation, William
1962-1979

Niccoli, Alessandro
1949-1950

Nichols, Rebecca
1991-Present

Noh, Joyce
1977-1979

Oberstein, Gerson
1942-1943

Olivero, Lilia
1952-1967

Orner, Ellen Ginzburg
1986-2010

Orner, George*
1963-2010

Ota, Junko
1975-1976

Otey, Cline W Jr.
1956-1966

Otey, Dolly Ann
1963-1968

Palmer, Jay
1947-1949

Parcells, Julie
1980-Present

Pariante, Victor
1943-1944

Park, Eunja
1971-1972

Parkinson, Judith
1964-1967

Patey, Edward
1968-2009

Pepper, Joseph
1942-1943

Pfieffer, William
1929-1931

Bottom Row.
Paula Childress,
soprano Ruth Drucker,
Greg Mulligan,
Mary Woehr.

Middle Row. Ken Goldstein,
Craig Richmond, orchestra
manager Mark Volpe,
David Bakkegard,
Joseph Birscuso.

Top. Arno Drucker.

Pfister, Ralph Rene
1955-1956

Picone, Benjamin
1953-1954

Plasschaert, Camille
1946-1947

Ponall, Charles
1966-1968

Portela, Guillermo
1964-1974

Radin, Jacob
1946-1948

Read, Thomas
1962-1963

Reisler, Jerome
1943-1944

Resnik, Simon
1964-1968

Richardson, John
1957-1962

Richmond, E. Craig
1971-Present

Ritter, Melvin
1942-1943

Robofsky, Abraham
1926-1928

Roby, Paul
1988-1989

Rodgers, Janet
1965-1966

Roerentrop, Fred
1916-1932

Rollman, Edgar
1916-1926

Roman, Julio
1948-1970

Rosenberg, Louis
1919-1922

Rosenker, Michael (CM)
1962-1964

Rosenstein, Max
1919-1929

Rouleau, Raymond
1920-1922

Rowney, Jas. B.
1916-1928

Rutter, Malcolm (CM)
1965-1966

Ryker, Leslie
1974-1975

Samuels, Jack
1916-1920

Sandler, Myron
1942-1943

Sanger, William
1952-1956

Saslav, Isidor (CM)
1969-1981

Schaffer, Peter
1955-1956

Schkolnik, Iiya (CM)
1944-1945

Schnabel, William
1921-1927

Schroeder, Gibbs
1936-1938

Schwartz, Emmanuel
1919-1922

Schwartz, Sandra
1971-1972

Schweitzer, Isidoro
1942-1943

Scroggins, Christina
1979-Present

Semiatin, Theodore
1921-1922

Semo, Adrian (AC)
1973-2003

Senofsky, Berl
1948-1949

Setzer, Elmer
1940-1948

Sevely, Jeno*
1942-1944

Shaffran, Sam
1943-1944

Shaftel, Josef
1942-1943

Shapey, Ronald
1950-1951

Shor, Sylvia Angel
1940-1983

Siebel, Laura
1957-1958

Siebel, Wolfgang
1957-1958

Siegal, Fritz (CM)
1955-1956

Simpson, Earl Levy*
1919-1920

Sinanian, Georges
1942-1943

Sisson, Paula
1976-1984

Skerlong, William L.
1951-1954

Slutsky, Leri
1980-2006

Smelansky, Leon
1950-1951

Smith, Kevin
2015-Present

Sokolove, Harry
1916-1923

Sokolove, Herbert
1927-1929

Sokolove, Julius
1921-1932

Solomon, Joseph
1929-1936

Somerville, Beauna
1945-1948

Sorask, Robin
1936-1937

Sosner, Benjamin
1924-1949

Stancl, Václav
1952-1960

Staples, Alan Powell
1949-1950

* Principal musician   (CM) Concertmaster   (AC) Assistant Concertmaster   (P) Piccolo   (EH) English Horn

Stefanovic, Ivan
1991-Present

Steiner, George
1936-1940

Steingard, David
1967-1969

Steinhardt, Laszlo (CM)
1956-1960

Sternberg, Albert
1945-1946

Stewart, Nelson
1989-1990

Stoler, Meyer
1936-1937

Strange, Richard
1936-1939

Suarez, Thomas
1978-1979

Svilokos, Andrew
1960-1962

Swindells, James
1956-1962

Szabó, Zoltán
1962-1963

Taitz, Bernard
1926-1937

Tanaka, Yasuoki
1970-2010

Taylor, Dorothy
1944-1946

Taylor, Jody
1966-1979

Taylor, Wayne C.
1971-Present

Tengwall, Ruth
1951-1957

Thachuk, Dolly Ann
1957-1962

Thaviu, Samuel (CM)
1942-1943

Tomasow, Jan (CM)
1950-1951

Totenberg, Roman (CM)
1943-1944

Trautwein, George
1951-1952

Tretick, Stephanie
1975-1979

Troyer, Ellen Pendleton
1991-Present

Turk, Jacob
1916-1942

Umber, James
1990-Present

Underwood, Charles
1975-Present

Van Hulsteyn, J.C. (CM)
1916-1936

Van Hulsteyn, Ruth
1940-1985

Van Sant, Karen
1972-1981

van Tongeren, Helen
1950-1956

Velten, Robert
1943-1944

Villine, Vincent
1936-1939

Wade, Bruce L.
1973-1993

Wagner, Carolyn
1952-1953

Waller, Franklin
1920-1926

Wasser, Sylvia
1944-1945

Wasyluszko, Andrew
1983-Present

Weiner, Michael
1929-1931

Whitelock, Katherine
1937-1939

Wicks, Eric
1960-1968

Wilkison, Ronald
1970-1971

Williams, Elizabeth
1951-1952

Wolf, Samuel
1956-1960

Yaroshuk, Frank
1946-1947

Yuzefovich, Igor
2005-2014

Zaraya, Melissa Schock
1967-2014

Zech, Julius
1916-1922

Zelditch, Louis J.
1921-1929

Zigelnik, Leon
1942-1943

Zinn, William
1944-1945

Viola

Andy, Elmer
1945-1972

Ayestas, J. Humberto
1962-1978

Barker, Julia
1977-2008

Barten, Michael*
1957-1960

Bauch, Arthur*
1946-1948

Blacklock, Nancy
1963-1967

Bochau, Charles
1919-1921

Bomus, Joan
1952-1960

Braun, William
1916-1921

Breithaupt, Zeddie
1928-1937

Breslaw, Irene
1971-1972

Brown, Harold
1945-1946

Brown, Karin
2002-Present

Brown, Lila
1981-1982

Chaves, Noah
1974-Present

Cheatham, Paul
1922-1925

Cherry, Abe
1942-1943

Chesner, Jack H.
1944-1945

Clodfelter, Joseph
1966-2000

Colberg, Christian
1993-2011

Collins, Keith
1936-1938

Conrad, Rolf H,
1954-1958

Cooke, Edmund
1936-1960

Cooperstein, Irving
1936-1950

Cox, John H.*
1955-1956

Creamer, Kenneth
1940-1946

Dodson, C. Milton
1921-1931

Dorman, Israel
1916-1919

Dumm, Thomas*
1974-1978

Elitzak, Harold*
1952-1956

Elson, Joseph
1943-1944

Essers, Hendrick*
1920-1935

Falk, Nina
1972-1974

Farquhar, Lydia
1940-1950

Feldman, Sara
1937-1973

Fenstermacher, Leroy
1964-1967

Ferguson, Paul
1970-1977

Field, Richard*
1979-Present

Figelski, Cecil*
1944-1948

Finkelstein, Morris
1919-1921

Fishberg, Theodore
1949-1957

Flagg, Russell Jr.
1951-1952

Francis, James
1973-1984

Gillam, Jeanne
1951-1953

Glick, Jacob
1947-1949

Grossman, George
1942-1944

Hammerbacher, George M.
1920-1937

Harris, Reid
1975-1979

Hecker, Charlene
1957-1958

Hemmick, Lloyd H.
1928-1929

Hill, Kristin
1970-2005

Hollman, W. Hart
1970-1973

Holston, Alvin
1936-1947

Holzaphel, Carl*
1932-1957

Hymanson, William*
1942-1943

Illions, Seymour
1952-1953

Iovane, Anthony
1957-1987

Jacob, William
1958-1962

Jeanneret, Marc*
1972-1973

Kahn, Myron
1960-1969

Kaplan, Maurice
1919-1920

Klima, Arthur
1973-1977

Labman, Murray
1951-1952

Lamboley, Geraldine
1974-1975

Langley, Allan L.
1943-1945

Lesinsky, Samuel
1921-1927

Lessing, Samuel*
1927-1937

Lewis, Arthur*
1968-1972

Liebman, Ethel
1944-1945

Linhard, Ferdinand*
1916-1936

Loughran, Hugh
1968-1971

Lysy, Oscar
1962-1963

Minkler, Peter
1985-Present

Montoni, Raymond*
1956-1957

Motter, Margaret
1973-1975

Mueller, Andrew
1916-1937

Mueller, Charles Sr.
1931-1932

Myer, Sharon Pineo
1978-Present

Newman, Rebekah
2013-2015

Nissenson, Harold
1940-1943

Odendhal, Emil
1932-1933

Paeff, Spinoza*
1949-1952

Pellman, Benjamin
1947-1971

Pellow, J. Boyd
1949-1950

Perich, Guillermo*
1960-1968

Primavera, Joseph
1950-1951

Reicheback, E.
1932-1937

Russ, Malcolm
1974-1975

Sander, Christiane
1973-1974

Segall, Irving
1960-1962

Shoop, Betty
1953-1960

Skernick, Abraham*
1948-1949

Slutsky, Genia
1981-2011

Smith, Charles W.
1928-1931

Sokolove, Herbert
1931-1932

Soloman, Alexander
1942-1943

Solomon, Stanley
1945-1946

Somogyi, Joseph
1963-1967

Stadnitsky, Joseph
1919-1931

Steinwald, O.P.
1916-1932

Steltenpohl, Lisa*
2014-Present

Stewart, Delmar
1977-Present

Stewart, Jeffrey
1978-Present

Susemihl, John
1919-1920

Tretick, Stephanie
1978-1979

Turow, Stanley
1927-1928

Wallfisch, Ernst*
1973-1974

Weiner, Michael
1921-1926

Weinrebe, Robert
1944-1945

Wicks, Nancy
1966-1969

Wilke, Eric
1936-1938

Woehr, Mary
1983-Present

Wolf, Samuel
1963-1982

Zinman, Mary
1988-1995

Cello

Akeley, Tom C.
1950-1952

Ancher, Marcel
1927-1930

Anderson, Eva
1963-1995

Argiewicz, Bernard
1947-1950

Aue, Margaret
1947-1951

Baker, Rita May
1942-1947

Besrodny, Boris
1942-1944

Blatt, Robert
1964-1967

Brown, Virginia
1967-1968

Calvani, Ilis
1955-1956

Chardon, Yyes*
1954-1956

Clay, Robert
1956-1957

Clodfelter, Judith M.
1967-1970

Cohen, Charles
1931-1932

Colletti, Charles
1943-1944

Davidoff, Judith
1951-1952

dePasquale, Francis
1942-1943

Doolittle, Mary Hill
1937-1943

Dorman, Samuel
1931-1937

Eidam, Mary
1937-1940

Eisenberg, Maurice
1916-1918

Evans, Susan Cohen
1979-Present

Fasshauer, Carl Jr.
1948-1949

Finkelshteyn, Ilya*
2002-2009

Flacco, Albert
1936-1937

Franzosa, Antoinette
1944-1945

French, Louise
1953-1962

Froehlich, Max
1944-1946

Furthmaier, Albert
1916-1918

Gingerich, John
1984-1985

Goldstein, Fred
1952-1953

Grosser, Herman
1942-1943

Gruppe, Paul
1946-1947

Hamburger, Siegfried
1919-1937

Hamburger, Sydney
1916-1937

Hamer, Sidney
1949-1950

Heitman, J. Bernard
1919-1921

Hennig, Frank
1945-1946

Horvath, William
1950-1951

Howell, Rosemary
1944-1945

Hradetzky, Eva
1963-1964

Isomura, Sachiya
1977-1979

Jarvinen, Dorothy
1946-1947

Joachim, Heinrich*
1958-1962

Jump, Dorothea
1952-1962

Kalkhof, Bernard
1945-1946

Kapuscinski, Richard R.*
1948-1952

Katz, Albert*
1954-1955

Kauffman, Irvin
1960-1964

Kay, Richard*
1956-1958

Kayaloff, Anna
1943-1944

Kayaloff, J.A.
1951-1952

Kayaloff, Jean A.
1949-1950

Kellert, Gabriel C.
1953-1962

Kirsch, Lucien*
1940-1942

Knieling, Louis F.
1919-1920

Koschura, Stefan
1951-1958

Kouguell, Alexander
1948-1949

Kuykendall, James
1967-1966

Lamp, Karl
1949-1950

Laskow, Julius
1954-1955

Lee, Chang Woo
1978-Present

Li, Bo
2001-Present

Low, Seth
1986-Present

Lu, Pei
2011-Present

Lumm, Alexander
1955-1967

Maas, Gerald C.
1942-1944

Manheim, Andre
1919-1921

Mauricci, Peter
1976-1985

Mellon, Esther
1977-Present

Mendelssohn, Felix Robert
1942-1951

Morand, Denise
1948-1979

Neal, Marjorie
1947-1950

Neikrug, George*
1946-1947

Niedelman, Mischa
1932-1936

Novak, Luba
1955-1960

Orazi, Ennio
1955-1960

Ostling, Kristin
1995-Present

Patterson, Jerome
1966-1967

Pearlman, Tricia
1966-1967

Petracca, Michael
1943-1945

Richardson, Louis
1947-1949

Roche, Gita
1992-2001

Rosanoff, Marie Roemaet*
1942-1946

Rosansky, Leo
1950-1952

Salvo, Andrew D.
1954-1955

Saunders, Joseph*
1947-1954

Scholz, Edwin
1960-1962

Schwartz, Louis
1916-1937

Shallin, Elliott
1956-1967

Shambaugh, Linda D.
1967-1968

Shapinsky, Aaron
1942-1943

Sher, Yuri
1983-1998

Simonowitz, J.L.
1922-1924

Sims, Jules
1925-1928

Skidmore, William R.
1974-1977

Skolnick, Paula
1970-2015

Skoraczewski, Dariusz*
2000-Present

Slatkin, Mischa
1952-1954

Spahn, Joseph
1930-1964

Spielman, Samuel
1951-1960

Stehl, Richard
1952-1954

Stern, Samuel Maurice
1920-1923

Stofberg, Zolic
1930-1935

Stolarchyk, Linda
1968-1975

Stolarchyk, Peter
1967-1992

Stone, Louise W.
1944-1945

Strassner, Gloria*
1952-1954

Sykora, Frank
1945-1962

Teie, David
1979-1982

Toroni, Wallace J.
1952-1974

　　　　* Principal musician　　　(CM) Concertmaster　　　(AC) Assistant Concertmaster　　　(P) Piccolo　　　(EH) English Horn

Left. Bart Wirtz.

Right. Steven Barta, Phillip Kolker.

Virizlay, Mihály*
1962-2005

Virizlay, Tricia
1967-1972

Wahlin, Eric H.
1946-1947

Wallace, Paul
1962-1963

Weimer, Patricia
1977-1979

Whitney, Grace
1968-1977

Willaman, Kenneth
1962-1999

Wirtz, Bart*
1916-1951

Yampolsky, Miron
1974-1977

Zimbler, Maurice
1950-1952

Zukowski, Boleslaw
1945-1948

Zundel, Olga
1946-1947

—————

Bass

—————

Alejo, Carlos
1967-1983

Barney, Robert*
1972-Present

Baughman, Isabel
1947-1960

Blech, Edward
1916-1918

Bloch, Henry
1942-1943

Bowman, Rea B.
1945-1947

Caster, Frank
1950-1951

Childress, W. Hampton III
1982-Present

Corsale, Vincent
1942-1947

Craver, Arnold
1972-1984

Cummings, Owen
1977-Present

Currier, N.W.
1943-1944

Edmonds, Isabel
1962-1967

Eidman, Charles A.
1916-1921

Eney, Frank
1929-1943

Epstein, Philip*
1946-1949

Ferrell Turner, Elizabeth
1966-2002

Glash, Joseph
1950-1951

Goliger, Joseph
1957-1958

Granofsky, Nicholas
1956-1982

Gravagno, Emilio
1962-1967

Gregorian, Arnold
1984-2014

Gribanovsky, Dmitry
1949-1950

Groat, Stephen
1990-1992

Hodges, Keith
1958-1960

Huang, Mark
2003-Present

Jensen, Jonathan
1983-Present

Karasek, Karl
1922-1927

Kouba, Jan
1946-1947

Lacey, Alexander
1958-1966

Lamagna, Michael
1944-1945

Lansinger, William M.
1927-1958

Lazzaro, Alfio
1943-1957

Levithan, Peter*
1942-1944

Linhard, J. Andrew
1919-1922

Litolf, Rocco*
1949-1972

Mackay, Cameron
1944-1945

MacLenner, Robert
1936-1937

Malin, Selwyn
1948-1950

Mathews, John*
1960-1982

Matthews, John Fenton
1947-1949

Mihalik, István
1967-1996

Millen, Harry I.
1951-1952

Moffett, Edwin*
1916-1948

Montemayor, L.V.
1920-1935

Pauli, Peter M.
1948-1957

Perlman, David
1960-1962

Pohrebynsky, Jack
1949-1950

Rahmig, Paul
1916-1918

Riccardi, Robert
1964-1966

Robinson, Kenneth
1947-1948

Rossi, Elgio
1950-1951

Ruzicka, William
1931-1933

Ryan, George
1945-1946

Schlecker, Richard
1966-1977

Schwinck, U.S.
1927-1937

Scott, Henry
1968-1972

Shachner, Harold
1947-1949

Sheets, David
1996-Present

Smith, George
1932-1935

Spitzbarth, Paul
1923-1930

Stahl, Eric
1982-Present

Stanley, Michael
1972-1974

Staszhy, Robert J.*
1943-1946

Strazza, Alfonso
1951-1953

Tartaglia, David
1989-1990

Totten, Clarence J.*
1943-1944

Varallo, John
1958-1970

Voulkan, Simon
1942-1943

Walter, D.C.
1916-1957

Williman, Leonard
1936-1937

Wilson, Barbara
1962-1964

Top Row. David Bakkegard, Bill Kendall, Bruce Moore, Herbert Greenberg.

Bottom Row. Emily Skala, Mark Sparks, Mary Bisson.

Wood, Raymond
1953-1956

Zinn, Louis
1942-1943

Ziporlin, Leon*
1944-1945

Zschunke, William J.
1945-1947

――――――――

Flute

――――――――

Berg, Jacob
1950-1957

Bohl, John C.*
1916-1931

Burgess, John
1942-1943

Camparone, Frank
1944-1945

Combs, Mardele (P)
1964-1965

Cramer, Frederick
1937-1938

Day, Timothy*
1974-1987

DiSevo, Oreste (P)
1953-1954

Foster, Eugene
1943-1944

Giese, Richard
1952-1953

Goldsmith, George G.
1943-1944

Gottlieb, Samuel
1928-1930

Gowen, Lloyd (P)
1954-1955

Grimes, Caroline
1962-1964

Hirsh, Harry*
1944-1945

Hoffman, Henry
1971-1972

Iula, Robert*
1916-1931

Johnson, Britton*
1945-1976

Just, Victor
1931-1943

Kämper, Marcia
2005-Present

Kniebusch, Carol (P)
1966-1969

Knox, Chelsea
2015-Present

Lake, Bonnie (P)
1957-2005

Landgren, Sara
1984-1985

LeRoy, Rene*
1943-1944

Magg, Kyril
1973-1974

McKee-Day, Robin
1978-1985

Mikita, Andrew (P)
1965-1966

Parker, Brooks (P)
1944-1945

Philipp, E. Augustus*
1919-1937

Richter, Michael (P)
1931-1946

Robillard, Wilford (P)
1945-1971

Rowe, Elizabeth
2000-2003

Sager, Marisela
2004-2005

Self, Susanna
2003-2005

Sinatra, Spencer (P)
1951-1953

Skala, Emily Controulis*
1988-Present

Sokoloff, Laurie (P)
1969-Present

Sparks, Mark
1987-2000

Stocker, Marc
1986-1987

Wojtysiak, Adam (P)
1940-1944

――――――――

Oboe

――――――――

Aranow, George Jr. (EH)
1950-1976

Burk, Charles Jr.
1943-1944

Chieffo, Eugene
1962-1963

Criss, William*
1946-1947

Genovese, Alfred*
1953-1956

Ghebelian, Oscar (EH)
1948-1949

Gomberg, Ralph*
1945-1946

Gruenebaum, Fred
1963-1964

Halpern, Sidney
1954-1955

Hewitt, Stevens*
1964-1965

Hooper, Melissa
2014-Present

Jansons, Andrejs*
1960-1962

Jurgensen, Edmund*
1936-1939

Kral, Galen
1962-1967

Kramer, Paul
1952-1953

Kummer, Keith* (EH)
1962-1999

* Principal musician   (CM) Concertmaster   (AC) Assistant Concertmaster   (P) Piccolo   (EH) English Horn

MUSICIANS

Labate, Bruno*
1943-1944
Lammers, John*
1916-1937
Lewis, Charles
1950-1951
Lisicky, Michael
2004-Present
Marvine, Jane (EH)
1978-Present
Miller, Mitchell*
1939-1941
Moore, DeVere (EH)
1949-1950
Morris, Charles M.*
1948-1949
Morrow, Bernard
1944-1945
Mullenix, Carlos W.*
1944-1945
Needleman, Katherine*
2003-Present
Ostryniec, James
1970-2005
Philipp, Ernest (EH)
1916-1942
Prietz, Rudolph
1920-1926
Raho, Lewis Gino*
1940-1942
Rapier, Wayne*
1956-1960
Rappolt, Priscilla A.
1967-1970
Rizzo, Ross
1947-1948
Schnabel, William* (EH)
1926-1962
Scruggs, Shea
2009-2010
Shallin, Joan
1955-1962
Smith, Wm. E.
1929-1930
Snyder, MacLean
1945-1947
Starr, Leslie
1983-1986
Still, Ray*
1949-1953
Thorstenberg, Laurence
1951-1952
Turner, Joseph*
1965-2008
Vas Dias, Humphrey
1953-1954

Woods, Pamela Pecha
1976-1978

Clarinet

Abato, Cosimo
1945-1946
Barta, Steven*
1976-2015
Bettelli, Aldo
1962-1963
Bishop, Neil
1949-1950
Bratman, Morris (BC)
1932-1962
Clearfield, Elvin (BC)
1947-1948
Cohen, Franklin*
1970-1976
Couf, Herbert (BC)
1946-1947
Fiorani, Angelo*
1923-1959
Freeman, Stephen (BC)
1960-1961
Gennusa, Ignatius N.*
1951-1970
Grden, Albin
1956-1958
Grisez, Georges (BC)
1943-1946
Grochmal, James
1927-1929
Hasty, D. Stanley*
1946-1948
Jenken, William
1998-Present
Kummel, Fred (BC)
1931-1933
Lester, Leon
1936-1937
Ma, Lin (Eb)
2015-Present
Miller, Gordon (Eb)
1946-1998
Palanker, Edward (BC)
1963-2014
Patterson, Rob*
2000-2002, 2015-2016
Prencipe, Pasquale (BC)
1949-1952
Reda, Frank Jr.
1946-1947
Renz, Adolph
1919-1920
Seibert, Daniel D. (BC)
1927-1930

Sigismond, Albert
1947-1948
Silfies, George*
1948-1951
Strange, Gilbert*
1916-1946
Strange, William*
1916-1918
Wolfe, Christopher (Eb)
1963-2015
Ziegler, John*
1919-1929

Bassoon

Bernstein, Josef (CB)
1951-1953
Broemel, Robert
1968-1970
Checchia, Anthony
1948-1951
Cole, Robert
1947-1948
Coleman, Herbert
1944-1945
Connors, Ellen
2012-2013
Coombs, David P. (CB)
1982-Present
Corey, Gerald*
1962-1972
Dawson, Robert M.
1945-1946
Del Negro, Ferdinand (CB)
1940-1942
Geiger, Charles Jr.
1916-1937
Gobrecht, Edward
1953-1962
Goltzer, Harold*
1940-1942
Greanya, Benjamin
2013-2014
Green, Julie
1970-Present
Hebert, Emil L.*
1944-1945
Jackson, Schuyler
2014-Present
Kellner, Sigmund*
1919-1937
Kolker, Phillip*
1972-2010
Krueger, Richard*
1916-1918
Lannutti, Arthur
1940-1954

Letellier, Louis*
1942-1943
Maciejewicz, Walter
1946-1947
Masucci, Sabatino (CB)
1942-1945
Mosbach, Joseph H.*
1943-1944
Nabokin, Jacob
1943-1944
Orosz, Julius S. (CB)
1967-1982
Palermo, Frank (CB)
1953-1967
Petrulis, Stanley*
1957-1962
Plaster, Richard
1951-1952
Popper, Michael
1962-1968
Rickman, Brent
1968-2007
Schwartz, Frank*
1954-1955
Segal, Cyrus
1952-1953
Skinner, Louis A. (CB)
1945-1951
Stein, Walter D.*
1945-1948
Tucker, Frank (CB)
1942-1943
Weisberg, Arthur*
1955-1957
Willoughby, Susan*
1965-1967
Xie, Fei*
2007-Present

Horn

Abbott, Kenneth W.
1945-1947
Antonelli, Pietro B.
1943-1958
Bakkegard, David*
1977-2011
Barnes, Byron
1973-1977
Beard, Richard
1945-1947
Bisson, Mary
1983-Present
Chernin, Bertrand
1945-1955
Cook, William
1960-1962

Corrado, Donald*
1952-1953
Deering, Charles
1963-1966
DePasquale, Joseph
1958-1962
Diori, John
1940-1942
Donaruma, Francisco
1974-1976
Evans, Ted M.
1942-1944
Finck, Gabrielle
2007-Present
Fisher, Hans
1940-1945
Gelwasser, Louis
1920-1937
Getz, Jeanne
2014-Present
Glaze, Martha
1973-1974
Gorell, Frank*
1942-1943
Graham, Beth
1998-2013
Grant, Edward E.
1944-1945
Horner, Anton*
1916-1918
Horner, Joseph
1916-1918
Johnson, Sune*
1942-1944
Kendall, William
1967-1998
Kenny, Thomas G. Jr.*
1949-1958
Klang, William
1960-1976
Knop, Jerry T.*
1945-1952
Kreuger, Raymond
1976-1997
Landgren, Peter
1979-2007
Laughton, Kirk
1981-1983
Lawson, Walter
1947-1975
Maniloff, Leon
1932-1937
Marks, Ferdinand G.
1920-1922
Martinet, Leigh
1948-1949

Mayer, Abby S.
1955-1958

Misare, Charles*
1944-1945

Moore, Bruce
1976-2015

Moore, Thomas J.
1962-1963

Munds, Philip*
1997-Present

Ogilvie, Clarence
1951-1953

Olson, Julian
1963-1972

Piazza, Jerry T.
1948-1949

Pierce, Robert O.*
1958-1982

Preller, Frank
1919-1920

Reissig, Richard
1955-1962

Rhodes, Ronald
1958-1960

Roberts, George E.
1946-1948

Rosemark, Paul*
1936-1938

Ryva, Anton Jr.
1954-1955

Schumann, Frederick
1919-1920

Seiffert, Stephen
1962-1963

Tryon, Denise
2000-2004

Vernon, Keith
1956-1958

Vitocolonna, G.
1940-1942

Weyforth, Theodore
1916-1935

Wilhelms, Helmuth*
1916-1932

Trumpet

Balio, Andrew*
2001-Present

Bowling, Glen
1963-1966

Bowser, Ira
1950-1952

Burke, James*
1943-1950

Byerly, Harold
1947-1949

Cioracek, Peter
1960-1961

Come, Andre
1956-1957

Converso, M.F.*
1929-1931

Corbin, Clifford
1944-1945

Darke, Ryan
2011-2012

DeGangi, Dominick*
1952-1969

Dieterich, C. Theodore
1919-1935

Feldmann, D. Raymond
1916-1918

Fischer, Joseph E.*
1946-1970

Fishman, Martin*
1960-1961

Fitzgerald, Langston J. III
1970-2002

Freeman, Arthur
1962-1963

Friedman, Maurice E.
1922-1927

Golman, Bennie
1942-1943

Gomberg, Leo A.*
1942-1943

Heller, Fred W.
1921-1935

Hepler, Nate
2013-Present

Hernandez, René
2002-Present

Hoffman, Edward
1982-2009

Hutchens, Gail
1966-2004

Imbergamo, John
1943-1955

Kratz, Nelson C.*
1919-1935

Kretschmer, Jonathan
2010-2011

Luftman, Adam
2005-2007

MacCluer, Joshua*
2000-2001

Marino, Felice
1943-1944

McElfresh, Charles
1940-1944

McGregor, Rob Roy
1970-1981

Mirr, Edward
1945-1946

Mueller, Charles Jr.
1932-1935

Mullinix, Clarence
1945-1946

Pearson, Shepard S.*
1916-1942

Pearson, Willard
1978-1979

Penzarella, Vincent
1957-1960

Smith, Daniel*
1986-1987

Snedecor, Phil
2007-2009

Tison, Don*
1969-2000

Traugott, Erich*
1950-1952

Volpe, Clement
1955-1956

Wennerberg, Karl E.
1942-1943

Wise, Wilmer
1965-1970

Wright, Ira J.
1944-1962

Yukl, Charles*
1931-1936

Trombone

Barber, Robert
1940-1942

Bricker, Robert A.*
1966-1967

Campora, Randall S. (BT)
1985-Present

Carlson, Eric
1980-1985

Clark, Hale (BT)
1956-1971

Clarke, Albert E. Jr.
1942-1943

Danck, George
1926-1927

Davidson, Mark*
2010-2011

Dudley, Christopher*
1988-2013

Edelman, Douglas*
1967-1970

Engelkes, John (BT)
1980-1981

Farnham, Dean
1957-1962

Fetter, David*
1970-1987

Freitag, William F.
1916-1918

Garstick, George*
1945-1950

Gaul, George*
1916-1918

Griffith, Ted (BT)
1960-1963

Hartmann, James
1944-1945

Hill, John D.
1956-1957

Hook, Jack
1964-1979

Janssen, Roger M.
1965-1966

Jarosk, Adolph
1921-1927

Johnson, A.J.
1919-1920

Kerr, Arthur
1953-1956

Kidwell, James Kent
1962-1964

Kimmel, Joseph*
1919-1935

Kupferberg, William
1952-1953

LaVere, Aaron*
2014-Present

Lieder, Adolph
1931-1942

Manson, Eugene
1945-1950

Marcellus, John
1964-1965

Melick, John Jr.*
1951-1966

Mittag, Karl
1916-1920

Nigh, Marvin A.
1950-1952

Olin, James*
1976-Present

Packard, Albert G.
1928-1929

Petesky, Louis
1943-1944

Rodriguez, Joseph*
2013-2014

Salomone, Louis
1928-1930

Smith, Susan
1986-1988

Strange, Lester*
1936-1937

Tavaglion, Dominick
1943-1944

Vance, John
1986-Present

Vernon, Charles (BT)
1971-1980

Warms, Gerhard*
1942-1943

Wiessner, Benjamin
1923-1926

Yeo, Douglas (BT)
1981-1985

Zam, Charles
1946-1956

Zeman, Edward*
1940-1942

Zimnoch, Francis T.
1944-1945

Tuba

Bedurke, Carl Richard
1945-1952

Brown, Warren Daniel
1974-1983

Ditzel, Henry
1921-1945

Donatelli, Philip
1952-1953

Fedderly, David
1983-2014

Horner, Seth
2014-Present

Pirko, Louis
1956-1974

Schmidt, Fred
1916-1920

Wall, Lafayette
1953-1956

Timpani

Duffy, Albert
1963-1966

Hart, William S. Jr.
1940-1953

Kain, Dennis
1966-2012

Kennick, Robert
1960-1963

Riehl, Adolph K.
1916-1942

Wyman, James
2013-Present

　　　　* Principal musician　　　(CM) Concertmaster　　　(AC) Assistant Concertmaster　　　(P) Piccolo　　　(EH) English Horn

Left. Bonnie Lake.

Right. Eric Stahl.

Percussion

Ames, F. Anthony
1966-1968

Asrael, Paul*
1920-1942

Behrend, Jark
1945-1946

Bosserdet, Paul*
1948-1951

Bratman, Carroll C.
1930-1937

Cohen, Nathan
1932-1937

DeLeon, William
1955-1960

DePeters, David
2001-2003

Galm, John K.
1964-1965

Granofsky, Frank
1942-1948

Jones, Douglas
1948-1951

Kaiser, Edward*
1940-1946

Kennick, Robert*
1948-1988

Kuehn, Don
1968-1973

Le Page, Leo J.
1967-2001

Leavitt, Joseph*
1946-1948

Locke, John
1980-Present

Luedtke, Glenn
1960-1963

Marks, Louis
1923-1930

Marshall, William
1916-1918

Meyer, Sylvio
1932-1935

Miraglia, Prospero
1931-1935

Prechtl, Brian
2003-Present

Robertson, Hugh*
1949-1952

Seamon, Ellis
1964-1965

Soistmann, Charles
1944-1946

Soroka, John
1973-1978

Stonefelt, Karolyn*
1963-1964

Stratemeyer, George
1953-1962

Van Hyning, Howard
1960-1962

Weyforth, William
1919-1935

Williams, Christopher*
1978-Present

Harp

Adams, Dorothy
1960-1962

Bottalico, Rosemarie
1963-1978

Fuller, Sarah
2012-Present

Glamann, Betty
1944-1947

Harrison, Joan
1960-1962

Iula, Felice
1916-1919

Lindquist, Karen
1974-1981

Mason, Eileen
1978-2002

Morton, Helen Mitchell
1936-1937

Nicoletta, Frank
1942-1944

Pfeil, Walter
1962-1963

Pizzo, Joseph
1943-1960

Robertson, Bertha T.
1920-1935

Rosenfield, Joyce
1963-1964

Schuster, Sarah
1981-1988

Shank, Nancy
1957-1960

Stainton, Frances
1942-1943

Walschot-Stapp, Astrid
2005-2007

Piano

Chappell, Jeffrey
1980-1987

Drucker, Arno
1970-1997

Evans, LeRoy
1932-1958

Johnson, Lura
2012-Present

Lyon, Milton
1931-1935

O'Meagher, Heather
1958-1964

Shub, Louis
1964-1975

Librarian

Cooke, Edmund R.
1942-1953

Ferraguto, Michael*
2015-Present

Fischer, Joseph*
1960-1989

Gruender, David
1989-1997

Kreuger, Raymond
1997-Present

Palermo, Frank
1958-1967

Plaine, Mary Carroll*
1985-2015

Willaman, Kenneth
1970-1999

BSO Discography

Rachmaninoff, Symphony No.2
Massimo Freccia
BSO recording BS-01
February 1955

———————

"Symphonic Souvenirs"
Tchaikovsky Symphony No. 4
Handel, Concerto Grosso
    for string orchestra, Op 6, No. 7
Mendelssohn, Violin Concerto
Rachmaninoff, Rhapsody on
    a Theme of Paganini
Boris Blacher, Variations for Orchestra
James Buswell / Leon Fleisher /
    Peter Herman Adler
Dominion RI 1437
1963

———————

Britten, Diversions on
    a Theme for Piano Left Hand
Ezra Laderman, Concerto for Orchestra
Leon Fleisher / Sergiu Comissiona
Desto DC-7168
1974

Thomas Jefferson Anderson, Squares:
    An Essay for Orchestra
Talib Rasul Hakim, *Visions of Ashwora*
Olly Woodrow Wilson, *Akwan*
Paul Freeman
CBS Records 'Black Composers Series'
    M 33434
1975

———————

Mendelssohn, Symphony 3
Sergiu Comissiona
Turnabout 10043
1975

———————

Mendelssohn, Symphony 4
Symphony No. 5
***Fingal's Cave* Overture**
Sergiu Comissiona
Turnabout 10044
1976

———————

George Walker, *Mass*
Sergiu Comissiona
Albany B00FOQUS0W
1977

———————

Allan Pettersson, Symphony No. 8
Sergiu Comissiona
Polar POLS 289
1978

Tchaikovsky, *Nutcracker* (Selections)
Sergiu Comissiona
Turnabout QTV 34752
1979

———————

Tchaikovsky, Symphony No. 4
Sergiu Comissiona
Vanguard VA 25006
1980

———————

Ravel, Boléro
Berlioz, *Le Corsaire* Overture
Enescu, Romanian Rhapsody No. 1,
Rimsky-Korsakov, *Capriccio Espagnole*
Sergiu Comissiona
Vanguard VA 25005
1980

———————

Leslie Bassett,
    Echoes from an Invisible World
Henry Lazarof Concerto for Orchestra
Sergiu Comissiona
CRI Records 677
1980

———————

Respighi, *Roman Festivals*
Pines of Rome
Sergiu Comissiona
Vanguard VA 25004
1980

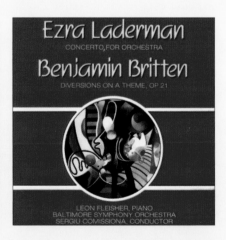

Saint-Saëns, Symphony No. 3, "Organ"
Frederick Minger / Sergiu Comissiona
Vanguard VA 25008
1981

Ravel, Concerto for Piano Left Hand
Alborada del Gracioso
Rapsodie espagnole
Leon Fleisher / Sergiu Comissiona
Vanguard VA 25014
1982

Brahms-Schoenberg,
    Piano Quartet in G minor
Sergiu Comissiona
VOX ACD 8196
1984

Alfven, Swedish Rhapsody No. 1
Enescu, Romanian Rhapsody No. 2
Kodály, *Háry János* Suite
Sergiu Comissiona
VOX Cum Laude D-VCL 9073
1984

Berlioz, *La Marseillaise*
Overture to *Benvenuto Cellini*
Excerpts from *La Damnation de Faust,*
    Roméo et Juliette, Les Troyens
David Zinman
Telarc 80164
July 1988

Barber, Cello Concerto
Britten, Symphony for Cello
    and Orchestra
Yo-Yo Ma, David Zinman
Sony Classical 44900
February 1989
Grammy winner: Best classical performer,
    instrumental soloist with orchestra

Christopher Rouse, Symphony No. 1,
    Phantasmata
David Zinman
Nonesuch 9-79230-2
August 1989

Elgar, *Enigma* Variations
***Cockaigne* Overture**
Salut d'amour
Serenade for Strings
David Zinman
Telarc 80192
October 1989

Rachmaninoff, Rhapsody on
    a Theme of Paganini
Tchaikovsky, Piano Concerto No. 1
Horacio Gutiérrez / David Zinman
Telarc 80193
February 1990

Schumann, Symphony No. 1, "Spring"
Symphony No. 4
David Zinman
Telarc 80230
April 1990

Tchaikovsky, Symphony No. 4
***Romeo and Juliet* Fantasy-Overture**
David Zinman
Telarc 80228
July 1990

Schumann, Symphony No. 2
Symphony No. 3, op. 97 ("Rhenish")
David Zinman
Telarc 80182
January 1991

Berlioz, *Roman Carnival* Overture
***Les Francs-juges* Overture**
Symphonie fantastique
David Zinman
Telarc 80271
April 1991

Stravinsky, *The Firebird*
Petrushka, Fireworks
David Zinman
Telarc 80270
June 1991

Michael Torke, "Color Music"
Green, Purple, Ecstatic Orange, Ash,
  Bright Blue Music
David Zinman
Argo / London 433 071-2
October 1991

_____

Rachmaninoff, Symphony No. 2
Vocalise
Sylvia McNair, David Zinman
Telarc 80312
June 1992

_____

Elgar, Symphony No. 1
Pomp and Circumstance
  Military Marches, Nos. 1 and 2
David Zinman
Telarc 80310
July 1992

_____

Barber, Adagio for Strings
Overture to *The School for Scandal*
First Essay
Second Essay
Music for a Scene from Shelley
Symphony No. 1
David Zinman
Argo / London 436 288-2ZH
October 1992

_____

Copland, *Billy the Kid* **(complete)**
Danzón Cubano, El salon México
Rodeo (complete)
David Zinman
Argo 440 639-2
June 1994

_____

Rachmaninoff, Symphony No. 3
Symphonic Dances
David Zinman
Telarc 80331
August 1994

Yo-Yo Ma: The New York Album
Stephen Albert,
  Concerto for Violoncello and Orchestra
Bartók, Viola Concerto, opus posthumous
Bloch, *Schelomo,* **Hebraic Rhapsody**
  for Cello and Orchestra
Yo-Yo Ma / David Zinman
Sony Classical SK 57961
September 1994
Grammy winner: Best classical contemporary
  composition – Albert
Grammy winner: Best instrumental soloist with
  orchestra

_____

Dance Mix
John Adams, *The Chairman Dances*
Dominick Argento, "Tango,"
  from *The Dream of Valentino*
Bernstein, "Mambo"
  (Symphonic Dances from *West Side Story***)**
Michael Daugherty, *Desi*
John Harbison, *Remembering Gatsby:*
  A Foxtrot for Orchestra
Aaron Jay Kernis,
  New Era Dance for Orchestra
Libby Larson, *Collage: Boogie*
Robert Moran, *Points of Departure*
Christopher Rouse, *Bonham*
David Schiff, *Stomp*
Michael Torke, *Charcoal*
  (7th movement from *Black and White***)**
David Zinman
Argo / London 444 454-2
April 1995

_____

Russian Sketches:
Glinka, Ruslan and Ludmilla **Overture**
Ippolotov-Ivanov, *Caucasian Sketches*
Rimsky-Korsakov, *Russian Easter* **Overture**
Tchaikovsky, *Eugene Onegin* **(Polonaise)**
Tchaikovsky, *Francesca da Rimini*
David Zinman
Telarc 80378
July 1995

_____

Ives, *Three Places in New England*
"Holidays" Symphony
They Are There!
David Zinman
Argo / London 444 860-2
May 1996

Michael Daugherty,
  Metropolis Symphony, Bizarro
David Zinman
Argo / London 452 103-2
January 1997

_____

Barber, Violin Concerto
Bloch, *Baal Shem:*
  Three Pictures of Chassidic Life
Walton, Violin Concerto
Joshua Bell / David Zinman
London 452 851-2
April 1997
Grammy nomination: Instrumental soloist
  performance with orchestra

_____

Gershwin, Piano Concerto in F Major
Ravel, Piano Concerto in G Major
Hélène Grimaud / David Zinman
Erato 0630-19571-2
1997

_____

Bernstein, Symphonic Dances
  from *West Side Story*
Facsimile
Fancy Free
Candide **Overture**
David Zinman
Argo / London 452 916-2
September 1997

_____

John Tavener, *The Protecting Veil*
Wake Up … And Die
Yo-Yo Ma / David Zinman
Sony Classical 62821
August 1998

_____

Beethoven, Violin Concerto
Bernstein, Serenade for solo violin, strings,
  harp, and percussion
Hilary Hahn / David Zinman
Sony Classical 60584
1999